THE
EMPEROR
AND THE
ENDLESS
PALACE

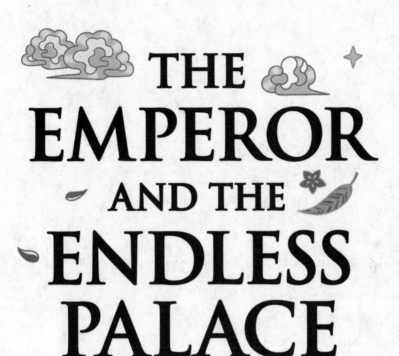

THE
EMPEROR
AND THE
ENDLESS
PALACE

JUSTINIAN HUANG

mira

ISBN-13: 978-0-7783-0523-1

The Emperor and the Endless Palace

Copyright © 2024 by Money Boy LLC

Good Life

Words and Music by Adam Schmalholz, Caleb Nott, Georgia Nott, Steven Zhu

Copyright © 2016 Columbia Records, a Division of Sony Music Entertainment

International Copyright Secured All Rights Reserved

Used by Permission

Reprinted by Permission of ZHU

For questions and comments about the quality of this book, please contact us at
CustomerService@Harlequin.com.

TM is a trademark of Harlequin Enterprises ULC.

Mira
22 Adelaide St. West, 41st Floor
Toronto, Ontario M5H 4E3, Canada
BookClubbish.com

Printed in U.S.A.

In loving memory of Kenneth

Forever singing to his guitar on the Playa del Rey

LET ME LOSE MY MIND. IT'S THE ONLY WAY TO LOVE.

—ZHU

What if I told you that the feeling we call love is actually the feeling of metaphysical recognition, when your soul remembers someone from a previous life?

How would that change the way you look at each stranger, knowing that they could be the epic romance across all of your lifetimes?

—

HE SHICAN
1740

Until I met him, I always thought that fox spirits could only be women.

They say that fox spirits resemble beautiful women because of their astonishing ability to confound and enchant any man they wish, from desolate beggars to legendary emperors. But it is also said that these irresistible spirits are born as mere mortal foxes…the same shy woodland creatures that one might spot peeking innocently from behind a thicket of trees.

But if one of these humble foxes lives long enough to reach a certain age and wisdom, it might begin searching for a human skull. Whose skull it is does not matter; what is important is that the procured skull fit snugly over the fox's own head, surely not an easy find. And if it does indeed find this well-fitted skull, this old fox might begin to wear it each sunset as it worships the Northern Dipper in the night sky.

And if this fox's dedication and desire is great enough as it gives praise to the constellation, it might begin to grow more tails, one after the other. It may take eons of this adoration of the stars, but one day, many years after it first entered this world as a blind pup, the fox will attain its ninth and final tail.

With this ninth tail, the fox is reborn, a divine spirit at long last! Meat and blood and cartilage and hair will sprout from its skull as it is gifted human form, able to walk among us in disguise, to enjoy the privileges of our flesh.

Yet, despite its years of devoted worship, when the fox spirit receives its divinity, something inside it inevitably turns evil. Its newfound powers of persuasion and perception could be used for the betterment of society and human progress, but as it turns out, these powers are as easily flipped as a coin.

Perhaps this turn is a testament to the true nature of the fox... or perhaps indeed it is a testimony to the fickle nature of power itself. Because once this newly christened fox spirit enters our fray, with it comes death and disaster to mankind. Beautiful as it is merciless, the fox spirit's malice is unrelenting, its once feral barks transformed into melodious laughter over the spoils of its power.

Yes, where there has been the folly of man, look for an ambitious fox slinking away.

Believing in fox spirits is not the leap—everyone knows someone who has encountered one. No, the question is not whether fox spirits exist. The question is: If one comes for you, can you resist it?

As children, my brothers and I would wait eagerly as our uncle polished off our father's stores of white liquor, just to hear him drunkenly retell tales of his dalliance with a fox spirit. When our uncle was a young man studying for the imperial examinations, he was seduced by an older woman of unearthly beauty who consumed him whole like a fat dumpling. By the time he discovered her true identity, it was too late: all of the hard-earned money that our clan had saved for his projected illustrious career he had squandered instead on hedonistic flights of fancy all for the pleasure of the fox spirit.

Needless to say, he never passed any imperial examinations.

Back then I was still the favored son, and after my uncle stumbled into the night my father would always take care to remind me that many men who should have been great blamed their failures on fox spirits.

What should I do if I meet a fox spirit? I once asked my father.

He frowned. *If you are an honorable man, you will never come across one.*

I am of the humble He Clan, the eldest of four sons. My given name Shican means Teacher, a nod to the great scholars that number among our ancestral tree. But like many things about me, the name was unearned; really I was a willing student instead.

I was quiet from birth, my mother always saying that I rarely cried, I only observed. She once dropped me as a child and I sustained a small cut on my hand. But instead of wailing like any other infant, I instead stared intently into the blood pooling in my palm, as though it were a new world encased in a dark ruby.

My father, a pragmatic merchant, liked that about me at first. He said that silence is a defining attribute of an honorable man. Father was quiet, too, and he thought that this was a trait he had passed on to me. But my father's silence and mine were different: his was a satisfied blankness, whereas mine was a curious void eager to be filled.

Had you asked me as a child, I would have said I did not realize I was quiet, because the thoughts in my head were numerous and clamoring. *Go,* they would say. *Go and look for it.* I spent those early years yearning for something foreign yet also deeply familiar, like a dog that has never tasted meat.

We lived on the outskirts of our village and each night I could see the trees from my window, swaying back and forth. I must have been around fourteen when I started to sneak out at night to wander those woods. I am not sure what I was looking for. Fox spirits, perhaps, but anything really that poked a hole into the mundanity of my life. I might have asked my uncle to join me with his merry company, but he had drunk himself into the ground a few years prior.

Every night that I could, I crept a bit farther into the woods. It always struck me how the very nature of light, and lack thereof, completely changes a place. During the day, the woods near our village were bathed in warm sun and full of twittering birds, cheerful and inviting. But at night, the air smelled strange and the trees took different forms.

It was not long before I discovered that there were other boys from our village who also walked the woods at night, for reasons I dared not fathom. So at first I would stay far away, and if they did notice me, we simply acknowledged each other from a comfortable distance.

For a year I walked the woods and observed the other boys. I noted that they would often pair up and disappear. Some of them I actually did recognize, particularly one named Zheng, whose father did business with mine. He had even come to my father's business quite a few times and we always acted as though we shared no nocturnal activities.

Zheng was a few years older than me. He had a long, elegant nose, clever eyes and upturned lips. He and his father were lumber traders; I had heard his father had him working manual labor with their woodcutters, and I believed it. Zheng was strong and sturdy, with broad shoulders and swarthy skin, a bronze contrast to us other alabaster sons of the merchant class. When he came to our store, he would occasionally catch me staring at him and furtively smile back, which would send me running upstairs.

I began to suspect that Zheng was timing his midnight walks to match mine, and I kept a regular routine to encourage him. One night, I did not see him at all. I walked in the woods to where the trees were denser than the moonlight and sat there, waiting. Somehow, I knew he would come.

And he did. Zheng emerged from the shadows. He sat next

to me in that effortless confident manner of his, leaning against a peach tree.

I cleared my throat. *Are you also looking for spirits?*

Surprised by this, Zheng laughed. *Looking for spirits is pointless. They only come to you if they want to be found.*

Then why do you walk the woods at night?

Zheng did not reply, but instead reached above him toward one of the tree's branches and plucked a large peach. Its bold fragrance startled my nose and its burnt hue seemed to illuminate our surroundings. He took a sumptuous bite, smacking his lips as its syrup rolled down his chin. He handed it to me.

As I took a bite, running its juices over my tongue, he reached over and parted my robes at my waist. In the still, cool air, I was exposed. As he leaned down to take me into his mouth, I continued to eat the peach, my eyes closing as sticky sensations washed over me.

Afterward, Zheng and I walked back to our village together, side by side. As we reentered the clearing, I felt like I had finally stepped into a new world. Zheng grinned at me, and I smiled back.

But there was a lone figure waiting for us at the edge of the village. My father. He looked at me, then at Zheng, and then back at me. Zheng quickly departed as I slowly followed my father back to our home.

From that night on, my father never spoke directly to me again. Zheng and his father never came back to our business. Some nights I would hear my mother trying to gently persuade my father to be lenient, but this was in vain. *Many sons who lay with other men go on to bring great fortune to their clans,* she would say, but my father was unmoved. I suppose I understood. I have never blamed him.

When my brothers and I turned of age, my father handed his company to my younger brother instead of me. At eighteen, I hugged my tearful mother goodbye and mounted my old horse, leaving my village for one far away called Tiaoxi, where I opened a small inn.

In the following years, I still walked the wilderness many a night in search of fox spirits. And yes, I often settled instead for the mortal comforts of another man's embrace. But when I finally did meet one, it was not a creature of the night.

No, the fox spirit stood there before me in the radiant light of day.

His name was Jiulang.

DONG XIAN
4 BCE

A few months after the Princess Feng Yuan was accused of witchcraft against our Emperor and ordered to commit suicide, a rumor spread like summer mold throughout the Endless Palace that there would soon be a shift in the Court. *Shift* was an alarmingly odd word, so my colleagues and I did what we did best as low-ranking imperial clerks: jockeyed with what little influence we had.

Luckily for me, I'd always been told that I wielded a rather large influence, and I was particularly adept at jockeying with it.

I started with my usual stable boy, because there is always a surprising amount of intrigue to be gleaned from whom is riding with whom. The irony was not lost on me as the fair youth straddled me with his limber thighs, bucking up and down as though I were his noble steed galloping over rough terrain.

Please, my lord, he moaned as he held on to my shoulders for dear life. I wasn't sure exactly what he was pleading for, and I certainly was no lord. But being addressed as one felt good, and I in turn did know a face of ecstasy when I saw one. Hence, I thrusted deeper inside him until I could feel my essence about to overflow, and then I flipped him face-first onto the mat in my chambers and pounded his pink plum until it was quivering around my happily depleted influence.

Afterward, as he was licking me clean, the stable boy mentioned that he had been charged with a new horse.

Whose horse? I asked, instantly alert. This particular stable boy groomed the Emperor's own prized horses, so undoubtedly this new horse would belong to someone in the Emperor's inner circle. My suspicions were confirmed when the fair youth said that he had never met its owner, clearly someone too important to be in the same vicinity as a servant.

The horse is armored, though, the stable boy said as he slipped back into his robes. He nearly tripped over an unbothered Miaomi, who was preening her blue fur in the sunlight.

Armored? I responded, stroking the palace cat's chin as she idled by me. *You mean it's a soldier's horse?*

He nodded as he tamed his tousled hair back into a servant's bun. *A massive stallion, no less! From the Far North. Red as wet rust. A real stunner.*

I gave the stable boy's shapely backside a thankful spank as he left my chambers, my mind bubbling. Whatever this shift in the Court was, it involved a soldier. Perhaps someone returning from battle?

After a quick wash, I found a scrap of food to feed an impatiently mewing Miaomi. Early on in my residency at the Endless Palace, I'd started feeding leftovers to the slinky stray cat whenever she came by my quarters, and eventually she was returning every day during my afternoon break to claim whatever bits of meat or rice that I had saved for her.

I had no idea where this blue cat actually lived, but that day I needed to send her on her way earlier than usual. I grabbed my robes. Now that I was armed with my stable boy's exclusive intelligence, I knew exactly who to see next.

A little to the left, Lord Pang groaned through gritted teeth. Now, here was an actual lord, far outranking me, but as I had come to discover since my arrival at the Endless Palace two years prior, many powerful men have a penchant for being overpowered.

I had him pressed against the silk screen door of his office, no doubt creating a curious shadow to any passersby outside in the halls of the Imperial Army administerial offices, but I had few qualms. I saw Lord Pang in his office regularly at his behest, and it was likely his subordinates were accustomed to curious shadows whenever I visited.

Deep inside the lord, my fingers gamely shifted to the left, and sure enough I felt that magic little node hidden within all men. I pressed down upon it, eliciting another stifled moan from the older man, tapping in rhythm with each of his spasms. He leaned his face in toward me as though to kiss me, but I slapped him ferociously across the cheek as hard as I could muster. He gasped with glee as I backhanded his other cheek and spat on him, leaving his face red. Then I hooked my imbedded fingers and swirled them inside him as he pleasured himself, until I felt that dependable warm splatter land upon my exposed chest coupled with a stifled cry from above.

Lord Pang let out a satiated sigh as I withdrew from him, and he slumped down onto the floor of his office. Out of his pocket he pulled out a clean cloth, which I gratefully used to wipe myself down as I slipped back into my robes. *What were you saying earlier, Dong Xian? A new soldier in Court?* Despite his heft, he had a high nasal voice that grated upon my ears. The pasty older man certainly was a far cry from my vibrant stable boy, but he was just as game to trade information for my influence.

*Yes, my lord. I am wondering if you have processed anyone return-
ing from battle as of late?* I handed him back his handkerchief. *I
have reasons to believe that they have something to do with the rumored
changes in the Endless Palace.*

The lord shook his head. *Dong Xian, if there was a soldier who
commanded such sway over the Court, they would not come under my
purview.*

I was at first disappointed, with soiled fingers for naught. But
I realized that there was indeed a clue here, even if I had overlooked it before. *Sway?*

Having securely retied his robes, Lord Pang sat down behind
his desk and waved me off. *Think bigger, Dong Xian. My office
handles the bureaucracy of the little people. You are encroaching upon
a circle in the very upper echelons of the Endless Palace, perhaps even
within the orbit of the Dragon Throne.*

As I hurried back to my duties on the far other side of the
Palace, I was so excited that I nearly tripped more than once.
Here I was in possession of a lead that very likely pointed di-
rectly toward the center of our universe, the Emperor himself.
I felt like I had finally discovered the hidden pathway toward
my ultimate destination.

It was finally time to pay Old Yang a visit. But first, I needed
to procure a jug of decent wine.

It had been a few weeks since I had visited with my teacher,
Yang Xiong, the elderly court philosopher who normally talked
in abstract musings wrapped in witty riddles. While at first balk-
ing at his esoterica like most of the Court, after a few dreadfully
dull sessions I mercifully discovered that once he had had some
liberal pours of yellow wine he reentered the common tongue
of us plebeians…as a bit of a gossip, actually. As my mother once
told me, there are few knots that strategic wine cannot unravel.

The harmony of the Court need be recalibrated, Old Yang said bluntly, as we sat in the shade of the courtyard foliage shielding ourselves from the sun, thankful for the massive tree that towered above us. Yang's private garden was the traditional thinking place of the Emperor's philosophers, and its intimacy allowed us to speak more freely.

I dutifully refilled the elder man's cup, waiting for more morsels. He took a hearty gulp. *Strange times, now. Accusations of witchery afoot. Consorts and eunuchs scheming. The wind-water balance of the Endless Palace is inauspicious. Curiouser and curiouser, indeed!*

I had a sudden recall of the Princess Feng Yuan prostrate in front of the entire Court, begging for mercy from the Prime Minister. Inauspicious is a word more terrifying than famine. Dynasties have fallen from even the prediction of inauspicious times.

No clemency was shown to the Princess Feng Yuan. She was stripped of her numerous titles and exiled to a faraway ruin. Once one of the most respected women in Court and lavished with the most decadent riches, it was there she was given a final gift: a gold silken rope with which to hang herself.

This was the macabre conclusion to a scandal that had struck the Endless Palace like a southern typhoon. Rumors and hearsay are the currency of bored officials, and we were all wealthy that month. Perhaps it was the sheer downfall that made this affair so profound: the Princess was by all accounts a virtuous saint, renowned for her humility and selflessness. For her to suddenly be exposed as a witch…it was all so deliciously morbid.

But the whispers within whispers, the dangerous truths that no one dared to speak aloud but instead only shared through knowing glances, were that these allegations were of course egregious lies! What had really happened was that the Princess Feng Yuan's lifelong rival, the Grand Empress Dowager Fu—grandmother to our Emperor—had finally triumphed in the two women's decades-long game of switching hands.

But truth doesn't matter here in the Court, and ethics are rarely rewarded. To survive here, we move to the current of the ocean, knowing we cannot dictate the waves.

Yes, as far as I was concerned, these machinations were meant to stay distant maelstroms. When I first entered the Court, I promised my father that I would keep my head low and work diligently. That is the honor that wreaths the Dong Clan: greatness through our austerity. Beyond it being a favor to my father, I think that is why the celebrated philosopher Yang humored a green teenager like me with not much to contribute to his sort of conversation. As a friend of my father's, Old Yang knew that my people were austere and rejected extravagance, and that was his credo as well.

But that didn't mean I wasn't curious.

One's station in the Endless Palace was not necessarily carved in stone, but rather could be as fluid as ripples on a river. One simply had to be in the right place, closer to the center, to create an impact with far-reaching effects.

By the center, of course, I mean the Emperor.

Thus, in the two years after I swore my life to the Court, I became a devoted student of it as well. Through my own brand of carnal research, I studied how it flowed, because everything in the Palace—from the lowest scullery maid's morning duties to a private audience with the Prime Minister—flowed around the Emperor.

Yet, direct access to him was near impossible; I had never even seen him in person. The Endless Palace lived up to its name, as it covered 1,200 acres of sprawling land, lake, and hill and had a population of hundreds. All of us who lived on these sacred grounds had one singular life purpose of selflessly serving the Emperor and his Dynasty of the Han.

Yes, despite its size and splendor, the palace was a labyrinthine prison, with endless traps around every corner. To be seen as overtly reaching beyond one's station was ill-advised.

There was one person, however, in my immediate orbit who had a regular audience with the Emperor. And perhaps this person could help me connect the dots among an accused witch, a mystery soldier and the Emperor.

Teacher Yang, I interrupted the philosopher, who was still droning on about wind-water imbalances. *But how does the Emperor fare in these uncertain times? He consults with you regularly, yes?*

Yang Xiong paused and made rare eye contact with me. In the years since my father introduced me to the old philosopher, I had made sure to tread carefully and respectfully with him, especially since my very first interactions with Old Yang had been particularly embarrassing. I had been waiting for a chance to invoke the Emperor out of concern...not opportunity.

The philosopher was quiet for a moment and I prayed my face looked properly concerned.

Finally, Old Yang, choosing his words more carefully than before, said, *The Emperor is an exceptionally bright and promising leader. Much like with his father and grandfather before him, my conversations with him fill me with hope for the Dynasty of the Han. But even an Emperor is also a man, and a son...and a grandson. And our Emperor's greatest attribute is his filiality.*

I could read between his lines. It was well understood that in many senses, the Emperor still yielded to his mighty grandmother. After all, it was through her design that he sat upon the Dragon Throne at all, considering his father had been only a regional prince. Taken away from his courtesan mother at birth to be hand-reared by the Grand Empress Dowager Fu, the Emperor at twenty years of age was by all accounts her puppet... and would likely remain one until she died.

Of course, all of this would be treasonous to say aloud. Yet, we all knew.

I looked up at the sky, still trying to sound innocuous. *Teacher Yang, do you know if the Emperor has received any new visitors of late? Perhaps someone in the military?*

When I glanced back down at him, Yang was silent, but he was studying me with strange eyes. *Curiouser and curiouser, indeed, Dong Xian*, he finally said. *You overreach.*

After that he would say no more. Perhaps his silence was statement enough.

Not long after that conversation with Yang Xiong, I was summoned from my desk in the Imperial Offices.

It was a morning that couldn't decide whether it was sunny or rainy, though my attention wasn't on the weather. I was scrutinizing the many discrepancies in the grain and salt tributes from the State of Chu. It was clear that something unsavory was happening in these numbers, but that was hardly unusual to encounter in my line of work in the Court.

Corruption abounded in the Empire, and I learned very quickly that my job was to record these discrepancies, but never to report them. It seemed as though the problem was systemic and pervasive, and it was getting worse by the month.

Dong Xian. Someone suddenly called my name, startling me from the problematic numbers. All the other clerks turned to look at me in surprise. We were rarely interrupted during our records keeping.

The stone-faced eunuch who had appeared in our office was a tall man named Shi Li. I'd heard bloody stories of his ruthlessness as a sword-bearing hand of the throne; he certainly looked the part, with powerful arms that could crush a skull. His features were masculine and made unique by his lack of any facial hair: no eyebrows and eyelashes, let alone a beard and mustache. He had said my name, but he knew who I was—when I looked up, his eyes were already trained on me.

Trying my best to stand steadily, I followed him out of the offices. I heard the anxious murmurs amongst my colleagues.

Where are we going? I ventured once we were outside.

Shi Li stared ahead. I figured he wouldn't answer. *The Unicorn Pavilion*, he replied gruffly.

I connected dots. The Unicorn Pavilion was the domain of the Grand Empress Dowager Fu, architect of the Princess Feng Yuan's ruin and grandmother to the Emperor. There was no reason for her to ask for an audience with me. No benign reason, at least.

My mind continued to race. Such a summons usually ends with a beheading. My legs quivered like river reeds as I followed Shi Li, as my mind raced with the possibilities. What had I done? How could I beg forgiveness? What will become of my clan? I grew up hearing stories of entire clans eradicated from the face of the earth over the errors of a single member.

I remembered my conversation with Yang Xiong. Had some ambitious maid overheard us and tattled? Or had Old Yang himself balked at my boldness and betrayed me? I blinked away tears as I silently prayed mercy from Heaven.

The Palace grounds had never felt so endless. We walked in silence through courtyards and pathways for perhaps half an hour. When we finally reached the entrance of the Unicorn Pavilion, I hesitated until Shi Li unceremoniously shoved me into the darkness inside. Without looking, I instantly fell to my knees, touching my nose to the floor.

I thought, again, of the Princess and what they'd done to her. Her hair had been half torn out in bloody patches as she sobbed in front of the Court before they dragged her out. What would they do to me, a nobody?

I stayed in this pathetic position for what seemed like a lifetime, waiting to be addressed. But there were no words, nothing. Finally, I lifted my head.

Reclining on an ornate dais of flowering pear wood and white jade, the Grand Empress Dowager Fu looked back at me, her sharp eyes glittering in the dimness like distant bonfires. As I faced her, she leaned forward ever so slightly, as if to get a better look at me. Then, her lips curled upward into a sharp smile, revealing two neat rows of gleaming silver teeth.

Outside, the steady beat of a distant drum reverberated in my ears.

RIVER
PRESENT DAY

First, feel the beat of a hypnotic bass in your head. A real club banger, one that fingers your soul.

Do you hear it? Good. Let it wash over you like aural pleasure.

Now, imagine a world where the gay Asian man is god.

Before you in a grand arena is a sea of pulsing, sweating, golden-skinned men, dancing to the mind-fucking beat under blinding rainbows of light. Electric potential hums in the air, punctuated with sudden blasts of cold mist, a welcome shot of icy relief in this otherwise stifling pit of musk and meat. On stage, the men are muscled like Mongol Empire warriors, with enough abs and pecs to conquer all the lands many times over.

Except it's not your imagination. Welcome to the Yellow Peril Party in downtown LA.

"River! Hold my drink!" I snap out of my reverie and turn away from the crowd. Calvin hands me a half-empty glass of something aggressively fizzy. He smirks, and has to yell at me over the music, "Close your mouth, unless you want something in it!"

I watch him fumble through his fanny pack that he has slung over his shoulder. He holds out two thick pink pills with something imprinted on them. I take a closer look and realize they've been stamped with the peach emoji, never looking more like a bubble butt than right now.

Calvin offers me one. I hesitate, then I shake my head. I've already gone too far tonight.

He looks disappointed but shrugs it off as he pops both into his mouth. With one slick motion, he peels off his tank top, his sculpted chest puffed out. Some of the boys around us smile, acknowledging his smooth athletic body with unabashed interest. His long bangs flop casually around his eyes, dewed with moisture. He slings his arm around me and we gaze back out at the crowd of men. My glasses fog up with steam and I push them back up my nose.

"What do you think of your first circuit party?" he hollers into my ear.

"There's so many of them!" I yell back.

"Us, River. There are so many of us!" With that, Calvin flashes me another huge smile, his teeth wet and sharp, and springs into the crowd without warning. I pause a moment. What the fuck, I shrug. I pull off my shirt and run after him.

We are in a stadium with easily five thousand other men. Known to many simply as Peril, the Yellow Peril Party is one of the biggest circuit parties in the world, catering to Asian men and those who love them. As Calvin explained to me in the Lyft over, each Lunar New Year, boys come from all over—New York City to Seoul to Bangkok—and congregate in LA to, well, bang cocks. His joke, not mine.

To think that, twenty-four hours ago, I didn't even know what a circuit party was.

On stage, the DJ flexes his juiced biceps more than he pushes buttons. The go-go boys gyrate next to him, wearing neon jockstraps and giant wings made of bright yellow stretch balloons. I know this sounds fairly ridiculous, but trust that in person it is spectacular. I'm momentarily transfixed on one of the dancers in particular. I'm guessing he is Japanese, and he is goateed with a jawline that could smash diamonds. An anime stud come to life. I catch his eye and he runs his tongue along the length of his mustache. Holy shit.

I feel my phone buzzing in my pocket and take it out. It's a text from Garden.

Where r u? Why did u just leave?

I quickly stuff the phone into my back pocket, clamping down a sudden nauseous wave of guilt. Calvin grabs me from behind and we grind to the throbbing beat.

Damn, he seems to be having a lot of fun. He oohs and aahs like a kid every time the lights change. I bite my lip. When is the last time I felt that happy? I can't remember.

"On second thought," I holler to him, "maybe I will take one of those pills."

Calvin's mouth drops open with delighted surprise, and he begins to search frantically in his fanny pack. I take a moment to assess him and my surroundings, somewhat amused by this evening's strange turn of events.

What had started as an impromptu and very random Grindr hookup somehow has landed me in a massive rave in downtown LA about to take ecstasy for the first time. When I arrived at Calvin's apartment in Koreatown earlier tonight, I had expected only a quick blowjob to release all the pent-up stress of Lunar New Year obligations.

But with his devilish wink and lips that somehow magically vibrate, this Calvin turned out to be particularly convincing.

"Come with me tonight to Peril," he had said once I told him that I was new to all this. "Let me initiate you."

"What's Peril?" I'd asked.

Oh, if only I had known.

"Aha!" Calvin pulls his hand out of his fanny pack and triumphantly holds up a stray pink pill like it's the cure for cancer. "I knew I had one left."

I reach for it but he snatches it back, playfully shaking his head. He sticks out his tongue and places the pill on it. I get the cue. Taking a deep breath, I lean toward him. A circle of spectators forms around us as we make out under the dazzling lights. With his tongue, Calvin expertly maneuvers the pill onto mine. Instantly, a stinging, repulsive taste of metallic chemicals stabs my mouth. I back away from Calvin, resisting an urge to spit it out.

"Trust me," Calvin says, laughing, "you'll learn to love how it tastes." He is clearly beginning to feel its effects; he seems to glow from within. "It's strong!" he says. "Give me your wallet if you feel like you might lose it. It'll be safe in my bag." I hand him my wallet and keys.

With that, he grabs me. His eyes are like neutron stars as he kisses me over and over again, running his hands over my body.

At some point, not long after, I feel a frenetic lump in my throat that starts to swell and swell until it becomes a ball of exquisite pleasure that engulfs me.

Sights, sounds and sensations blur around me. Everywhere I turn, there are more bodies, dancing to the secret choreography of a lust ritual. Random thoughts race in my mind, but mostly I'm thinking that I just want to kiss Calvin With The Vibrating Lips some more. I turn around to look for him…and he's nowhere to be found. I shudder as my entire body hums. Then I realize my cell phone is buzzing.

I take it out of my pocket and see who is calling. At first, the characters on the screen make no sense, like I am staring at an alien language. Then the letters reassemble and I can read them. A sinking feeling.

Garden again. Seven missed calls. A string of unanswered texts. She hates when I don't reply immediately. She probably always assumes the worst, except usually I ignore her only when studying for the MCAT.

But tonight? Tonight she can assume the worst. I let it ring till it goes to voice mail.

I'm sorry, Garden.

I put my phone away and when I look up, it's like I've entered a new dimension of discombobulated vibrations and colors. Nothing feels normal; everything is exploding. I try to stabilize myself. What was I doing before?

Where's Calvin?

I look around frantically, but he's nowhere to be seen in the crowd. I have never missed someone more in my life. I just want to feel his body around mine again. I need to look for him. I begin to make my way through the crowd of sweaty men, some of them pawing at me as I brush past.

"Are you okay?" Someone pulls me on the shoulder as I walk past him. I turn to a backlit being, unable to make out any of his features, save for a gold eyebrow piercing that shimmers at me like a ring of Saturn. I shake my head and try to keep moving, suddenly feeling a mounting panic inside me. I think I need to go to the restroom. I look around until I see it in the far corner, a black hole light-years away. I break away from Saturn and continue pushing my way through the solar system.

When I finally get there, the base stench of male bodies crash-lands me back onto Earth. The restroom is crowded and dank. Men go into stalls up to four at a time. At the sink, I take off my glasses and splash cold water onto my face, but it doesn't help. I feel like a volcano is awakening inside me.

Again, I feel my phone ringing in my pocket. I stumble back

outside, greeted once again by the deafening throng and mob of bodies. It all begins to hurt.

I need to go home. The bass throbs.

I don't feel well. The lights blaze.

What have I gotten myself into? I crash into someone and they shove me off, snarling at me. I feel my way to a wall and lean against it. As reality turns into plasma soup, I close my eyes as my body melts.

And melts.

And melts.

Maybe this is what dying feels like.

I blink, and I sit up.

I don't know how much time has passed but I am on the upper balcony bleachers overlooking the arena. My heart has stopped racing. It is quieter up here. I am leaning against someone warm and comforting. He hands me a bottle of water. "Calvin," I say, relieved. I turn my head around to thank him.

But the man behind me isn't Calvin. He is a stranger, but strangely familiar. I see that he has a gold eyebrow piercing. He is dressed in all black, in a sleeveless shirt that shows off his cut arms, each of his biceps symmetrically accentuated with a thick vein. I might still be rolling a bit, but he is undeniably beautiful, his high cheeks indented with soulful dimples.

I take a drink of the water. "Thanks," I say.

"Feel better?" He has a deep resonant voice and speaks English with a Chinese accent, similar sounding to my parents'. Around his left wrist, he wears a bracelet of green stones that look like Buddha beads.

You're from China? I was born in Taipei, I say in Mandarin.

He smiles, amused. "But your Chinese is so bad."

I laugh. "Yes, I moved here when I was a baby and I have an embarrassing American accent, I know." I look around. "How did we get here?"

He shakes his head, amused. *You don't remember. I saved you.* When he speaks Mandarin, it sounds like moonlit poetry. Whenever he talks, he plays with the Buddha beads around his wrist.

"You did?" I hand him back the water. "Was I that bad?" I look down at my phone. It's shut off.

"How much did you take?" He still sits behind me, intimate and protective.

"Just one. It was my first time. Probably overdid it." I slowly stand up, though I'd rather sink into him forever.

He stands up, too. "Be careful. Take care of yourself." He turns to walk away.

There's something about him…

Wait, wait. I grab him by the shoulder. He stops and turns back to me. *Stay with me a while.* I sit back down on the bleachers and pat the space beside me.

He looks at me as if conflicted, as if deciding. Then he sits down next to me, thumbing the stones on his bracelet. He notices me looking at it.

"It's jade," he says. "Very old green jade." He singles out one of the stones, and I notice that unlike its perfectly polished neighbors, this one in particular is a misshapen polyhedron, as if it was broken off something. "It protects you, keeps the badness away."

He takes my hand and grasps it, sliding the bracelet onto my wrist. *Wear it for now,* he says in his velvety Mandarin. The stones feel soothingly warm. "So you don't feel bad again."

As soon as his palm presses against mine, the drugs in my system seem to catch a second happier wind, because my body begins to tingle, as if every surrounding air molecule, trillions of them, is gently kissing my skin. I take a deep breath. "Wow."

He smiles. "You feel better."

"I'm River," I say. As our eyes meet, the music and lights and sweaty men below us erupt into a euphoric crescendo. And I don't know how else to describe a bittersweet feeling inside me—in this moment that I meet him, I realize I might be lonely for the rest of my life.

His name is Joey.

四

HE SHICAN
1740

His name was Jiulang.

It was a sunny day, but it was also a windy day, as though something looming was stirring up all of us. I was sweeping the scattered leaves from the entryway to my inn for the second time that afternoon, blinking the dust from my eyes. Near me at her trough, my old indigo horse, Dama, kept sneezing, similarly distressed by the weather.

Apparently, he had been calling my name for a moment before I heard him.

Master He.

But when I did hear his voice, it was like the sound of jade. *Master He.*

I looked up to see two figures, the sun shining behind them. And though he was backlit, his smile shone as he tilted his head forward respectfully. Behind him, the trees of the woods surrounding us swayed gently back and forth in the wind.

I blinked a few times until I could see him clearly. The speaker was a young man who looked no older than eighteen. He had a clever face with no trace of a beard, though his long hair had been tied into intricate braids cascading down his back.

Next to him was an older woman, I guessed perhaps his mother. She kept her eyes downcast and seemed as though she might flutter away if the wind blew any bolder. I looked back at the boy.

Dear friends, please come inside from this gusty day. This air is not good.

After they entered, I sat them down at my center table and scooped out my best leaves. The woman never spoke but the boy talked aplenty, engaging me with pleasantries and polite compliments as I prepared tea. My hands trembled ever so as I filled their cups. I did not understand why but he made me so incredibly nervous, even though I had never met him before.

Huang Jiulang.

I burned my tongue on a hasty sip of scalding tea, sputtering a bit. *Pardon me?*

The boy managed to keep his face straight, which I appreciated enormously. *You asked me my name, Master He. I am Huang Jiulang.*

I recovered quickly. *Huang Jiulang? Meaning the ninth in your family? Have you eight siblings?*

Jiulang smiled an unknowable smile. *Alas, it is just my grandmother and me.* His eyes flicked up at me, as if daring me to ask more.

Our eyes met. His were the color of amber.

I hastily looked down at my tea, lifting the lid to peer inside, hoping that the dependable normalcy of tea would calm me. But inside the liquid the leaves were inexplicably swirling around in a miniature maelstrom, as though the wind outside had crept into my cup. Indeed, the whole room seemed to be revolving. My head grew a bit light.

I took a deep breath and steadied myself again. If the boy

thought I was acting strange, he did not show it. I cleared my throat. *And how did you know who I was, Huang Jiulang? When you first arrived, you addressed me by name. I do not believe we have ever met.*

Jiulang took the hand of the woman. *My dear grandmother is ill. We live in the countryside, just the two of us. I came to Tiaoxi after hearing there is a physician here named Dr. Qi Yewang, and I was told you had a special relationship with him. I was hoping you could help us.*

The somberness of this dutiful grandson seemed to steady the room. And for a moment I was reminded of my mother, whom I had not seen in years. I thought of her face as she hugged me goodbye, both of us knowing we may well never see each other again. Feeling a sudden rush of emotion, I stood up to grab the kettle to refill their tea, but also to blink away the wetness under my eyes.

Please stay with me as my guests, you and your grandmother. I do know Dr. Qi, and I will speak to him on behalf of you. I have a spare room ready for both of you.

I turned back to him, to find him kneeling on the floor in front of me, seemingly speechless.

Stop, stop. I helped him up to his feet. Jiulang and I took his grandmother to their room, where we laid her down.

That night I was outside repairing a chair. The wind had finally stopped, but the same eeriness still clung to the air like humidity. Jiulang emerged at the doorway.

You are an honorable man, Master He. How can I ever repay you for the kindness you have shown? He leaned against the side of the door.

I glanced back at him. *A man's duty toward his elders is the very foundation of our society. As I am unable to take care of my own mother, I will do everything I can for your grandmother.*

He sat down next to me, watching me tinker with the chair. Unlike earlier today, he was quieter now. Under the moonlight, the density of trees encircling my inn watched over us protectively.

Forgive my forwardness, but this is an odd location for an inn, Jiulang finally said. *Beautiful indeed, but odd. Do many people pass through this way?*

I chuckled. *Not many at all. I used to own an inn in the city of Tiaoxi. But I moved farther out here about a year ago. As it turns out, I prefer trees over people.*

Jiulang looked out at the woods, too. *Most people fear the woods. It is a place where the world remains ancient. Yet, you are beckoned by it.* He was inching closer to me as he spoke. *Does it not get lonely out here, all by yourself?*

I did not know how to answer him. *I chose to move out here by myself. I make enough to feed my horse and the occasional guest, and I built this inn myself so I owe nothing to anyone.*

You and Dr. Qi Yewang are close friends, you said? Strangely, his lips didn't seem to be moving anymore, even though his voice was crystal clear.

Yes, I suppose we were. I was wondering where this was headed.

I heard something about Dr. Qi, the boy continued, softly unrelenting.

People hear things all the time. I shrugged unconvincingly. Upon his silence and my own curiosity, I relented obediently. *What did you hear?*

I heard he is of the Cut Sleeve persuasion.

Startled, I turned to face him. He was now so close I could smell his breath. It was sweet and flowery, but our conversation was veering toward poisonous territory.

Yet, I was entranced by him, by his gentle bluntness.

Perhaps he is. It is not for me to say, I replied.

With that, Huang Jiulang leaned back, as though satisfied for now. Somewhere in the distance, a chorus of owls began hooting, their cries echoing through the night.

What ailment afflicts your grandmother? I asked, hoping to change the subject.

Without warning, he placed his hand against my left chest, startling me. His touch jolted my body like a sudden blast of heat. For a moment his entire form seemed to change into something strange and animalistic, but it happened so quickly I felt betrayed by my eyes. He released his hand and continued as though it had not happened at all.

She has a heart condition, Master He, and is in need of a medicine called the Primordial Bolus. Jiulang went into details of her ailment, but his words blurred into the background as I felt a palpable heat rising inside me. What feeling was this? I felt compelled to flee but the moment I looked at Jiulang again, I felt an indescribable longing for him.

Tomorrow I will go see Dr. Qi, I said reassuringly, *and inquire of this Primordial Bolus.*

The look of appreciation on his face was like seeing the sun rise for the first time. *My grandmother has been sick for so long*, he said. *I have devoted my life to caring for her, but if she can be healed by Dr. Qi, we can finally leave our isolation.*

He looked up at the stars, his shimmering youth reflecting their light. He looked sad. *You ask me if I am lonely*, I said as I cautiously placed a hand on his shoulder. *It seems that you have been alone for a long time, too.*

He glanced back down at me, a small smile on his lips. *I do not feel alone now, here with you, Master He.* He then just barely leaned against my hand, the pressure of his body against it quickening my heartbeat.

With that, he stood up and retired to his room, saying he had to check on his grandmother. As he walked inside, I listened for each of his footsteps as they faded away.

Later, as I sat in my bed and thought about the day's events, I grew anxious. I had not seen my Dr. Qi in a long time, and I knew that visiting him again might come with an enormous cost. But if I could help this boy, I would have faced any tribulation. Nothing else mattered anymore except for him. I realized that I had been lifeless and worthless until I met him.

I lay down on my mat, blowing out the candle, though I would not sleep for many hours more.

I only had one thought: I would go to the ends of the earth for Huang Jiulang.

五

DONG XIAN
4 BCE

On one of our wine-drunk afternoons, the old philosopher Yang Xiong once explained to me the rivalry between the Grand Empress Dowager Fu and the Princess Feng Yuan, which began decades before the Princess's recent demise.

In their youths, the elder man began, *both women were the two most ravishing stars of the Endless Palace, only eclipsed by one another. The late Emperor Cheng was equally bewitched by his two favorites, but beyond both possessing striking beauty, they were otherwise entirely different people. Whereas the Consort Fu was clever and incorrigible, with sparkling wit and shifty designs, the Consort Feng Yuan was pure and unassuming as fresh-spun silk, a gentle girl beloved by all.*

Life, after all, is but duality, Old Yang mused. *The Emperor could flow between the fiery Fu and the placid Feng Yuan. Indeed, those were the days when the energy of the Palace was balanced. Not like today… Precarious situations abound. Tsk, tsk.* He began to mutter to himself. *Curiouser and curiouser, indeed!*

I poured more wine into his cup to encourage him back on topic.

I do believe this tenuous truce of the two consorts would have remained at stalemate, solely due to the uncalculating nature of the Consort Feng Yuan... The philosopher took a hearty gulp, then belched. *Alas, then the bear arrived.*

I leaned in, ready to unwrap a meaty metaphor. *Tell me, Teacher Yang, who was the bear? One of the Emperor's advisers? A conniving general?*

Yang Xiong cocked an exceptionally bushy eyebrow at me, then relinquished a rare smile. *Young man, I am referring to an actual bear.*

It was a hot spring day on which the Emperor and his favorite consorts, including Fu and Feng Yuan, were enjoying the merry entertainments of a traveling circus troupe. The jesters spun plates, blew fire and conjured shadows, much to the chattering delight of the ladies. But the showstopper event was the ferocious battle-to-the-death melee of the wild animals.

The party gasped as leopards gnashed at tigers, and cobras spat venom at mongooses. The Consort Fu cackled in pleasure at the bloody sight, while the Consort Feng Yuan averted her eyes, pitying the sad beasts.

Suddenly, disaster struck. A particularly voracious bear broke free from its cage and lunged directly at the Emperor and his imperial party. Everyone, led foremost by Fu clutching her jewels, fled. There was bedlam in all directions.

Everyone...that is except for Feng Yuan, who, despite her slightness and her fragility, boldly strode toward the charging bear. All the witnesses screamed, expecting the worst.

Fortunately, the animal handlers reached Feng Yuan before the bear did, and they quickly impaled the wretched creature with their spears. The Emperor himself rushed to his consort's side and demanded to know why she risked her life so. The young lady buried her face into his chest and replied, "I once heard that if a bear catches a person, it won't attack another. If it means that my Emperor would be safe, I would sacrifice myself many times over."

THE EMPEROR AND THE ENDLESS PALACE · 43

Already admired by all as a virtuous woman, the Consort Feng Yuan's selflessness in the face of certain death instantly elevated her to a saintlike status that she enjoyed for the rest of her life. But as the Emperor embraced his favorite and showered her with exultations, a hunched figure glowered at the happy pair from a distance.

The Consort Fu was publicly shamed by her petty cowardice in the presence of this lofty martyrdom. And in that moment she made a silent vow that no matter how long it took, no matter how difficult it might be, she would destroy Feng Yuan in the end.

Indeed, it was this vow that ended up shaping our Empire for the next thirty years, to this very day. For it is Fu's own grandson who sits upon the Dragon Throne today as our Emperor, while Feng Yuan rots in an unmarked grave.

The philosopher Yang paused to scratch his thigh. I offered him more wine, but he waved me off and stood up to leave. *You see, young man, that the Princess Feng Yuan did escape the bear that fateful day, but her true predator was the woman who would become the Grand Empress Dowager Fu.*

This foreboding story rang in my ears as I knelt on the cold floor of the Unicorn Pavilion, punctuated by the reverberating beat of a distant drum.

Peering out at me from her shadows, the Grand Empress Dowager Fu beckoned me to stand. She was swathed in magnificent green-and-gold robes, and whenever she moved, the many gems studded into her raven-black hair twinkled like starlight. I quickly glanced around me.

The Unicorn Pavilion was not the largest hall I'd seen in the Endless Palace, but it certainly was one of the most luxurious. Except for the sad patch of cold floor under me, every other surface was draped with the hides of great beasts, their mouths gaping wide open as if in silent scream. Intricately woven silk screens were placed behind her, framing her with a painted backdrop of lush forest imagery.

You may rise. Her echoing voice startled me, but I tried to hold myself still. I could feel my hands and feet shaking, but I forced myself to steady them as best I could.

I slowly rose and lifted my head, knowing that at any moment a blade could appear and chop it off. I stole a glance at the powerful woman before me. Thirty years might have passed since the bear incident, but she was still a luminous woman of her age, though her beauty was hardened and deliberate as a dagger.

I am eternally at your service, Your Imperial Majesty, I managed to say.

Dong Xian, son of Dong Gong, of the Dong Clan of Yunyang, she said. Not a question nor a greeting, but rather a declarative statement that affirmed she knew exactly who I was, who my people were and where I came from.

I nodded, hoping she couldn't see the icy-cold beads of sweat accumulating on my forehead. *Yes, Your Imperial Majesty. I am... he.*

She chuckled, an odd guttural sound reminding me of skipping stones on a river. *You can refrain from formalities after the initial salutations. We both know who you are talking to.*

She suddenly rose and walked to her desk, motioning me to join her. Bewildered, I sat down on the seat across from her, wondering if any beheading had ever begun with such civility. She motioned again to a servant, and a cup of flowering tea was promptly poured for me, its perfumed scent wafting into the air. The tension in my veins began to subside a little. Whatever this was, it didn't feel immediately perilous.

She took a sip of her own tea and I did the same, looking at the exquisite carvings on the surface of the wood table. It was a frolicking scene, depicting randy fox spirits mirthfully chasing after mortals in lush fields.

The servant placed a small coal in a pipe and handed it to her. She puffed and the coal sputtered as smoke unfurled around her. *I'm told that your father is one of our most respected court administrators,* she said.

Your generous words honor my family. I will tell my father and he surely will be humbled.

No need. Normally, I don't pay heed to Court administration. I mention it only because it serves to our advantage.

Our advantage? A slow dawning of realization began to glow in my mind. I kept quiet, not daring to surmise.

How long have you been in the Endless Palace, young Dong?

I came when I was eighteen years of age. It has been just under two years.

Suck, inhale, blow. Billowing smoke. *And your station? How do you find your duties?*

It is the honor of lifetimes to serve the Emperor.

She chuckled again, then coughed. *Indeed, serving the Emperor, like your father did, and his father before him. Obediently taking records. Click, click, clicking away at numbers on your abacus. An honorable life, no doubt.*

I realized that the drumbeat, or whatever it was, had ceased. It was silent now, except for the flickering of candles between the Grand Empress Dowager and me. I had kept my eyes down, but glanced up again. She was actually leaning forward, peering at me intently, reading me like a tablet.

Do you know what the Court says about you, Dong Xian?

This was by far the most terrifying question of my life. I tensed again. *The Court says things about me?*

She grinned, once again revealing her teeth, bright as polished iron. It was alarming to see a mouth of metal on an otherwise pin-perfect woman. I hoped my face didn't openly react. *Surely you know by now, young Dong, that the Court has an opinion of everyone, down to the stable boys. What else is there to do in this gilded box of ours other than observe the other pieces?*

I'm sorry, my lady, but I don't know what they say about me.

Well, for one thing, you are turning our court philosopher into an alcoholic.

My face turned red as I stammered, *I... I didn't mean any—*

No need to apologize, child. I find him much improved now. He used to be so self-righteous and tiresome, but now he just dawdles in his garden.

Despite myself, I giggled. She joined in with her metallic laughter.

There now, he relaxes, finally. Your Grand Empress Dowager isn't so frightening after all, is she? She waved a hand and suddenly the eunuch reappeared. *A pipe for our new friend, Shi Li.*

I watched as Shi Li measured and crushed some leaves into a pipe, then sprinkled a silver powder on top, something I'd never seen before. Without asking, he stuck it into my mouth, lit it, and both he and Fu watched me as I inhaled. I didn't dare not to.

I sputtered as an intense hit of smoke coursed its way into my lungs. It tasted of something...sweet on the verge of rot. Peaches, perhaps. It had a heady effect and—I don't know how else to put it—I suddenly became aware of my tongue for the first time.

What else does the Court say about me? The bold question shot out of me like a sneeze.

She nodded encouragingly. *Two things. First, that you are overly ambitious and terrible at hiding it.*

Perhaps, but how terrible? Here I am, having tea with my Grand Empress Dowager. The careless words continued to just tumble out of me.

Fu beamed with pleasure. *Indeed you are, young Dong. Indeed you are. Have you met my grandson?*

The Emperor? No, I am but a lowly clerk. I would have no possibility of meeting him.

She sighed. *My beloved grandson is in trouble. The demands of the Dragon Throne are enormous for a boy of barely twenty years. Your Emperor isn't well, you understand, Dong Xian?*

It was well known throughout the Palace that the Emperor was often sick, though no one seemed to know the cause. But to hear him talked about like a mortal, when he was by definition a god amongst us, was fascinating. I nodded sympathetically. *But as he descends from your esteemed lineage, my lady, I know he will bring glory to the Dynasty of the Han.*

She leaned in again. *He needs a friend. Someone he can trust. Someone I can trust. The Empire is in a fragile period, with usurpers lurking in the shadows. These first few years of his reign are crucial. Treachery and corruption plague the Court like locusts.*

Thinking about the unsavory numbers that I dealt with each day in my clerking duties, I nodded in silent agreement. Then, a shadowy figure emerged in my mind: the unnamed soldier. My face must have shifted because she narrowed her eyes at me and asked, *What are you thinking, child?*

My lips continued to defy my caution by feeding my curiosity. *My lady, has our Emperor recently received a new guest? Perhaps a soldier? Is that what spurs the new rumors around Court?*

Fu arched her brow and I instantly wondered if I should take it back. But then she scoffed and leaned back, her words dripping with disdain. *Heed my advice, child: Focus on the singular advantage that Heaven gave you. You are no politician or strategist, you are a foolish kitten dragging around a dead rat just to show it off. Cease your inept meddling and just do exactly as I say from this moment forward, do you understand?*

I understand, my lady. Her criticisms stung, because they were familiar.

But then, her energy shifted, and her face went soft, her eyes widening as she leaned back toward me. *Liu Xin needs someone who understands the precarious situation we are all in, and who is will-*

ing to do whatever is needed to protect Heaven's Will of the continuation of our Dynasty.

Liu Xin? It occurred to me that this must be the Emperor's birth name. I hadn't even realized that Emperors had names. I was sure I looked dumbstruck about this all, but I managed to reply, *Whatever my Grand Empress Dowager wishes, I will do my best to fulfill it.*

She sat back, looking satisfied. I took another puff of the pipe, watching the shiny powder on top crackle. Whatever was in it, it was like inhaling a caress. As I exhaled blissfully, I suddenly felt strong, rough hands placed on my shoulders. I looked up to see Shi Li standing behind me, though looking straight ahead at Fu.

My mind had become dulled and heavy, as though I were in a memory of a dream. *Your Imperial Majesty, you had said that the Court says two things about me? What of the second?*

The older woman cocked her head to the left. I thought that she was thinking, but it was actually a command. With a deft motion of his hand, Shi Li slipped my robe off my left shoulder, exposing my bare skin underneath. If I was alarmed, I couldn't feel it. I couldn't feel anything except an involuntary heat building inside me.

Shi Li began to slide his hand down, past my shoulder, past my collarbone, over my nipple and down my chest. His touch seemed to reverberate through me, humming against my skin. I looked up at him, his expression still solemn but now softer, then at Fu questioningly. She took a puff, and as the smoke snaked out from between her gleaming teeth, she nodded gently.

Certain attributes. Certain prowess. I had heard about this talent of yours, but I need to confirm whether you are up to the task at hand.

With his other hand, Shi Li pulled down the other side of my robe, exposing my bare chest. Both of his rough hands traveled down my front as I let out a soft gasp by reflex. The room, and the smoke, seemed to swirl around me. I realized that I'd been drugged, or perhaps enchanted.

But a searing lust, spiked with confusion and shame, overcame me as Shi Li's wandering hands wrapped around my influence.

I closed my eyes, as I heard Fu gently murmur, sounding as though she were far, far away...

Besides, I like to watch.

六

RIVER
PRESENT DAY

As Joey and I leave Peril, a hint of dawn ignites the sky. Like the last two leaves on a tree in autumn, we had sat on those bleachers for a long time, watching the raucous throng of shirtless men below. When the crowd was about half-gone, Joey'd tapped me on the shoulder, saying, "Let's get out of here."

Once we are outside the building, we pause in front of the parking area as Joey pulls out a pack of cigarettes and lights one. Somewhere nearby, a car alarm blares. I look around, taking note of our surroundings. On one side of us there are restored warehouse buildings decorated with colorful murals, staple structures of the Arts District that house chic coffee shops and interior-design stores. Directly across the street are rows of tattered tents huddled together, their unhoused occupants probably cursing at the loud swarm of fucked-up men disturbing their sleep.

DTLA is a gilded place: between its pockets of manicured yuppie bubbles there are still large swaths of poverty, drug use and crime in its historic Skid Row. It was a scary place to us when we were kids, and that was why my mom used to threaten my sister and me when we were misbehaving that she would send us "to Downtown, where the bad people are."

As I look at this mysterious man named Joey, the glistening skyscrapers towering behind him, I wonder if we are those bad people now.

He offers the cigs to me, and I shake my head. I'm shivering, as my tank top is still soaked through with my sweat. Joey takes the black hoodie he was holding and wraps it around me. "Thanks," I say. "For everything."

"How are you going to get home?" He has a way of talking that is hard to read.

I turn to him, genuinely curious. "So what's your deal anyway? You wander around circuit parties by yourself, rescuing messy people?"

He smiles, and I could fall into his dimples. Then he replies, "Who said I was alone?"

That catches me off guard. "Oh! I see…"

"River! I've been searching all night for you!"

Joey and I both turn to see Calvin jogging toward us, still shirtless and inexplicably wrapped in several feet of twinkling fairy lights. He pants as he gets to us, untangling himself.

"Oh, sorry, Calvin. I was looking for you, too," I say, but already I see Calvin shifting his focus to Joey, who looks a bit amused by my awkwardness.

Calvin gives Joey a look down, then winks at me. "Apparently not very hard. Don't blame you." Then he takes a closer look at Joey, as if recognizing him. "Hey, aren't you…? Sorry, you look very familiar. You're not on OnlyFans, are you?"

I know it is just harmless flirting, but I am keenly aware that Calvin is better looking than me, and I suddenly wish he hadn't found us. "Calvin, this is Joey."

Joey nods at Calvin. "Are you two friends?"

Calvin theatrically puts his arm around my shoulder, smiling devilishly at Joey. "We are boyfriends. But we play together."

I am about to correct Calvin but I stop myself when I think I see a flash of jealousy in Joey's eyes. His tell is that his cheeks turn rosy peach, and rosy peach is now my new favorite color. I bite my lip and say nothing.

Joey throws his cigarette to the ground, stamping it out. "I'm supposed to go to the afterparty..." he says, sounding uneasy.

Calvin lights up like a firework. "A homepa?" he exclaims, "I love me a homepa. Is it the one in the Hills?"

Joey nods. "My friend Winston is hosting it... Do you two want to come?"

Calvin gives me a c'mon look. I have a long list of questions in my head, but before I even think about everything, I hear the words slip out of my mouth.

"Let's go."

Calvin is already calling a car.

Once we are in our Lyft, Joey sits shotgun while Calvin and I sit in the back. Calvin asks the driver to turn up the radio and then leans over to me. "So how did you meet this hottie anyway?" he whispers so coarsely that I worry that Joey will hear.

In front of us, Joey seems to be sleeping. He's definitely the quiet type. I speak softly into Calvin's ear. "I wasn't feeling well, and he took care of me."

Calvin cocks an eyebrow. "And they say chivalry is dead. Well, if I've clocked him right, your knight in shining tank top is somewhat famous."

"What do you mean?"

Calvin checks to see that Joey was still sleeping before continuing. "I'll let you find out for yourself. You at least know who Winston Chow is? We're about to go to his house."

"Winston Chow...? You mean the tech billionaire?"

"Yes, that Winston Chow. Every year he hosts the exclusive

AF afterparty for Peril, and it is impossible to get invited. For most people." Calvin pulls rock star aviator sunglasses out of his pocket and puts them on as he chuckles. "Damn, River, did you expect your night to go like this?"

We are driving up Laurel Canyon, entering the hills of Hollywood. The old roads up here are twisty and treacherous, but that doesn't concern the Teslas and Audis that zip up and through them, teeter-tottering near bare cliffs. The houses are architectural candy, nestled between heritage trees. If Los Angeles were a club, the Hollywood Hills would be the champagne room, on a VIP balcony overlooking the mega sprawl below.

I turn around as the early morning spills across the city like a toppled glass of orange juice. "It's not night anymore, Calvin."

The car makes a sudden sharp left turn and we drive down a private lane that is framed by dense foliage, with whimsical red lanterns hung overhead, swaying as we pass under. Joey stirs awake and looks back at Calvin and me. I smile and he nods back, not unfriendly. He takes a small remote out of his pocket and clicks it. In front of us, a wood and cast-iron gate overgrown with climbing roses opens, and instantly I hear the invitingly thumpy beat of a dance party.

The driver parks and we hop out of the car. Calvin and I follow Joey as we enter the compound, which looks like an old Hollywood manor out of a black-and-white film—except that there are yellow laser lights shooting out of all its windows, like it's being abducted by aliens.

Standing at the front door as bouncers are two absolutely breathtaking Asian women wearing ornate qipao, one holding a clipboard and the other a gold tray of what look like clear plastic bags. As we approach, they wave at Joey cheerily.

"Look who it is, the wandering boyfriend. Daddy was wondering where you'd been, Joey baby," teases the one on the right in a crimson red qipao decorated with roses. Roses has a deep voice and as I approach, I realize both of them are drag queens. She pokes Joey on his chest playfully with her pen and then looks at Calvin and me. "Welcome to after-Peril, puppies!" she purrs as she motions to her companion's golden tray.

I take a closer look at the tray and discover that each plastic bag is full of colorful pills and powders, a kaleidoscope of bad choices. I'm about to shake my head, but Calvin quickly takes two and stuffs one in my pocket. He's pretty sharp, this Calvin.

Joey looks at me. *Ready?*

Calvin laughs, "Hey, I'm Korean. English only."

From inside the manor, I feel an energy radiate. I nod at Joey. He pushes open the door.

We are greeted by a heady throb of loud electronic music and body heat. My eyes adjust to the dimness inside, and the first thing I see is a massive black crystal chandelier directly in front of me. The chandelier has apparently crashed down onto the marble floor of the foyer and shattered into smithereens. I look up, and sure enough its severed wires slowly swing back and forth from the high ceiling, propelled by an occasional bright spark of electricity that zaps out of the frayed ends. The pulsating song that is blasting through unseen speakers is a brooding track of whiny guitar riffs and mesmeric drum beats.

The palatial interior of the mansion is a mix of contemporary Asian and Western motifs, but with an overall palette of a luxuriously dark blood red. There are about fifty intimidatingly attractive men in the foyer, socializing around the broken chandelier. I seriously wonder if its downfall was intentional because no one seems to be concerned.

Kicking away stray fragments of crystal with his shoe, Joey leads the way deeper into the manor as we follow him. Nearly everyone at least acknowledges him as he passes. As we enter a gargantuan kitchen of sleek steel with a massive window that overlooks all of the Hills, Joey stops next to a cute boy, maybe Filipino, who is bartending for the other partiers.

"Where is he?" Joey asks the bartender.

The bartender looks us over as he responds, "Where do you think? Daddy's always upstairs." He motions to the booze in front of him and grins. "Want anything?"

Calvin slides in, already thumbing through his goodie bag of complimentary drugs. "Hey, handsome, I'll have two vodka sugar-free Red Bulls if you got it." He pops a baby blue pill into his mouth.

Joey leans over to me. "Are you feeling better? Do you mind waiting down here?"

"Yeah, do your thing, don't worry about me." I do feel better, though I don't want him to go. I suddenly have a strange foreboding feeling about this.

Calvin points out the window to the backyard, where there is a massive infinity pool that seems to pivot into the sky. "How deep is your pool, Joey?"

Joey laughs. "It's like the ocean." He gives me a small wave and leaves us.

Calvin is already pulling me outside, where the sun's beams set us aglow as it finally breaks the horizon. It's a new day. The pool area in the back is where the real action is; it's packed with beautiful men of various shades of bronze, all of them wearing Speedos that seem locked in a fierce competition to see which is skimpiest.

We find seats that face the rising sun. Calvin hands me one of the drinks and I take an absent-minded sip. I try to see if my phone will turn on. It does, though the battery is blinking low. As it finds reception, a torrent of real life floods onto the screen. Emails from my professors, notifications from TikTok, breaking news from the *LA Times* and…more texts and missed calls from Garden.

I read through them, hearing her voice as she goes from worry to anger back to worry. The last text she is threatening to call Mom. It was sent an hour ago.

I stand up abruptly, which cuts off Calvin, who had been leisurely chatting away. I must look concerned because his face falls. "What's wrong?"

I look around the seat for anything that I might've dropped. "I gotta go... I have stuff at home I need to handle."

"Are you kidding me? You can't leave now! This is the legendary—"

I snap. "I don't care what this is! This isn't my life. These aren't my people. This is... This is just a hookup that has gone on too long." Calvin blanches instantly. Several people turn to look our way at my outburst.

Calvin's usual veneer of bravado melts away as he takes off his sunglasses, his eyes genuinely sad. "Hey... Don't be like that. I really like you, River."

I feel terrible in this moment, and the only way to solve it is to leave as fast as possible. "You shouldn't like me, Calvin. I'm a dead end."

Without looking back at him, I walk back into the mansion. "Bad vibes, sis!" I hear someone hiss at me.

I'm frantically walking toward the front foyer, wringing my hands. It's been years since I've had a panic attack and I feel one building inside me. Breathe, River, breathe! Then I feel something on my wrist.

Joey's bracelet. I look down at it as my panic dissolves, as I roll its pointy central stone between my fingers. He had given it to me at Peril. *Wear it for now,* he'd said.

I stop and look to my right, considering the stairs leading to the second floor, where Joey had gone.

I can't leave without giving this back. Clearly, it means a lot to him.

The stairs lead up to darkness, though I hear muffled sounds from above. Once again, I have a distinct feeling of something looming and ominous. But I shake it off.

Holding the bracelet in my hands, I slowly walk up the steps.

七

HE SHICAN
1740

The rhythmic beat of a funeral drum throbs in my head.

I find myself not in a room, but in a dark space, a formless vacuum except for the clouds of smoke that dance around me, pulsating to the beat.

An endless place.

Someone cackles. I turn to my right to see a massive pair of disembodied lips framing silver teeth, hovering in the air. The lips curl upward into a gleeful snarl as the gleaming teeth part to emit another rumble of menacing laughter.

A rough hand appears out of nowhere from behind me, reaching over my shoulder to slide its way down my chest like a slinky snake, the scratchy sensations sending shivers up my spine.

I am roughly flipped around and there is a man lying on his back in front of me, his muscular legs splayed open, his face obscured in shadow.

And where his manhood should be is instead a glinting mirror, reflecting back at me the image of a scared young man who looks exactly like me.

But I know he is not me.

A searing lust is coursing its way into my groin. Without thinking, I thrust myself into the invitation between his sculpted thighs, ready to claim him, ready to fill him with my influence.

But instead, the ground beneath me gives way, and I plunge headfirst into a void of brilliantly bright light. Screaming, I fall into the blinding chasm, surely plunging to my death.

But when I do land, I land upright on my feet, unharmed.

I am now in an arena full of the carcasses of magnificent dead beasts, hundreds of them, their eyes glassy and lifeless.

I stand still, too afraid to move. I stand there for what seems an eternity.

Then, all at once, their eyes suddenly animate to life, their heads turning to stare at something behind me.

I turn to look as well. Behind me stands a tall and powerfully built being, backlit into black, with a massive sword slung over his shoulder.

Before I can react, the being grabs me by the throat and lifts me high up above him as I helplessly kick the air, struggling in vain against his power.

With a brutally possessive grip, his hand tightens around my neck—tighter and tighter as I choke for air. But the more

he squeezes, the more I am consumed by a shameful but overwhelming desire.

As the beats of the funeral drum intensify with my lust, I feel
myself starting to arrive, a faltering dam no longer capable of
restraining its turbulent river.

Right as I burst apart, I hear his words:

The truth is…you belong to me.

With a jolt, I woke up from a familiar dream that was all
smoke and carnage. Blinking away unsettling images of animal carcasses and gnashing teeth, I wondered why I was shivering all over.

Then I realized I was naked, and that I was outside. I was
half buried in a heap of fallen leaves, surrounded by trees. It was
early morning, the sun not yet risen, and I could hear my old
rooster crowing in the distance.

I stood up, looking around me, noting that I was still painfully erect with morning virility, even though my still-warm
seed had spilled all over my thigh.

At first, I thought I was alone, then I heard a twig snap.

I looked down and saw a wild hare chewing methodically on
a leaf, staring up at me with somewhat judgmental eyes. I must
have sleepwalked into the woods the night before, I realized. I
could not help but feel disappointed with myself. It had been a
long time since this had happened.

I gathered a bundle of shrubbery to shield what was left of
my dignity, and began gingerly walking in the direction of my
rooster's calls, the moist mud caking onto my feet.

Fortunately, neither Jiulang nor his grandmother was outside
when I reached my inn, though Dama did shake her mane at
me from her trough, acknowledging my strange predicament. I
slipped into my bedroom on the ground floor from a side door,

and washed off the dirt of my night-walking episode. From my guests' room upstairs, I heard no sign of movement, and was grateful they were still asleep.

Later, I crept to their door, creaking it open to check on them for breakfast. To my surprise neither of them was there. At first, I had a sinking feeling that they had gone for good, but then I noticed their few belongings were still sitting on the floor.

I saw that there was a note left on the table in the room. I picked it up to read it, though some of the characters were strangely written and hard to decipher.

Master He,
I have taken my grandmother on a morning stroll as the early air is good for her.
We will be back by noon. Thank you again for your hospitality.
Your humble servant,
Huang Jiulang

Satisfied with this, I grabbed my cloak and mounted my horse to set off for Tiaoxi, where Dr. Qi Yewang resided. If there was any apprehension about seeing him, it was clouded by my re-invigorated eagerness to greet Jiulang with good news when he and his grandmother returned.

Tiaoxi was about an hour's ride from my inn in the country-side, and usually I made the trip only to pick up occasional sup-plies. But today there was a spring in my step, and even my old horse seemed to trot with intention. The strange winds of yes-terday had vanished, replaced by the tranquil fragrance of ap-proaching spring.

I held my face up to the sun, feeling its warmth upon my face and feeling, for the first time in a long time, happy.

However, at the edge of my mind, that smoky dream lin-gered. It was a dream I had dreamed before, yet as with the nature of most dreams, its fine details had largely dissipated from my memory upon waking. I strained to remember.

There was a man in it who was missing a part of his body... a limb, perhaps?

Dama snorted and tossed her indigo mane, as if scolding me for daydreaming. Obediently, I tried to clear it from my mind, but my mind so rarely did as I told it to, and it suddenly occurred to me that the last time I had this dream was also the last time I had sleepwalked into the woods, however long ago.

And when had this last sleepwalking episode occurred? It was hard to say, since my solitary days tended to blur together anyway. Then it suddenly struck me that I had not sleepwalked since I had last seen Dr. Qi. The revelation startled me, and added to the anxiety I already had about seeing him. Perhaps even the thought of him had triggered an episode last night?

As my horse and I approached Tiaoxi, I came across more and more people, some of whom I knew. I nodded at those acquaintances in greeting. I was not sure if it was just in my imagination, but I got a few looks of surprise in return from them. I had not returned to the city in a while, I realized.

Tiaoxi was a bustling trading port, named after the generous river that forks through it. Though it started as a humble fishing village in ancient times, about a century ago it was stricken with a disease that threatened to spread to the surrounding states. To tackle this problem, doctor and shaman alike from all over the Middle Kingdom were sent to Tiaoxi to study and conquer the illness, which they were able to do after much strife and loss of life.

Though that illness had been long since defeated, the medical tradition and the legacy of those healers continued in Tiaoxi, which became renowned for its community of physicians and practitioners who were sought after even by royalty. Dr. Qi was perhaps the most celebrated of them.

His clinic was situated in the city center along a calmer portion of the river where all the fishmongers hawked their catches out of their boats. Upon arriving and dismounting Dama, I pushed our way through the crowd of people haggling over plump fish and crabs, retracing the steps with ease.

When I reached his door, I stopped and looked up at the old wooden building that he had converted into his clinic. It had been more than a year since I had set foot inside. I took a deep breath and knocked, but the door had been ajar and popped open instantly. I took a step inside.

He was sitting at his desk, his back to the door, when he heard me enter. *Just a moment,* he said, his head bent deep to his documents. He always had bad eyesight, and would read as though his nose were feeling for the words.

Dear Dr. Qi. It has been a long time, I said, wanting to break my tension.

Upon hearing my voice, he sat straight up and paused for a few seconds. Then he set down his papers, stood and turned around. We stared at each other face-to-face, taking one another in.

He Shican, he finally said.

I smiled. *You look well, Qi Yewang.*

Dr. Qi Yewang walked toward me and we clasped hands. He had aged more than I expected in the past years, and he had gained a little weight that was not altogether unpleasant on him, but he still had the same kind and intelligent face. He motioned to his table and we sat down. A servant came in to pour us both tea.

My eyes wandered over to the back of his clinic, where his magnificent apothecary cabinet stood against the wall. It was an impressively large chest of hundreds of intricately labeled drawers, each the size of the palm of a hand, that went all the way up to the ceiling.

A sliding ladder stood in front of it. Yewang had been building it, I remembered, when I first met him, wandering into his clinic by chance. I had a sudden flashback of lazy afternoons where I lounged on that sturdy ladder, opening random drawers and hearing Yewang's gentle explanation of the rare pharmaceuticals nestled inside each of them. *Petrified caterpillar. Dragon dung. Pregnant seahorse—male. Vine of the Thunder God. Human fingernail preserved in arsenic.*

He must have noticed me staring at it, because he turned and looked at it, too, perhaps sharing the same memory. He turned to me and we were quiet again.

I never expected you to come back in here again, Yewang said finally.

And why not? I replied, looking down at my tea. *We have no quarrel. I hope my continued fondness for you is reciprocated, Yewang.*

Yewang did not reply at first. He cocked his head at me, as if studying me. Finally, he took my hand back into his. *Does this mean you have returned to me at last, Shican?*

Blanching a bit, I shifted uncomfortably and he noted this. He quickly withdrew his hand. *Dear Yewang, I come to you today for your services as a doctor. And as an old friend.*

Yewang processed this. *An old friend. I see.* He said it politely, though I could see a flash of pain in his eyes.

I felt a sudden wave of regret disturbing him like this, but staying determined, I pushed on. *I have a friend who is in need of a specific medicine, and obviously you are the most qualified person to consult for this.*

He nodded. *Well surely, I will help as much as I can. What is this medicine called?*

I was relieved to see that he was handling this professionally. *It has a strange name, and I had never heard of it before yesterday. It is called the Primordial Bolus. Do you know of it?*

Yewang had been raising his teacup to drink from it, but upon hearing the name, he paused midway. *Sorry, can you repeat that?*

I said the name again, intrigued by his reaction.

Primordial Bolus, Yewang said, in a rather mystified tone. *Pri-*

mordial Bolus. I could see the mind turning behind his clever eyes. *And who asked you for such a medicine?*

A new friend, I said, hoping it sounded casual. I had wanted to avoid this topic. But already he was scrutinizing me closely.

Shican... he replied with a concerned tone. *How are you feeling? You look a bit strange in the eyes.*

I laughed good-naturedly. *I have missed your impromptu examinations of me, but please rest assured, Dr. Qi, that I am more than fine. It is my friend who needs your help. So what is this Primordial Bolus? Do you have it?*

Yewang stood up and I expected him to walk to his apothecary cabinet, but instead he walked over to his library on the other side of the room. His library was comprised of row upon row of texts, from ancient wooden tablets to crisply bound journals, on old shelves that seemed to buckle under this collective weight of knowledge. And while it may not have been as dramatic as his medicine cabinet, I knew that the pharmaceutical wisdoms inscribed on those pages were just as invaluable.

The doctor perused the titles, until he pulled out a tattered book, its binding unraveled and frayed. He blew on it and dust filled the air. He walked back over and placed it in front of me.

I leaned in and read the title. Recognizing the book but incredulous, I thumbed through the weathered pages before I finally looked up at him in confused amusement.

Yewang, I must congratulate you because you have finally managed to surprise me. Why, this is a book of children's fairy tales! I mused, laughing at his joke.

But Yewang was dead serious. He picked up the book and flipped through it until he found a passage. He tilted it up toward my face, his finger underlining the unmistakable characters.

I read them aloud: *Primordial Bolus.*

Placing it down on the table in front of me, Yewang sat back down, folding his arms. He looked troubled but did not say anything.

But why would the medicine be in a book of fairy tales? I pondered, confused.

He Shican, he said, his face angered, *let us speak plainly for once. You have brought inauspicious tidings today.*

Leaning down, the doctor carefully turned a single leaf of the book, revealing a full-page illustration of a fantastical creature with nine tails. Even at a glance, it was unmistakable what it was.

Dr. Qi then took my chin in his hands and once again examined my eyes, while his own widened in alarm. Finally, he released me.

When he spoke, his voice was choked with fear. *You must tell me right now, Shican! Where is the fox spirit?*

DONG XIAN
4 BCE

After my visit with the Grand Empress Dowager Fu, I didn't know what to expect. That evening, as I deliriously stumbled back to my chambers, I wondered if I'd soon be whisked away to the private residence of the Emperor. But actually, nothing changed. The first month passed, then another. Where was he?

Over the following weeks, my life folded back into its humdrum routine. Several acquaintances did delicately ask me about Shi Li's ominous summoning at the Imperial Offices—my colleagues had all been talking about that incident for a few days—but I just repeated what Fu had told me to say: *The kind and benevolent Grand Empress Dowager wants to honor my father for a lifetime of service, and asked me what sort of fruit we should serve at the ceremony.*

What sort of fruit? It was a flippant lie and I felt silly each time I said it. It was clearly meant to be facetious, though why I couldn't figure out. Fu's level of deception made mine look like a child's game.

But without anything concrete, such as my severed head on a

platter, the hubbub about me soon died down, replaced by the latest chatter about Lord Song's alleged penchant for lying with his many daughters-in-law. I must admit, I hadn't minded the extra bit of attention.

As the door of opportunity slid shut, my circumstances grew more and more dire. I could no longer concentrate on my tasks in the Imperial Offices. I lost my appetite and stopped sleeping. I spent much of my time stewing in my chambers, complaining to Miaomi. As I starved, the blue palace cat had grown fat from my untouched leftovers, but she was a good listener as payment and patiently heard me out, as long as I kept rubbing her belly.

What if I hadn't performed to Fu's satisfaction? The memory of that visit was as smoky as the room we were in, but I could recall flashes of fervor, as I had mounted the surprisingly submissive Shi Li in front of the Grand Empress Dowager, who observed us like we were prized horses. The sight of naked Shi Li was both impressive and grotesque, as his otherwise powerfully muscular physique was only marred by his sad castration. I had averted my eyes to avoid looking at the mutilation, though I caught fleeting glances—particularly when he had been on his back.

Then I wondered if I wasn't the only candidate in the running. What if that dastardly Fu was auditioning half the Court? Who else might her eunuch have bent over for? This new suspicion made me fume. Like a boulder up a hill, I rolled the event over and over in my head, obsessing about what I'd said, what I hadn't said, what I'd done, what I hadn't done. Every detail I remembered took its own turn crushing me.

And yes, I did also wonder if instead of being discarded, I had been spared by benevolent fortune… Spared from a life where death might lurk around every palatial corner, where the riches would only be exceeded by treachery. I knew that desiring to be closer to the Emperor was gambling my fate on Heaven's chessboard. Proximity to the Dragon Throne often shortened lifespans. And if an Emperor fell, so, too, would his entire inner circle, even if by their own hands.

But my ambition was deaf to my fears, and I freely obsessed over finding another chance to prove myself. I might have been foolish about many things, but I was not foolish about myself. I knew my gifts were of the physical nature, in my appearance and my sexual talents. My best abilities had been put to the ultimate test, and if I did not pass, I had only myself to blame. I could not bring myself to accept the potentially devastating truth: Could it be possible that I had finally come so close to glory, stroking the edge of the sun, and then…fell short somehow?

Because up until then, I had fallen short my whole life.

Growing up in my hometown of Yunyang, I was like a forgotten valley between two majestic older brothers. They say it is better to be the first son of a humble man than to be the second son of a rich man, and here I was, the tardy and overlooked third.

First Son was a rising politician in our state, painstakingly groomed by our father since birth. Second Son was an enterprising merchant who often sailed to distant lands. And what of me? I once overheard my father grumble that by the time it came to me, he had run out of ink.

As soon as I began to utter words as a child, a hush would fall over the room whenever I attempted to speak. It was clear from an early age that I had a severe stutter. I didn't as much talk as I did expel halting bursts of noise, as though unseen hands were strangling me.

At first, I didn't realize that there was anything so wrong with it, because it was all I had known. But at some point, maybe when I was around six or seven, I realized that whenever I did release my broken speech and my father was present, I would be quickly ushered midsentence out of his sight. Though even that would put it generously, because it was around then that I also realized he never looked directly at me; I was never even within his line of sight.

He spent his every free moment with my two older brothers, who themselves seemed unapproachable and ancient to me as they were a decade older. I knew that I was not the same as them, and I was ashamed.

No one ever did figure out why I had this initial tribulation in my life, and if someone asked my mother, she would have shrugged in relief and said that I simply grew out of it by the time I was a teenager. I suppose to the uninterested bystanders, my stutter seemed to just gradually fade away. No one knew that the moment I could read I essentially stopped sleeping, and began instead a years-long nightly exercise that doubled as contrition.

My family, the Dong Clan, were not literary nor philosophical, and our elders were praised instead for their political shrewdness. We were not from scandalous nor adventurous people, at least not openly. Instead, my father prided himself on his acumen and relative proximity to power. From afar, he seemed to me a gregarious and nimbly witted man, qualities that did not come naturally to me. My early inability to express myself rendered me useless to this stranger.

People whispered about me, whispers that were louder and clearer than I could ever hope to be. Unexplained afflictions in privileged sons like me could predict bad omens for a clan. I found out later that my mother even consulted with sorcerers in hopes to seek a remedy. As for me, I did not wait for magics. I knew that this was my burden to correct on my own, and I was going to stamp it out with sheer determination.

In my childhood home, there was a spare study that no one ever really entered, except whenever it was converted into a bedroom for the occasional unexpected guest. It had an unappealing view, looking out onto the wall of an untended patch of our garden. But this study actually housed a rare artifact of scholarly prominence, which had been a betrothal gift from my mother's clan to my father as part of her dowry.

The gift was a decorative collection of poetry tablets, placed in this spare study and forgotten by my father. Three hundred and five classic odes were etched onto these many tablets, some of them dating back more than a thousand years, anthologized by Confucius himself.

As soon as I was skilled enough in reading, I would go to this little study each night, and I would read these ancient poems aloud to myself. I would read until I stammered on a character, and then I would repeat that word until I said it correctly, then start the ode over again. I repeated this simple process for nearly four years. I read and reread these tablets so many times that to this day I still have their poems all memorized in the correct order.

That is how I lost my stutter: not by magics but by methodical labor. But it wasn't all gloom. Despite the mental strain of the exercise, the poems themselves were often dreamy and romantic, the amorous verses of separated lovers bemoaning the distance between them.

> *Those who know me*
> *Say I have a sad heart,*
> *Those who do not know me,*
> *Say I am missing something.*
> *O endlessly blue Heaven:*
> *Who is this missing person?*

Raised by the yearning splendor of these old love songs, I was only further motivated to expel my shortcomings and find a way for myself into the world beyond my small province. Maybe, I thought, if I defeat my impediment I, too, can create a life that is epic enough to be immortalized as great poetry.

After four years of reciting these poems, my stutter left me without a trace. But I never told anyone about those long years of my poetic immolation. It felt better to pretend I just outgrew it, because...it was a lot of effort for something that shouldn't have been wrong in the first place. Better to just not call attention to it, I figured.

The cruel irony is that in all that time I spent practicing how to speak to him properly, my father had spent it forgetting I ever existed. By the age the hair began to grow on my face, he had risen in prominence in the Emperor's court and spent most of his time there. I was not a priority on his returns home, where he spent his time conjugating with his cronies, hosting diplomatic banquets and visiting my mother's chambers. The closest interaction we ever had was when I refilled his cup at dinner. Once in a while I'd get a pat on the shoulder as I helped him mount his horse to return to the Endless Palace, but not much else.

The Endless Palace! Each time I watched my father and his caravan disappear over the horizon, I would think of this faraway Palace and long to be there as well. But without the favor of my father, I had a better chance of growing wings and flying there. Without his endorsement, I was not meant for greatness.

I promised myself that if the door of opportunity presented itself again, I would be like a battering ram.

When I was seventeen, that door appeared. My father sent word to us that he would be accompanied by a guest of the utmost honor who would be staying at our home for one night. Our entire household began to plan for the arrival of the Prefect Grand Astrologer, adviser to the Emperor on metaphysical affairs of state.

But even more intriguing was his other duty, which my mother pointedly mentioned to me when we first received the news: The Astrologer was the proctor of an infamously difficult examination. Any man, privileged or common, who hoped to serve in the Endless Palace, could ask to take this test. A perfect score guaranteed entry to the Court as a clerk. And this test was a literacy test!

Heaven was finally heeding me. I had spent the end of my childhood locked in a library memorizing classic poetry for this very reason. If I could not win my father's favor, I would enter the Endless Palace by my own merits, and all the more better so. I furiously practiced my calligraphy for the next weeks. By the time I heard the shouts from our servants announcing my father's return, my hands were knotted with calluses.

That evening I nervously followed my mother into our banquet hall, readying myself to meet the man who might change the trajectory of my life. My plan was to take advantage of my proximity to the Prefect Grand Astrologer at dinner and petition him to let me take the test. I knew my father would likely be angry, but if I managed to charm the Astrologer, perhaps they would humor me.

But upon entering the hall, I was aghast to see that my two elder brothers had traveled home unannounced to surprise my father and our guest of honor. I watched from my mother's side as the visitor lauded praise over my father's accomplished sons. I was exiled to a table with young cousins far away from them.

The only acknowledgment I received was much later in the evening, when my father, red with mirth and drink, summoned me over to refill his cup.

As I approached the table my brothers, my father and the special guest were in the middle of an animated conversation. As I poured the yellow wine, the visitor, who was sitting next to my father, suddenly touched my hand. I flinched when I saw he was examining my calluses. He turned to look at me. He was a short man with long, wispy white eyebrows, perhaps in his sixties. He had a kind face with shrewd eyes, and I was surprised his robes were so simple.

Is this that other son of yours, Dong Gong? the man asked. *He certainly takes after his mother, doesn't he?*

Come now, Old Yang, just let the boy refill your glass, my father yawned as he gestured at me.

This was my chance to speak, though I wished I hadn't been holding a jug of wine like a servant. *Y-your Grace, you honor us by visiting our home. Yes, I am my esteemed father's third son, Dong Xian.* I could feel my father staring at me, a very odd sensation indeed. *Your Grace, I hope to request that you proctor the Literacy Test for me so that I might attempt to qualify as a clerk in the Endless Palace.*

Instantly, the air changed and I could feel something had gone wrong. My father palmed his forehead uncomfortably while my older brothers tried not to laugh. Old Yang looked regretful. *I am pleased to meet you, Dong Xian, but I must apologize because I am not who you think I am.*

My father looked like he was going to flay me after dinner. He laughed loudly. *Forgive my third son, Old Yang. He is acting stupidly on old information.*

Second Son chimed in. *Dong Xian, this is the honorable Yang Xiong, the Emperor's philosopher.*

First Son guffawed, his voice thick with wine. *Don't look so disappointed about it!*

I ran off before my father could think to strike me. But when I sat back down, I could see that from across the room, the philosopher Yang Xiong was still looking at me strangely. I was innocent back then, but there was something about the way he was looking at me that I instinctually understood.

I had until morning to test it.

That night I mustered up all my courage and slipped out of my chambers. I tiptoed through the quiet dark of our grounds toward the guest quarters. I could see that the Emperor's philosopher was still awake; his shadow was projected and magnified against the screen doors as he sat reading in his room. I held a bowl of peaches as I tapped gently at his door.

Come in, he answered.

My head bowed, I entered. *Sir, my mother sends this fruit from her garden, along with her regards for a restful night with us.* I placed the bowl on the table in the room. Once again, I felt his eyes on me. I was nervous, but held myself steady. I looked up, expecting to meet him in eye contact, but instead he was looking at my hands yet again.

Now I understand, Yang Xiong said, *why a son of Dong Gong would have hands in this condition. Your dedication to take the Literacy Test is admirable, as is your desire to serve in the Endless Palace. But despite its size and splendor, the Endless Palace is actually a labyrinthine prison, with endless traps around every corner. Dong Xian, why is this a life you want?*

Please, sir, I replied, *I wish to achieve greatness for the Han.*

Yang Xiong raised his brow. *Greatness? That is a lofty goal for a third son. In all the years I have known him, I had never heard your father speak of you until this trip.*

Hearing my shameful truth from an outside observer floored me.

The old philosopher sighed and laid a gentle hand on my shoulder with a paternal kindness that I had never before received. *Despair not. History is carved by men who did not have their fathers' favor.*

With that I kneeled in front of him. *Then you understand, sir, why I so desperately entreated you when I thought you might be the Prefect Grand Astrologer. The Imperial Literacy Test is the only option I have.*

The philosopher looked down at me, his face inscrutable. Finally, he replied. *I think you will get what you want, Dong Xian, but it will not be because of that test*, he said.

Without thinking, I reached out to part his robes at his waist.

The man leaped backward away from me. *What are you doing?* Yang Xiong cried, clearly stunned. I could only stammer incoherently in response as I leaped up to run out of his room. I had woefully misread the situation, and my idiocy would surely ruin me.

Wait! he called as I was bolting for the exit. I stopped and turned back to him. He had that strange look on his face again, the one I had misread. *Curiouser and curiouser, indeed. Sit down, young man, and share a peach with me.*

Cautiously, I sat down at the table in the room. Old Yang grabbed one of the peaches and tore it in half, handing me the side with the pit. I held it helplessly in my hands. Both ashamed and defeated, I cursed the stinging tears brimming onto my cheeks. *I am sorry, sir. I insult you with my dishonor.*

The philosopher sighed. *You forget that I said you would get what you want*, he replied. *I do not need a test to recommend someone to the Court, especially the son of a respected senior administrator. I will speak to your father tomorrow before I leave, but I am sure he will be agreeable as well.*

I was shocked. *Why would you recommend me, sir, when I've made such a fool of myself?*

He smiled unexpectedly for the first time. *Because I believe that those who dare to desire greatness should be mentored, lest they lead themselves astray.*

Hardly daring to believe my good fortune, I wisely kept quiet for once. *I am eternally grateful, Teacher*, was all I said as I bowed my head to him.

The philosopher was silent for a moment, but then nodded at me. *Do not so easily express gratitude when you have no idea what fates await you, Dong Xian. You seek greatness, but you know not the exquisite perils of when greatness decides to seek you.* With that, he took a sumptuous bite of his peach.

The next day, as he promised, Yang Xiong spoke to my father. Within a month, I packed up my life in Yunyang to make the long journey to the Endless Palace.

I was deep in these memories when Miaomi startled me by purring against my hand. We were both sprawled under the late-afternoon sunlight on my mat in my chambers, and the cat was wondering why I had stopped stroking her. But my one-sided conversation with her had given me insight. If there was anyone who might steer me back toward the Emperor, it was my original benefactor Yang Xiong. I would inform him what had occurred with the Grand Empress Dowager Fu and ask his counsel.

That evening I located Old Yang's attendant to ask if his master would grant me an audience in our usual meeting place. I was heartened when I quickly received an affirmative reply. At least in the philosopher, I still had a friend.

The following day I could barely concentrate as I rushed through my numbers, nearly swiping the stones off my abacus. The moment the afternoon drums tolled, I hopped up from my desk and sprinted to the philosopher's garden. I sat down under the shade of a tree and set up our usual setting of yellow wine, which I had plucked from the kitchens that morning, courtesy of one of the kitchen boys.

Finally, I heard behind me the familiar footsteps of Yang Xiong, the steady walk and deep, labored breaths, and grinned to myself as I filled up his cup. *It's been so long since I've had the pleasure of my teacher's company, I was beginning to wonder if he had abandoned me.*

But when the person sat down across from me, I realized it wasn't Old Yang. It was a tall young man, about my age, with amber eyes. And even though I had never met him, I instantly knew who he was. One knows when one meets a god.

He was the Emperor.

九

RIVER
PRESENT DAY

I kept my eyes open when I prayed.

When I was little, my mom always made sure our family arrived early to Sunday service so that we could sit at the front of the congregation. Dressed in our crisp finest, we were the model minority Christians of our mostly white church in the Pacific Palisades of Los Angeles, piously listening to Pastor Grayson's sermon.

My sister, Garden, hated our VIP seats. "So creepy," she'd always say as we approached the pulpit. She was referring to the life-size replica of the Christ on the cross at center stage, his face seemingly convulsed in eternal pain as he stared accusingly toward the video projector nailed into the ceiling high above.

But I saw something else when I looked at that statue. I didn't see pain and anguish. I didn't see glory and redemption, either. I spent so much of my childhood staring at it, trying to figure out what it was. You could see it in every vein on his face, in the clench of his jaw, unfurling along his arched body.

What was it? Always wondering, I never paid close attention to Pastor Grayson's sermons, only mindlessly mouthed the hymns, held my Bible open without reading it.

And I kept my eyes open when I prayed.

I didn't figure out what it was until many years later, when I was a senior in high school. My dad was in the late stages of his cancer, and my mom was spending a lot of time at church. I had dropped her off on a Tuesday evening in my old Acura when I realized she'd left her cell phone in the cup holder. I went into the chapel looking for her. Not seeing anyone except my old friend the Jesus statue, I wandered toward the church offices.

I heard them before I saw them. The receptionist wasn't there, and Pastor Grayson's door was slightly ajar, and through the crack I watched as he and my mom passionately kissed. I'd never seen her like that before, as though her blood had erupted into fire, as though she were finally alive. I backed away quietly.

Without saying anything, I placed her cell phone on the receptionist's desk and walked back into the chapel.

In there, I walked right up to the pulpit and stood face-to-face with that statue. I looked him in the eye, and in that moment we were one and the same. It was then when I finally realized what it was that this Son of God was feeling. Not pain, not anger, not the glory of salvation. No, this was actually a moment of explosive catharsis, an outpouring of hot truth so dangerously orgasmic that they had to nail the fucker to a cross lest he fall into the sun.

This true feeling is more than just nervy sensations of the body—it marks a cataclysmic revelation from which there is no turning back. But what is the revelation?

Hastily, I stepped backward away from the statue, nearly stumbling down the steps of the pulpit as I turned and bolted out of the church. I got into my car and drove east, out of our neighborhood, out of LA, speeding down the 210, until I ran out of gas at the base of the mountains, where I waited until Garden came to pick me up.

And I spent my life hiding from the feeling, scared of what it may bring. I was hiding when I entered the pre-med program at UCLA, even though I wanted to be a musician. But it had been my dad's dying wish. I was hiding when I dated good Asian girls who believed me when I said I was saving sex for marriage. I hid until one day a few months ago when I was at the college library and followed a boy who'd been eyeing me into the bathroom.

As he pressed me against the side of the stall, unzipping my pants with fast hands, I suddenly caught a captivating hint of that true feeling. I traced it with my fingers as it hummed along the arch of his back, traveling up his spine, where I felt it tingling at the back of his neck as I cradled his face and we touched lips. It teased me, promising there was more where it came from, as long as I kept looking.

I kept my eyes open when we kissed.

So, no, I'm not a clueless closet case who's in way over his head. I go up these steps in noble pursuit of the true feeling.

And I'm 95 percent sure that wasn't just a Molly monologue.

Somewhere, the DJ puts a BLACKPINK song over the mansion speakers. Winston Chow's staircase has no handrails and is a spiraling double helix made of clear Lucite, maybe because rich people like things to be overwrought. As I make my way up, I can see through the transparent stairs that the second floor is a dimly lit and extremely long hallway of shut doors.

Fidgeting with Joey's bracelet, I timidly reach the second floor, looking left and right. At first, there seem to be hundreds of doors, but then I see the strategically placed mirrors that give the hall an endless appearance.

I wonder if I am supposed to be up here, daring myself to open any of the doors. I think I hear some sounds coming from the impressively tall double doors directly facing the stairs. Plus, there's a neon yellow party hat looped over its handle. Seems welcoming.

I gently turn the handle and push my head in, and I recoil in shock at the sight.

In the middle of a huge ballroom that has been entirely wrapped in glossy black tarp, there is a group of perhaps twenty-five or so naked men in every form of sexual congress imaginable. They are backlit by strobing black lights, the only source of light in the room before I barged in, and already I am apologizing and about to shut the door when I realize—they aren't moving.

I prop the door open and walk into the ballroom toward the sculptures. They are all intricately sculpted of what looks like terra-cotta. The statues are life-size and spaced over an area that has to be the size of a volleyball court. Yes, they are all in various sexual positions, with varying numbers of direct participants as well as varying levels of kink, but the overall effect is magnificent.

I step closer to inspect one of the statues, and I am immediately drawn to the features of its face. Perplexed, I quickly move on to get a good look at its neighbor. And then the next. I run in a circle around them all, realizing that they share the same familiar face.

I don't know how else to put it, but all of the sculptures look a lot like...me.

"River!"

Suddenly, bright lights engulf the room, causing me to jump.

I wheel around and standing there is Joey. My hearts skips a beat when I see him again.

He has changed into white flannel pants and an unbuttoned Henley shirt that graciously reveals a top row of deeply cut abs. At first, I'm afraid he's angry, but he is smiling, so I relax. "There you are, Joey. I'm so sorry, I was leaving and then I realized I still had your bracelet."

His eyes light up as I hold his jade bracelet out to him. He walks over to me and puts his hand over mine and its cool stones click between our palms. Once again, that true feeling swells within me. Neither of us lets go at first, and we both laugh.

I wonder if he feels it, too.

The other door suddenly opens behind Joey, and standing there is a tall mature man, easily twice my age. He wears a simple button-up with a boxy Eastern cut and slacks. He looks familiar and then I realize that it is because I recognize him from the internet.

Joey lets go of my hand as Winston Chow puts a thick arm around him, intricate Yakuza-style tattoos peeking through the billionaire's sleeves. Winston is the tallest of us by far. He has the build of a retired football player, with a face that looks like it was chiseled out of a mountain. His long, thick hair is streaked with white, and tied up in a neat man bun.

"You must be River. Joey was just telling me about you." He reaches out his hand and we shake. "Welcome to my home. I'm Winston Chow." He has a deep baritone voice with a posh Hong Kong accent that echoes in the ballroom.

He doesn't smile much, but has a somewhat mischievous arch in his eyebrow. I nod respectfully as I say, "I know who you are. Thank you for having me. Your house is amazing." I've never met a billionaire before. Another first.

"Thanks. I just keep some of my LA things here." He walks past me. I turn to watch him observe the orgy of statues in front of us, his hands on his hips. "I see you found my temporary art gallery. I'm just storing this piece here for now. I have a condo in Taipei where I think it'd fit."

I clear my throat. "Well. It definitely is quite striking."

Winston nods. "Created by a very exclusive artist. I think it a very good investment."

Joey leans over to me. "Besides Peril, Winston is in town for an art event."

"Do you collect art, River?" Winston turns back to me, looking me up and down like he's sizing me up.

I chuckle. "Not really, no." I clear my throat. "I actually thought, when I first looked in here, that they were real people."

Winston suddenly laughs, a loud bark that shows off his big teeth, and I nervously join him as Joey looks down at his feet.

"An orgy! What sort of party do you think this is?" Winston walks past us and exits the ballroom, which cues both Joey and me to follow him out.

Joey sighs, looking annoyed for the first time. "Winston is joking, ignore him." He then earnestly points down the hall. "The real orgy is at the door at the end there, if you're interested."

I put up my hands. "No, no. I really did come up here to give you back your bracelet. And to thank you for everything. This has probably been the craziest night of my life."

Winston had been walking away but turns to us when he heard what I said. "Joey gave you his bracelet?" He arches his eyebrow and looks back and forth at us. "You sound like you're leaving, River."

I laugh nervously. "Yes, it's time for me to go."

"Which direction are you heading?" Winston is walking down the stairs, with Joey and me following him.

"Westside."

Winston looks at his bare wrist, and I watch as a hologram of a watch appears on it, like something out of Star Trek. "Well, Joey and I have a breakfast appointment in Malibu. I'll give you a lift."

"Oh, no, honestly," I say, as Joey looks on, inscrutable. "I'll just get a car."

"Just say yes, lah," Winston says, his bouncy Cantonese accent especially strong.

We step onto the first floor, which is now packed with people, all partying like it isn't eight in the morning. Winston quickly disappears into the crowd, which mobs around him. Joey leans over into my ear and says, "Meet us out front in ten minutes, okay?" He smiles at me and squeezes his way past the bodies in the same direction as Winston.

As I make my way toward the front entrance, I pass an open door and I'm pulled into a powder room so abruptly that I yelp out loud. I'm pushing the person off me until I realize who it is.

"Calvin!"

He's still wearing his sunglasses, but I can tell by the way he sways that he is really messed up. He closes the door behind him, and the ruckus of the party mutes down to a dull roar. He keeps taking deep breaths, huffing and puffing, then giggling to himself.

"Calvin, I'm so glad to see you. I wanted to say I'm really sorry—"

"Fuck, River!" Calvin laughs and mimics tearing out his hair. "Why you gotta be so real all the time? It's a party... Goddammit, just kiss me."

He grabs me and presses his lips onto mine. I let him do it. He stops, frowning at me, and shoves me back lightly. He pouts. "We were having fun together until that Joey guy arrived."

I think about the time. "Are you okay to stay? I can take you home..."

"Home is literally the last place I want to be right now." He holds up an empty plastic bag. It takes me a second to realize what it is. My mouth drops open.

"Calvin! Did you do everything in that bag?"

"No, I shared." He leans against the door. "Lots of cute guys out there are into me, you know. I was just waiting for you."

"Have a nice day, Calvin." I reach for the doorknob, ready to go.

Calvin moves aside, but not before he says, "By the way, I never told you about how I knew who Joey is."

"Yes, I know now. He's Winston Chow's boyfriend."

Calvin laughs. "River, you're so innocent. Maybe if you were being polite you would call him a boyfriend."

"Christ! Just say what you mean!" I have lost my patience.

"Joey is a money boy. An infamous one from China." He looks pleased with himself.

"What's a money boy?" I've never heard the term before but already I have a sinking feeling.

Calvin pushes my arm away from the handle and opens the door himself. As he exits, he waves goodbye.

"Exactly what it sounds like," he replies.

HE SHICAN
1740

You must tell me right now, Shican. Where is the fox spirit?

Dr. Qi Yewang slammed his hand on the table between us. For all the time I had known him, I had never seen him angry like this. *If there are fox spirits encroaching upon Tiaoxi, we must ward them off immediately. This city has seen enough tragedy.*

I reached out to him again, trying to placate him. *Yewang, please calm down! I promise you that this is no fox spirit. Perhaps he misspoke the name of the medicine. Let us not jump to conclusions.*

Yewang's brow furrowed but I felt his heat go down. *He? It is a man?*

I nodded reassuringly. *Yes, my new friend is a man. Come now, Yewang, who has ever heard of a male fox spirit?*

Yewang scoffed but remained calm. *Despite their appearances, fox spirits are not male nor female. They are simply whatever your heart desires.* He looked at me pointedly.

I quickly changed the subject. *Am I to believe that this is medical advice from the preeminent Dr. Qi? I am a bit stunned that a simple request for a prescription has led to these tall tales of spirits and fairies.*

I have always held you as a man of the sciences. Ignoring me, the doctor was once again studying my eyes. I stood up and started to walk away from him in annoyance, but he pulled me back quickly. *Sit, sit.*

I sat back down as he gestured to our teacups. Mine I had finished drinking while his was still full. *Medicines and magics,* he said, *they both follow the same principle: what comes unbalanced must be balanced again.*

He picked up his teacup and poured half of it into mine. In each of our respective cups, I saw our reflections. *And I can see an imbalance within you, Shican. There is a shadow in your eyes that is not of you. I fear for you.*

I studied my reflection in the cup. I believed him when he said that he was concerned for me, and perhaps I also might have believed there was something wrong with me—but I did not care.

Instead, I looked around his clinic, taking a deep breath to alleviate the tension between us. *Where is little Mei? I was hoping that an added benefit of seeing you today would be reuniting with your dear daughter.*

My intention had been to deter his focus away from me, and it worked. Yewang was caught off guard. For a second he seemed unsure what to say. Finally, he said flatly, *Sadly, she is not here today, Shican.*

I see. I stood up. *I am sorry for troubling you today, Yewang. It was not my intention.* I gathered my belongings, preparing to go. *It was good to see you, old friend.*

You are leaving? Yewang asked quietly, looking crestfallen.

I reached over and took his hand into mine. *I came for a medicine that does not exist, save for in a book of fables. I shall not take any more of your time. Please, take care of yourself and little Mei.*

I turned and walked to the door. Just as I was exiting, I suddenly heard Yewang speak. *The medicine does exist.*

I stopped in my tracks and spun around to face him. *It does?*

He took a deep breath, massaging his eyes with his fingers,

looking conflicted. *I should be able to concoct the Primordial Bolus. I have never done it before, but in theory it should be possible.*

Overjoyed, I rushed to his side, where I knelt beside his chair, looking up at him gratefully. *Oh, Yewang, do you really mean it? Is it actually possible?*

Yewang reached over and flipped through the pages of the book of fairy tales as he spoke. *You call me a man of the sciences, but what you do not know is that my grandmother was a holy woman, a mountain priestess from the Far South. It was she who first guided me in chemistry and alchemy. Without her, I would not be the doctor I am today.*

I bowed my head respectfully. *She would be proud to see it, no doubt.* Then I had a creeping thought. *Why are you changing your mind to help me?*

Because I can tell that you are going to do this dangerous thing with or without my help, and I would rather you have my help. He had on a small smile.

I leaped up and wrapped my arms around him. Though he stiffened at first, he then patted me on the arm. *All right, Shican, all right.*

I have truly troubled you, I said as he picked up the book and started reading it.

He sighed. *You are so eager that you do not even wonder what this medicine is for.* He held the book close to his face and read a passage as I looked over his shoulder.

> *Three hundred miles farther east is Emerald Mountain,*
> *Where much jade can be found on its south slope*
> *And green cinnabar on its north.*
> *There is a beast here whose form resembles a fox with nine tails.*
> *It makes a sound like a baby and is a man-eater.*
> *This beast is a divine spirit,*
> *But can be destroyed with primordial bolus.*

I threw up my arms upon hearing the last sentence. *Well now, Yewang, why would a fox spirit call upon you to create something that might destroy it?*

The doctor ran his finger along his beard, thinking. *Did he tell you why he wanted it?*

He came to me with his grandmother, I replied. *She is unwell and he was seeking medicines for her. Yewang, do you really still think that he is a fox spirit? A man-eater? I did not see any tails on him.*

Yewang closed the book and walked back to his library. As he reached up to place it back in its spot, his back turned to me, he said, *If I am to help you, then I intend to find that out myself.*

This startled me. *What do you mean by that?*

Moving quickly, he went over to his desk as he began to pack up some of his effects into his medicine bag. *You call me your old friend, and indeed I care for you as a true friend would.* He walked over to his apothecary cabinet and began to pull open drawers quickly, grabbing a pinch here and a handful there. *You come to me asking for a supernatural potion for a new friend who may or may not be a malicious spirit. Well, as your old friend, I would like to meet this person myself before I decide to help him.*

I knew already that there was never changing Yewang's mind once he decided upon something. Not sure what to do, I nodded, resigned. *He came to me because he did not feel worthy to come to see you himself. I am sure he will be eternally grateful for your generosity. You can examine his mother in person!*

Yewang grabbed his cloak from his chair. *Well. Let us go, then.*

I was taken aback; I had thought he was leaving for another appointment. *You are coming right this instant? It is midday.*

Yewang turned to me, annoyed. *If your new friend is actually a fox spirit, we should find that out as soon as possible. Surely your mother told you stories about fox spirits who brought ruin to the land?*

My uncle was the storyteller in the family, I said softly as a flash of his merry face appeared in my mind.

Yewang paused. I could not recall if I had ever told him about my childhood. *My mother used to tell us the story of Empress Daji,* he then said, *the evil fox spirit who two thousand years ago seduced the Emperor and destroyed his kingdom. But not before she depraved him and tortured thousands of innocent people, simply because she loved the sound of screaming.* He motioned to his servant to close up the clinic.

Bedtime stories to scare children into behaving, Yewang. I gathered my things as I followed him outside. *Besides, if a fox spirit is meant to bring calamity to all the lands, why would one have anything to do with me? I am but a commoner innkeeper with no station or power. I am no Emperor!*

DONG XIAN
4 BCE

The Emperor and I sat across from each other staring for a moment, and even the trees seemed to cease moving in the breeze. Then, I remembered myself, and leaped from my stool to quickly kowtow, bowing to the ground. *O Radiant and Holy Son of Heaven, I am eternally your servant!*

Where is the philosopher? His voice was soft, barely audible, but intense.

My forehead was still pressed against the cobblestones. *If the Son of Heaven may forgive me, but I do not know. I, too, was supposed to meet Yang Xiong here.*

And who are you?

If it pleases the Son of Heaven, I am Dong Xian, son of Dong Gong, of the Dong Clan of Yunyang.

Whether it pleases me or not, that is who you are. You may stand, Dong Xian of Yunyang.

I slowly rose, keeping my nose pointed to the ground. But I couldn't help but peek up at him again.

The Emperor was tall and slender in build, but with broadly

set shoulders. He had a short, thick beard, but his mustache was more scarce and wispy, betraying his young age. He wasn't looking at me, but into the distance with annoyance on his face.

I thought quickly. *Would Your Radiance like me to locate Yang Xiong? I can call for his attendant.*

He suddenly winced, clutching his side.

Is Your Radiance all right? I wasn't sure what to do. I looked around. I would have expected the Emperor to be constantly attended by an entourage of servants, but we seemed to be completely alone.

No. No, I'm not. His fist was balled up against the table. *I am constantly in pain, or I am retching from medicines that a legion of ineffectual doctors seem to get a sick pleasure out of forcing into me.* He finally looked at me again. *Do you suffer from pain like this?*

I shifted from foot to foot, uncomfortable with this unexpected frankness of his. *Not normally.*

You are a luckier man than me, then.

Son of Heaven, I have had a few strange months, but nothing has been stranger than being told by my Emperor that I am luckier than he.

He laughed suddenly. It sounded like bells. He looked me up and down, and then motioned me to sit down, which I did. Our faces level with each other once again, but this time both of us calmer, I noted how refined and pleasant his features were, particularly his amber eyes and his full lips. If I was staring, he seemed to notice because he looked upward to the sky, as though suddenly shy.

I spoke too soon earlier, Your Radiance.

Oh?

When I was a teenager, I fell off a horse and broke both my legs. Thankfully, I healed properly but I spent many months in bed in excruciating pain.

His brow furrowed in genuine concern at my lie. *As a child? That must have been very hard. How did you get through it?*

I memorized all of the Three Hundred Songs.

He let out a snort of disbelief. *You know, there are actually three hundred and five.*

Alas, Emperor, I didn't memorize the last five.

He shook his head, but was amused. Then, concentrating hard, he began to slowly recite:

It floats about, that boat of cypress wood...

I chimed in, knowing the poem well by heart.

Yea, it floats about on the river.

He nodded, impressed, and replied:

Disturbed am I and sleepless...

And we joined in together.

As if suffering from a painful wound.
It is not because I have no wine,
And that I might not wander and saunter about.

Cued by the poem, I lifted the bottle of yellow wine and poured a cup for each of us, handing one to him. We continued:

There are the sun and moon—
How is it that the sun has become small, yet not the moon?
The sorrow clings to my heart
Like an unwashed sleeve.
Silently I think of my case...

I let him finish the poem by himself:

But I cannot spread my wings and fly away.

I bowed my head ever so slightly to him as we both tipped the wine into our mouths. He was now staring deeply at me. I smiled back at him. He did not smile, but sat back in his chair.

So tell me, Dong Xian of Yunyang. Who are you?

I felt like I had leaped out of my body, watching from afar as I introduced myself to the Emperor himself, a living god in human flesh, the most powerful person under Heaven. I was sure I was dreaming, because it felt like a dream in the same surreal way that anything could've happened next.

We talked for a while, drinking the yellow wine together. He asked questions about me, what my home of Yunyang was like, and where I grew up and who my people were. At first, I thought this would seem dull for an Emperor, but it soon dawned on me that he probably didn't have casual conversation often.

He was intense but unassuming, and apparently not accustomed to humor, at least not my sort, because when I would say something lighthearted he always at first didn't seem to understand. But then his amber eyes would light up and he would laugh as though he were surprised he was laughing, and I would join in.

At one point I picked up his cup to refill it, but he reached out to stop me, and our fingers touched. His skin was warmer than I expected. Neither of us pulled back for a moment, and I noticed that he ever so subtly bit down on the inner flesh of his lower lip.

Nay, I should stop, as enjoyable as wine during the daytime might be, he said as he pulled back finally, stretching his arms and looking content. *My afternoon was supposed to be an austere lesson of classics with the old philosopher!*

I leaned in ever so slightly toward him. *I am sorely sorry for intercepting the Son of Heaven and leading him asunder.*

He laughed. *I think you and I are close in age, yet you have such a carefree spirit about you. It is quite refreshing.*

I do not have the weight of Heaven's Will on my shoulders, I replied. *If my Emperor ever does feel unwell as he was saying earlier, it is only because of the seriousness of his love and concern for his people.*

Funny, he seemed to realize, *actually I feel a great deal better now. Usually, my episodes last for days. Curiouser and curiouser, indeed, as Yang Xiong would say!*

Perhaps you have benefited from Old Yang's teachings after all, I said, grinning. *The old man has always endorsed to me the healing properties of drunken poetry.*

You give undue credit to wine and old poems, the Emperor responded, *and none to the unique pleasure of your company.* He then smiled at me for the first time, and it was a smile that lit up our surroundings like a warm hearth in winter. I briefly found myself lost in this inviting curvature of his lips.

What a blessing it is, I finally spoke with a bit of genuine awe, *to receive such kind words from Your Radiance.*

A rare interaction that is not just enjoyable, but also healing, is deserving of kind words. How often do you meet with the philosopher?

Yang Xiong is patient enough to humor me as a favor to my father. I see my teacher as often as three times a week, I seamlessly lied, trying to predict where this was headed.

How about the next time we meet it not be so happenstance? As he spoke, I wasn't sure which of us was moving, but our bodies were drawing closer together. *Yang Xiong should be delighted to take a reprieve, as I am sure the old man humors me just as much as you.*

There was something quietly intoxicating about the Emperor, at first disguised by his innocent features and surprisingly casual manner. But most of all I found myself immersed in his eyes, as they occasionally caught the sunlight and would flash like raw gold.

That was when an odd thought entered my mind: that I should tell him everything right now, about his grandmother's plot and my involvement in it. It confounded me, but there was something disarming about him that was leading me astray from everything that I had planned.

Then I thought to myself, who is seducing whom?

Your Radiance. I bowed my head. *I would cherish the honor of being your company as many times as you will allow it.* I paused, uncertain.

Then I decided. *There is something I should tell—*

But then his eyes glanced up, looking behind me. I turned as well to see rows of nearly forty eunuchs filing into the small courtyard, their heads appropriately bowed nearly to their knees as they shuffled toward us. A group of them carried a magnificent wooden palanquin adorned with phoenixes inlayed with precious gems, a chariot fit indeed for an emperor. I was somewhat amused that I was being interrupted by the very procession I had initially imagined would have arrived with him in the first place.

An elderly servant approached us. His round blue cap was a uniform that I knew to signify higher rank among the Emperor's attendants. Though he did bow, I noticed he stood upright as he addressed us.

Holy Child, pardon the intrusion. He had a high, nasal voice that did not suit his stout frame, and he occasionally wheezed for breath. *The Prime Minister requests to be of audience to you.*

Without protest, the Emperor stood as servants rushed to bring the palanquin to his side. *Then we should see him right away, Uncle,* he said to the head eunuch. He did not say anything else to me, but just before he climbed into his chariot, he nodded subtly at me. I understood.

As swiftly as they appeared, the Emperor and his attendants were gone in a rapid scurry of deft feet, leaving me dazed in the bright sunlight. I let out a long, overdue exhale, my heartbeat finally easing.

I grabbed what was left of the wine, shaking the bottle near my ear to hear a respectable sloshing inside, and strode victoriously out of the courtyard to celebrate my good fortune.

However, as I rounded the corner, I was caught off guard

when I saw that a large figure was leaning against the walled perimeter of the courtyard. I froze in my steps and cautiously looked in that direction.

It was a man, perhaps twice my age and a good head taller than me. As I turned to him, he stood upright, displaying powerful shoulders and long hair that cascaded down his back. From a distance, he looked every bit a mythic hero.

But it wasn't his appearance that captivated me the most. It was what he was wearing. He was in full military regalia, with a massive gleaming sword slung behind his shoulders.

Whoever this man was, he was a soldier.

RIVER
PRESENT DAY

As I exit Winston Chow's mansion, I squint to allow my eyes to adjust to the cloudless sunny day. The Lunar New Year marks the beginning of spring on the Chinese calendar, and already I can feel an arid warmth returning to Los Angeles.

I shut the front doors behind me, relieved to finally be headed home. The party inside showed no signs of slowing down, but all I can think about right now is my bed. My head feels hollow and I am sore all over. I look around but I don't see Joey, or Winston for that matter. At first, I think I am alone, but then I see the drag queen bouncer from earlier, wearing her rose-patterned qipao.

Roses is taking a break, leaning against a tree and smoking a cigarette, looking breathtaking as ever in her skin-tight red qipao. I wave at her and she motions me over.

"Hey, sweetie, do you happen to have any PrEP?" she drawls.

It takes me a second to realize what she's talking about. "Oh, you mean pre-exposure prophylaxis? Sorry, I don't have any."

She raises an eyebrow. "Pre-expose what? What are you, some sort of doctor?" She offers me a cigarette and I shake my head.

"Not yet. I'm studying for med school, though."

She rolls her eyes good-naturedly. She wears gold contact lenses. "Yes, a real doctor would never turn down a smoke."

I take a deep breath. "I've got a question."

She presses a brightly manicured finger against my lips, the pointy tip of her nail digging into my septum. "Sis, if you're another fan looking for a SuperSoul moment with me, this is not the gig. Everyone's descending into K holes and suddenly thinking I'm their fairy drag mother or something."

I laugh. "No, it's not that deep."

"Okay, baby, then what is it?"

"Can you explain to me what a money boy is?"

She leans back dramatically, blinking at me. "Are you sure it ain't that deep? Shit. Why on earth are you asking that?"

I open my mouth to speak but nothing comes out. She suddenly gets a look of epiphany on her face. "Oh, sweetie. I see. Yes, a money boy is what they call gay escorts in Asia. You didn't know about Joey, I guess. I think in his case it is...a bit more complicated."

I try to shrug it off. "It's not like that. I just heard that about him and I saw how he was with Winston, so..."

Roses studies me as I stammer, then cradles my cheeks with her hands. "They are usually that beautiful for a reason. Or the reason is why they are beautiful. Choose one, whichever lets you hate them less."

"Maybe I will have a cigarette, actually."

She smiles and sticks another cigarette in her mouth and lights it. She tucks it between my lips, smudged red with her lipstick. As I take a drag, she points a finger at me. "Who cares about money boy this, billionaire that? You are here! No one's ever seen you before this morning, and already you're in the most VIP of circles. Clearly, you belong here. And you know what?" She pushes my glasses up my nose and smiles at me. "I bet that's what is actually overwhelming you. The realization that you do belong."

She throws her cigarette butt onto the ground, stamping it out with her stiletto. Then she cackles. "Girl, looks like you got your SuperSoul moment after all!" Her face lights up as she sees someone behind me.

I turn to see a sleek black car pull up from behind the house. The window in the back rolls down and Joey sticks his head out. "Hey, River, let's go!"

The drag queen kisses me on the cheek. "Go ahead. Use a condom since you ain't got no PrEP."

As I approach the car, Joey waves at her. "See you later, Jujubee!"

I've never seen a vehicle like this before, with no distinguishable maker. I'm not a car person, so I could only say that it looks like the Batmobile redesigned by Apple. Joey opens the door and I'm surprised to see it is laid out like a limo inside, with four long seats facing each other. Sitting at the far end of the car is Winston Chow, who is talking on the phone. I scoot as Joey moves to the side seat.

The door shuts by itself and we start to drive out of Winston's complex. I look up to see there is no driver. The car navigates up onto the main road and starts the winding route down to Hollywood.

"Where are we headed?" the car asks, in a surprisingly zesty Russian accent. I give my address.

Winston is talking in rapid-fire Cantonese, which I don't understand. Joey is looking down at his bracelet, fiddling with it again. I wonder if he's always this shy, or if he just doesn't feel like talking. He sees me watching him and he smiles. "How are you feeling?"

I unintentionally yawn. "I'm sure it's pretty obvious. I'm beat. How are the two of you still alive?"

"We're just jet-lagged and still on Asia time."

Winston ends his call and the cell phone deactivates, disappearing from his palm. Another hologram. We've reached the base of the Hills, turning onto Sunset Boulevard. "So, River, what are you? ABC, I'm guessing."

"I was born in Taipei, where my family is from. But I came here when I was a baby."

The older man is studying me again, like he did in the ballroom. "You aren't like Joey's other friends. How'd you two meet again?"

Joey interjects quickly. "I told you already. I was looking for you on the dance floor at Peril, and we bumped into each other. He didn't look well so I watched over him until we found his friend."

Winston smirks like a man not easily fucked with. "Just like that. Two lost souls collide." Joey rolls his eyes, starting to lose patience, but Winston continues. "How common would you say your face is, River?"

I don't think I understand the question but I can feel my face burn hot instantly. Joey snaps, "I know you think you're being intriguing when you say weird shit like that, but it just makes you look like a dick."

Winston scoffs and leans back. "You seem like a smart kid, River. If you ever make something of yourself, don't let the people on your payroll make an ass of you. Especially if he was giving blowjobs in a dirty bathroom in Shenzhen when you discovered him."

Silence engulfs the car. I shrink a bit into my seat as Joey and Winston fume in their respective corners. The car drives us through Beverly Hills as I wonder if I should just get out at a stoplight.

But the car, which may or may not be able to detect human awkwardness, starts playing a classic Red Hot Chili Peppers song. We cruise between the high-rise apartments of Westwood as its top retracts—of course the iBat is also a convertible.

Eventually, we pull up to my house in the Palisades, in a cul-de-sac overlooking the Santa Monica Canyon.

I reach out a hand to Winston. "Thank you, Winston, for everything."

He stares at me for a second before returning the handshake with a firm grip. "Maybe we will meet again." He doesn't seem very enthused about the possibility.

I climb out of the car as Joey follows me. He walks me to my front door. "Listen, I hope I didn't cause any awkwardness…"

"No," Joey says curtly, "he was being an ass and needed to hear it."

"Joey…" I don't quite know what to say. "If you need any help, or if your situation is bad…"

Joey shakes his head and gives me a sad smile. "We all do what we have to do to get what we want. I'm no different. You don't need to worry about me."

He opens his arms and we hug, his muscular arms squeezing me tight. I inhale deeply and he smells like sex on fresh linens.

"Maybe I'll see you around," I say.

His face darkens a bit. "Actually, I'm leaving tonight. Back to Asia."

"Oh!" It's like a blow to the stomach. "So soon. Do you come back often?"

His face says no.

He takes me by the hand and repeats what he did at Peril, sliding his green bracelet off his wrist onto mine. Before I can refuse, he says, *I want you to hold on to it for me.* He grins. *It always finds its way back to me, so maybe we will see each other again soon.*

Once again, neither of us wants to let go. I want so badly to kiss him in this moment, but then he quickly releases me and turns to get back into the car. The door closes and I watch as Joey and Winston Chow drive away, disappearing around the corner, and out of my life. I stand there for a while.

"Where the heck have you been?" Garden asks from behind me, her voice making me jump.

I turn around to see my sister as she peers out the front door of the house. She is in a mood, and I don't blame her. I have never ghosted her for an entire day. Not wanting to argue, I head into the house, sidestepping past her. "Riv, who was that?" she demands again, following me in.

Before I shut the door, I look one last time in Joey's direction, but he is long gone.

"I don't know, Garden."

HE SHICAN
1740

How do you know when you are in love? I learned early on that for people like me, there are no grand gestures, no bold declarations painted across the sky. There are only little hidden moments, intense yet fleeting as shooting stars, that quickly burn away into night.

As for Dr. Qi Yewang, I knew we had fallen in love the moment I realized it was inevitable I was going to end up hurting him. It happened as he looked into my eyes one day, gently kissing each of my fingers, one by one. This would become our tender ritual. He would always kiss my fingers this way, and in return my heart would twist and bend for him.

I had met him about a year after I first moved to Tiaoxi, when I was still operating my old inn in the city center. My life back then was starkly different from the forest solitude to where I had since retreated. This former inn of mine was bustling and always full of travelers, and I was celebrated as a hospitable host with an eye for detail and comfort. Every evening the tavern in my lobby was packed with rowdy regulars drinking and reveling together.

But despite these material successes, I was still dogged by those numerous voices in my head, the same chorus from my childhood that pushed me at night toward the wilderness. *Go!* they repeated over and over again. *Go and look for it.* And obediently, I would leave Tiaoxi each night to walk the woods by myself.

I began to neglect my duties as an innkeeper and my business suffered, my clients fell away. For some, this sort of failure would be a massive loss of face. Certainly, my father would have been ashamed. As for me, all it did was reinforce to me that my place was not here—that I belonged elsewhere. I began to make plans to leave Tiaoxi, but to where I still did not know.

One day I was walking by the river that flows through the city. At this point my old inn had been shuttered and I was making my living doing odd jobs here and there. As I walked past the fishmongers, wrinkling my nose from the pungent smell of their morning catch, I suddenly caught a glimpse of a little girl of perhaps seven years smiling at me from across the thoroughfare. I smiled back, and she beckoned me over playfully. Complying, I chased her through the crowd, until she disappeared into an old fisherman's hut. Not sure what this place was, I cautiously entered to see her perched next to a man who was attempting to build a ladder by hand.

Good morning! I had said. The man turned to look at me as the little girl whispered in his ear, giggling behind her shyness. The man stood, picking up the girl as she lovingly wrapped her arms around his neck.

Good morning, friend. He bowed his head forward politely. *I see you met my business promoter. Sadly, we are not open yet. We just moved in.*

What store is this? I said, looking at the old creaky architecture.

The man looked around as well. *This may surprise you, but it is going to be a clinic. I am a physician.* He gestured around him. *Sometimes people are anxious about seeing a doctor, so I thought it would be nice for my office to be homey and welcoming.*

I grinned at the little girl who was waving at me. *It certainly is those things. I am He Shican.*

Qi Yewang. And this is my daughter, Mei.

I nodded at the ladder he was building. *The wood you are using for the frame of that ladder is sturdy enough, but for the rungs might I suggest cherry tree? It might be more difficult to work with, but it is soft against the sole and its pink hue would complement the colors in here.*

Dr. Qi Yewang set down his daughter, who ran back outside. *That is a lot of knowledge about lumber.*

I shrugged humbly. *My far more accomplished father was an expert merchant of it.*

Yewang laughed. *Well, I could certainly use the advice. This is my fourth attempt at this ladder. I may just give up except I am worried one of these days I will fall while trying to grab something from my apothecary cabinet.*

I was already walking to the behemoth chest that stood against his back wall. *Now this, this is an incredible feat of carpentry,* I said as I inspected the many drawers, each meticulously labeled with old characters.

Yewang walked over to stand next to me. *Yes, you can clearly see I did not build it. It was passed to me by my teacher, who himself was gifted it by the great doctors who saved Tiaoxi from the plague. I suppose one could say that it is responsible for all of us being here.*

I reached out and ran my fingers along its weathered wood. *I am not from here, but indeed standing before it I am filled with awe.*

The doctor cocked his head at me. *Yes, I was wondering that. I would have known you if I had seen you before.*

He was looking at me so earnestly I wondered if I was mistaking his candor for something else. *You know, Dr. Qi, if you need help building this ladder, I am an amateur carpenter.*

Our smiles were twins of each other.

Very quickly, Yewang became my closest friend. Because I had limited funds after the closure of my inn, he invited me to stay with him. I slept on the floor of his clinic while constructing furniture for him, including that sliding ladder. I remember laughing as his daughter Mei rambunctiously climbed up and down our ladder, a testament to the durability of what we had built together.

And though he talked of her occasionally, I never met Yewang's wife. It was perhaps customary to introduce one's good friends to one's wife, but Yewang never seemed interested in introducing us.

It was each other's company that we cherished the most; many a night we would simply talk into the late hours, as I marveled at his brilliance and wisdom. I was never one to feel sorry for myself, but there had been a void in me after I left my family. Yewang became my family.

We were fishing on the river one day when he took my hand suddenly. The sun was shining brightly upon us, though the air was crisp and frigid, a sign of looming winter. Not saying anything, I watched him as he kissed each of my fingers, so lovingly and carefully that it made my heart twist.

Yewang… I began, not sure what to say.

Shican, before you say anything, he said, cradling my hand against his cheek, *I know a young man like you, with your whole life ahead of you, has little to desire from someone like me. But please do not hold my lips accountable. I have held them shut so long around you that they no longer know what they do.*

As I pulled him to me and we kissed, I already knew that I would end up hurting him.

This is an odd location for an inn, Yewang said stiffly as we approached a clearing of trees, his horse whinnying in agreement. I snapped out of my daydream, marveling at the difference in tone Yewang had toward me now compared to that day we were fishing.

I was just thinking, I replied, *about that first year we met.* I nudged at my own horse Dama to catch up with his.

Yewang was quiet for a moment. *What of it?* he finally said.

Yewang, I never apologized to you for how it all ended. I looked over at him, and though he kept his eyes pointed ahead, he did seem to soften a bit.

What is done is done, he said quietly.

I was sad not to see little Mei today at your clinic, I ventured.

The doctor looked down at the reins in his hands. *I no longer see my daughter,* he said quietly.

I put my face in my hands, the searing guilt washing over me like unforgiving sunlight. *Oh, Yewang, why did you have to tell your wife? Why did anything have to change?*

Yewang shook his head. *I have never had an issue seeing the truth about myself. My problem was that I refused to see the truth about you.*

In the distance beyond the clearing of trees, I could see the rooftop of my inn. *I am scared to ask further, Yewang.*

Yewang suddenly chuckled drily. *Actually, I think the problem is that you are not scared enough. Many a night when you thought I was asleep, I know you still went to walk the woods alone. What nefarious thrills do you seek in the night, Shican, where there are only shadows and spirits?*

Dama began to pick up her pace as she caught sight of her trough, eager to feed and rest. *I seek nothing,* I protested quietly. *Spirits only come to you if they want to be found.* We had arrived at my inn. I dismounted Dama and led both her and Yewang's horse to drink water.

Yewang climbed off his horse as well, watching me intensely. *Yes, or if they want something.*

I sighed, already regretting all of this. *Let us see if my friend is in. Try to be friendly with him. He is just a boy.*

We will see about that. Yewang followed me into my inn.

Sitting at my table, Huang Jiulang was waiting for us when we entered, as though he had been staring at the door for a long time. He leaped up when he saw me, instantly kowtowing again with his head to the floor. *Master He, I am so glad to see you have returned.*

Feeling Yewang's eyes upon both of us, I quickly brought Jiulang to his feet. *Huang Jiulang, may I introduce to you the honorable Dr. Qi Yewang.*

Jiulang turned to Yewang in astonishment. *You are Dr. Qi himself? I am humbled to be in your presence, sir!*

Dr. Qi had a small smile on his face. *No kowtow necessary. When Shican told me of your dilemma, I decided I would come consult with you in person.*

Jiulang was overwhelmed, his eyes suddenly wet. *Such generosity. I am undeserving, but I accept graciously on behalf of my poor grandmother.*

I was carefully observing Yewang during their exchange, and I could see that all of his angst had abandoned him. He, too, was instantly charmed by the boy, which relieved me. Yewang nodded reassuringly at Jiulang. *You are a good grandson.* He then turned to me pointedly though not without humor. *Especially at such a young age.*

I quickly interjected. *Is she well enough to walk? Do you want to bring her here, or shall we go to your room?*

Jiulang was already going up the stairs. *We walked this morning, and I think some more movement would be good for her. Let me bring her down.* He disappeared onto my second floor.

I turned to Yewang, who was sitting down at my table. *I can see you are less concerned already, Yewang.*

Yewang held his palms up, as though surrendering. *Clearly, he is just a harmless boy trying to help his grandmother. Perhaps he did get the name of the medicine wrong.*

Exactly as I said it, Yewang, I said with a snort. *I told you you were overreacting.* I was pleasantly surprised. This was incredibly unlike Yewang, as it usually took him a bit longer to trust new people.

He has a funny way of talking, does he not? Yewang commented. *Very old-fashioned and formal for someone of his age.*

Jiulang reappeared at the top of the stairs and began to guide his grandmother carefully down them. I joined them at the base as Jiulang and I both helped her to the table. Her body felt heavy, as though weighed down by unseen rocks. She trembled with each step.

When we sat her down, I finally got my first good look at her, since her head had always been bowed whenever I had talked to Jiulang before. She did bear resemblance to her grandson. What struck me was it was clear she once had been a great beauty, but apparently that beauty had been suppressed by her poor health.

Yewang set his medicine bag on the table and was looking through it, pulling out different medical instruments. *I will need a fire to cauterize my tools*, he said.

Jiulang stood before I did. *I saw where you keep the wood in the back, Master He. Let me fetch it while you rest. I can make some tea as well.*

Yewang nodded. *I will have some tea. Thank you, Jiulang.* He motioned at me. *How about you? Would you like tea, Master He?* There were traces of amused mockery in his voice.

I nodded at Jiulang and he exited outside.

Yewang took Jiulang's grandmother's hand in his and felt for the pulse under her thumb. Then he inspected her ears, looking into them carefully. But what caught my attention was her eyes, which had lost their cloudiness. Instead, they shone bright and sharp as bonfires, and she looked at me as if seeing me for the first time. *Yewang*, I said, tapping him on the shoulder.

The doctor turned to me questioningly and I used my fingers to tilt his face to look upon hers. Now Jiulang's grandmother flicked her eyes over to him, watching him meaningfully. Confused, Yewang touched his fingers to her lips, parting them gently. Both of us winced in revulsion when he exposed her teeth, which were silver as iron metal. *My dear woman*, he said to her gently, *what ails you?*

Jiulang's grandmother suddenly made a strange sound without moving her mouth, though she gritted her silver teeth as if in pain. Her eyes flashed once again. Yewang turned to look at me, his eyes widened with shock and fear. *Shican. Listen. She is trying to say something, but is unable!*

And indeed, as if bound by an invisible gag, Jiulang's grandmother could only make muffled, panicked noises. Her terrified eyes darted between Yewang and me, like those of someone unable to scream for help.

DONG XIAN
4 BCE

The soldier and I were silent. I saw his eyes scan me from foot to forehead, as if sizing me up for combat. He had been eating what appeared to be a peach, and as we made eye contact he threw it to the ground, spitting out its pit. Then he walked toward me in long, steady strides.

As he approached, I nodded, taking note of just how tall and large he was. I found myself leaning back slightly as a way to more subtly lift my head. *Good evening, sir.* I had no idea how to address him. Military men were rarely seen in the administerial wings of the Endless Palace, let alone in full armored regalia.

He stopped a few paces before me but was silent and expressionless, now gazing down upon me. Up close, he was even more astonishingly handsome. Bold eyebrows, an upturned mustache and a shiny scar across his right cheek were like elegant brushstrokes upon his angular face.

I cleared my throat, nervous. *How goes your evening, my lord?* I decided to try a better title so as to not risk offending.

Suddenly, he smirked, his coarse beard parting at his lips revealing sharp white teeth. *So you are Dong Xian. You're younger than I was expecting.*

I was taken aback, not just by the comment but equally by the rough candor of his speech. *Beg pardon, sir, do we know each other?*

He drew back and bowed slightly toward me. *Citizen Dong Xian of Yunyang, I am Jujun, Commander of the Imperial Armed Forces.*

Upon hearing his name, I knew exactly who he was now, though I was shocked to be meeting him in person. Everyone knew of Jujun, the Emperor's elder cousin. My mind was racing. But how and why was he back in the Endless Palace? I'd thought he had been exiled.

I did my best to feign placidity. *Commander, I am honored to make your acquaintance. Have you recently returned from battle?*

A couple years before I entered the Endless Palace, I had overheard my father gossiping with my mother about the Emperor's cousin Jujun effectively being honorably exiled to lead the Imperial Army. Apparently, there were concerns that he, too, had plausible claims to his younger cousin's throne, so he was sent off to hopefully die a hero in a faraway war.

Commander Jujun took off his helmet, and more thick tangled hair fell down onto his brawny shoulders. *After the recent witchcraft scandal, the Court has decided that the Emperor's inner circle must be in constant supervision. Therefore, I've returned home at the request of the Emperor to be his personal security detail.* He grinned again at me. *So to answer your question, I am still very much in battle.* There was a hint of peril in the curl of his mustachioed lip.

My usual conversations with my colleagues were steeped in the stilted politicking of the Court, so there was a roguish bluntness to this soldier that I rarely encountered. He was charismatic, which was surely aided by my awareness of the many victories he had garnered for the Empire. He certainly did not end up dying in war as many had expected—instead, he had become a hero of our people.

But…why was it all so secret? There should have been fanfare and celebration over Commander Jujun's return. At the very least, he had to have only recently returned, and the news of his reappearance would surely swarm through the Palace soon. For whatever reason, he had not been given his due hero's welcome.

Not sure what to say next, I decided on flattery. *Indeed, I and every other Han am indebted by the Commander's brave service. And I am glad that the Emperor has faith and trust in you, as I can see you are as honorable as you are brave.*

He stopped smiling. *Dong Xian, as the Emperor's personal bodyguard, it is my duty to assess any person who approaches the orbit of the Dragon Throne.* He began walking at a spirited pace and motioned me to follow alongside him as we departed from the courtyard area.

I understand, sir, only I am surprised that the Commander would take it upon himself to bother with a nobody like myself.

He suddenly made a sharp right turn, cutting in front of me. *Well, Dong Xian, I figured it'd be the best way for us to meet privately.*

We had come to a secluded place on the Palace grounds, a nondescript back alley where we were alone. It was certainly private. He turned to me. *After all, if you are indeed to become a new friend of the Emperor's, then as his bodyguard I am to look out for your safety as well.*

Before I could respond, Jujun suddenly leaned down toward me from his much greater height, until he was barely a finger's length too close, and I could smell his summer musk. I was backed against the alley wall. I cleared my throat, feeling a bit light-headed. His face lingered near mine. *Consider me at your service, Dong Xian.*

This was an unexpected perk.

And how can I be of service to the Commander? I had a few interesting ideas clouding my mind, and the husky tone of my voice betrayed them.

Swiftly, Jujun pulled away backward with a pleased snarl. He chuckled and shook his head at me. *Already you reveal yourself, boy. This is a disappointment. I was hoping you'd be more calculating than some back country pleasure woman.* He spat on the ground, still laughing to himself.

I mentally slapped myself for my sloppiness, and my cheeks burned hot. *You misinterpret me, Commander,* I said sullenly.

More laughing. *Somehow, I don't believe you are ever in danger of being misinterpreted, Dong Xian. You are about as subtle as a bitch in heat. But fear not, I am well aware of my effect on others. I will not hold it against you. Unless, that is, you want me to.*

His smugness was infuriating. I turned to leave, unable to face him any longer. He yanked me back with a violent pull on my shoulder, his hot mouth pressed to my ear. *Don't get so easily upset, boy,* he whispered in mock secrecy, his mustache scraping against my cheek. *If you can't be clever, then at least be agreeable. Plenty of the similarly lesser minded have survived in the Endless Palace by being simple and pretty.*

Knowing I needed to respond but unable to think of anything, I could only reply: *I thank the Commander for the advice.* But I had never been so angry before in my life, seething under my breath.

He was tying his long hair into a ponytail, his thick arms like two hills on either side of his head. *No need to thank me, just heed me. There is something admirable in admitting when you're not good enough.*

My anger spoke before I could stop it. *And I should listen to someone who was told by the gods themselves that he wasn't good enough.* Shocked, I bit down on my lips to clamp them shut, but it was too late.

I could see I had caught Jujun off guard, as his face fell for just a moment. But I gleaned much from the reddening of his face. Clearly, the Emperor's cousin agreed on some level with the rumors about his own claims to the Dragon Throne. It must have been such a sore spot to know that no matter how many songs they wrote about his victories, he would always be a mere mortal like the rest of us, while his younger cousin was the singular Son of Heaven.

Commander Jujun suddenly pulled his sword out of its hilt. It caught the sun and gleamed with blinding white light. I backed away from him, instantly afraid.

But he pointed its sharp tip toward the ground and began to slice into the damp dirt beneath us. He spoke, his soft voice now more refined and strangely melodic. *Though the Endless Palace is far away from the battlefields where its spoils are reaped, within its walls are designs far more brutal than blood and bone.*

I realized he was writing elegant calligraphy, and I was surprised that despite his boorish ways, Jujun had the sumptuous longhand of a classical scholar. As he wrote, he continued: *I am a friend to you today, Dong Xian, because I am taking it upon myself to warn you that you are about to be caught outside naked in a lightning storm during an earthquake. I will not be a friend to you tomorrow if you don't save yourself.*

That is a shame, because the Commander does not yet know that I am a most excellent friend, I replied with conviction, pleading my case. *I would say that a friendship between us is mandatory as we move forward to serve our Emperor together!* I subtly made my stance shorter so I could peer up at him more innocently. *Please, Commander Jujun, view me as you would a little brother in need of your guidance and mentorship.*

Jujun shook his head. *You are shameless, boy. You would never have my endorsement, because I see you exactly for what you are.*

And what is it you think you see, Commander?

He finished writing. His characters were stacked tightly in a square; they looked like a seal of a stamp or something of that sort. He looked up at me. *I see that you are insatiable. That all the world's riches could be strewn at your feet, and still you'd wonder why you can't have the stars.*

He stood back and we both looked down at the words he had carved into the dirt. I read them aloud: *As is Heaven's Will, a long and prosperous life.* I shot him a suspicious glare. *What does this mean?*

He traced a thick finger across the shiny scar on his cheek. *Memorize it. It is a promise made to Emperors that is so rarely kept.*

His cavalier words spooked me. *I was under the impression that the Commander was a true friend of the Emperor's,* I said uneasily, *yet he speaks in a way that is tinged with treason.*

Jujun held up his sword again in my direction, but this time I didn't flinch. He wiped the dirt off the blade and then sheathed it. *You are wrong yet again. I've been protecting him since he was born. He is our Emperor, but he is also my family.* He gestured back toward his words in the mud. *I remind myself of this promise whenever I encounter those who would harm my cousin, intentionally or not.* He sneered at me in disdain. *Even the dim-witted can be dangerous.*

Oh, so I am a threat now, Commander? I could barely contain the growl in my voice. I'd had enough of his condescension. *No longer a back country pleasure woman?* I took a step toward him. *You were huddled against that wall outside the courtyard the whole time, weren't you? As you spied on our conversation, no doubt, you would have heard the Son of Heaven request a regular audience from me. That is an imperial order I must obey, and it is your sworn duty as his guardian to facilitate it.*

Suddenly, Jujun placed a burly hand on my shoulder, startling me. *All right, Dong Xian,* he chuckled. *You have some fight in you, I see. But that only means you'll die a slower death.*

It was time for me to exit, and quickly. *Forgive me, Commander,* I said, *I am expected elsewhere.* I turned to go.

But the Commander tightened his grip around my shoulder and I felt my bones click. *It was clever to manufacture the appearance that the old philosopher arranged your meeting with the Emperor. But I know the truth, even if the Son of Heaven doesn't. I know you are working with that old bitch Fu. And when the time is right, I will be sure to make a bloody example out of you, boy. I have been studying the execution methods of the previous dynasties, the ones that have been deemed too barbaric by the Han. I think I will revisit certain exceptions for those who dare personally betray the Emperor's trust.*

With that, the soldier saluted triumphantly and turned to leave. *Now is your time to choose, Dong Xian, whether or not you want a long and prosperous life,* he called out as he disappeared around the corner.

I stood there for a long time after he walked off, the hot sun beating down on me as I perspired from both heat and panic. But then I took a deep breath, forced myself to calm down and headed back to my quarters to think more about this new revelation.

I rolled the dilemma round and round in my head:

How do I get rid of Commander Jujun?

RIVER
PRESENT DAY

The sky is dim when I wake up in my bed, and my skull feels like it's been scooped empty with a melon baller. Groaning, I rub my head as I wonder if it is morning or evening. I look over at the clock. It is 6:47 PM.

I am standing under the hot stream of water in my shower when it suddenly strikes me. "Give me your wallet," Calvin had said at Peril right as I'd taken his pill, "if you feel like you might lose it." I slam my palm against the tile in frustration. What a mess I've been. I had also handed him my keys. I sit down in the shower, considering whether I should just drown myself.

How will I get my shit back? Also, I'm an idiot who let the boy of my dreams get away. Because I am stupid, awkward, with no game. Always. A closet case scared of his own shadow.

Wow, this must be what a comedown feels like.

After I dry myself off, I look in the mirror. Maybe it is from dehydration and dancing, but I look like I've somehow lost five pounds in one night. Embarrassing to admit, but this cheers me up just a tad.

Next to my sink is Joey's jade bracelet. I pick it up, rolling its jagged central stone between my fingers. I slip it on my wrist. I can't tell if it is all in my head, but even now when I'm sober, the bracelet still feels like it hums at my touch.

My stomach growls like a bear. I need to eat.

I walk downstairs toward the kitchen, and I hear the TV on in the adjacent living room, playing the local evening news. My sister, Garden, is sitting in front of the TV, smoking an e-cig as she works on her laptop, probably coding something for work. She doesn't turn to look at me as I open the refrigerator, but I can see her fidgeting with her prosthetic leg, which means she is annoyed.

"I'm sorry for missing your calls, G." There's nothing in the fridge except a few cans of fizzy water and an opened container of old Greek yogurt. Typical, since Mom left.

"There are some leftovers warming for you in the oven," Garden announces without turning around.

"Oh. Thanks." I open the oven and see some pizza and chicken wings, hopefully the sign of a truce. I burn my fingers on the plate before I grab a mitt and transfer it onto a tray.

I walk over to the living room and sit down next to my sister as we watch the news. I shovel the food into my mouth, reveling in the greasy carbs and protein, and feel better instantly. "So...how was your day?" I ask with my mouth full.

"Let's talk about you instead," Garden replies tensely. "Where the hell have you been? You had me really worried." Garden takes a drag of her e-cig. I watch the plume of smoky vapor swirl around her. I've always been a little intimidated by my sister, who has a commanding presence that I envy. Our dad used to say—in typical Asian parent flippancy—that "River might have both legs, but Garden has the kick."

I try to shrug nonchalantly. "I was just...you know, out and about."

Garden scowls at me. "Don't gaslight me like that. You can't just disappear all night and then come back in some spaceship on wheels and expect me to accept that explanation."

I groan as I chew the cartilage off a chicken wing, not in the mood for one of her lectures. "G, you're my kid sister, not our mom. What's the point of being orphans if you're going to be such a buzzkill?"

"Don't call us orphans!" Garden snaps. "Mom's still around."

I gesture around us. "Well, where is she, then?"

Garden looks down at her lap, her face darkened. I instantly feel bad.

"Hey," I say, putting a hand on her shoulder. "Look, I'm sorry, okay? I didn't mean to worry you."

She shakes her head, still upset, though she's calmed a little. "It wasn't just yesterday. You've been randomly disappearing like that for months now. You think I don't notice? Riv, my bedroom is right above the garage! I hear you coming and going at all odd hours of the night!"

I pause, wondering what to say because she's right. Ever since I hooked up with that random boy at the UCLA library those few months ago, I've been doing a lot of random hookups, courtesy of Grindr. But I still haven't come out to her.

I bite my lip, knowing that it is time. "Hey, Garden, there's something I need to tell you." I take a deep breath as our eyes meet.

"I think...no, I know...that I'm gay."

My sister lets out a big exhale. Then she gives me a small smile...finally.

"It's okay, big brother," she says. "I know."

I lean back, surprised. "What do you mean?"

"Riv, I used to find your porn on our desktop all the time when we were teenagers. I've known for a long time. I was just waiting for you to tell me."

I'm stunned. "Whoa. Did you ever tell Mom or Dad?"

Garden shakes her head. "Of course not. But I'm glad you finally told me."

Without thinking, I reach over and pull her into a hug—the first hug the two of us have shared in a while. We hold each other like that for a long time.

When we release each other, there are tears in our eyes. "Thank you, G," I say softly, "for accepting me."

"I will accept you no matter what, River," she says. "But that doesn't mean I won't worry."

I nod. "I understand now. I'm just...finding myself, you know? Exploring."

Garden looks conflicted by this. "Do you remember," she asks, "when you called me to pick you up from the San Bernardino Mountains?"

I chuckle darkly at the memory of my revelations with our old Jesus statue. "Like it was yesterday."

"When I got to the base of the mountains, you were having a massive panic attack, screaming about Mom and Donald. I sat next to you and listened to my life fall apart even more. I will never forget that look on your face as you told me that Mom was cheating on our dying dad with our pastor."

I wince at this. "Damn... I'm sorry I put you through that. You were just a kid. You still are."

"No, River," she replies firmly, "that's not my point. My point is everyone talks these days about going off and finding themselves. But no one ever seems to care about what they might lose in the process."

I think about her words, not quite sure what they mean. But I nod sincerely.

"Okay. I hear you, G. I really do."

"So tell me, who was this cute guy who dropped you off?" she asks, smiling a little.

I beam. "He's pretty hot, right? His name is Joey." I show her his bracelet on my wrist. "He gave me this."

Garden laughs. "Well, at least you have good taste. What's his deal?"

I chuckle, shaking my head. "The whole thing is so improbable that I'll just say it. He is Winston Chow's boyfriend. But he might be a money boy, too. Which I still need to Google."

Garden is staring at me aghast. "Winston Chow?" she finally manages to get out.

"Yeah, you know, that Hong Kong entrepreneur who—"

Garden pointed past me in the direction of the TV. "Yeah, I know who he is, dummy, and he's right over there!"

I whip my head around to look at the news segment as my sister grabs the remote control and turns up the volume. We watch schmaltzy b-roll of Winston Chow—ringing the bell at the New York Stock Exchange, shaking hands with the President of China, floating weightless in a spaceship with the entire planet Earth visible behind him—as the reporter narrates.

"Famous for bankrupting Elon Musk, multimedia tycoon Winston Chow is hosting tomorrow in Los Angeles what he calls the most important historical art and artifact event in modern times. Chow has invited the world's foremost artifact dealers, art brokers and blue chip collectors to showcase for the first time what he says are the lost treasures of China. He calls this showcase the Reign Incarnate Gala."

The news segment cuts to a clip of Winston, leaning casually against the very same Russian car that drove me home this morning. Behind him I can recognize the Pacific Coast Highway in Malibu. He looks dashingly handsome under the California sun, though I can only glower at his smarminess.

"When the last Chinese dynasty fell at the beginning of the twentieth century, we didn't just lose our ancient heritage," Winston declares, his gleaming hair an unmoving perfect mass in the brisk ocean breeze. "We also lost countless pieces of history representing invaluable significance to our people, stolen from us in unjust wars by colonial looters. But thanks to the global efforts of a brilliant team of curators, scholars and investigators, I am proud to present the Reign Incarnate Gala, where we will reintroduce the lost treasures of China to the world."

The segment cuts back to the reporter, standing in front of the Griffith Observatory, which has been swathed in massive dark red banners inscribed with gold Chinese characters, transforming the classic Art-Deco landmark of LA to an embodiment of Eastern extravagance.

"Tomorrow is the big night," hams the reporter, "where the who's who of the international art scene will gather on the roof of Griffith Observatory to watch the unveiling of the lost treasures of China, and to ring in the Lunar New Year!"

Garden mutes the TV. We stare at each other in disbelief.

Finally, I break the silence. "But Joey told me that he was leaving for Asia tonight…"

Garden scoffs and opens her laptop as she types furiously, searching Reign Incarnate Gala. "Is that all you're going to think about? Boys? River, what sort of people have you gotten involved with?"

Undeterred, I realize something as I look down at Joey's bracelet. "If Winston is still here, then that means Joey might still be in—"

Our doorbell suddenly chimes, and both Garden and I jump. She looks at me, incredulous.

I walk over to the front entrance, hardly daring to believe it. Could it be that Joey is still in LA? Through the opaque glass of the door, I can see the figure of a man standing outside. My heart begins to beat like a drum. "Coming!" I say. I grab the handle, take a deep breath and open the door, hardly daring to believe it.

The door opens, and Calvin is standing there. He has taken a shower and changed into a loungewear tracksuit with a hoodie. He is also wearing a sheepish smile.

"Calvin!" I exclaim, genuinely stunned.

"Who is it?" Garden calls from the living room.

Calvin lifts up his hands, and he is holding my wallet and my keys. Of course. My home address is on my driver's license.

I take them from him as he shifts from foot to foot, looking a bit embarrassed. "Hey, River, I might owe you an apology for acting messy yesterday… I get a bit intense on E sometimes. I texted you today but you weren't responding so I figured I'd just drop your stuff off."

I am so surprised that at first I just stand there gawking at him. But I quickly remember myself and swing the door open wide, motioning him inside. "I've been asleep all day. That's so cool of you to bring my stuff back. And you don't need to apologize. Come inside, it's cold out."

He walks in, admiring the foyer. "Nice place."

I shrug. "My mom is married to a pastor. They make a lot more money than you'd expect." I motion him to follow me. "Come to the kitchen. I'll crack open one of his prized bottles of wine."

As Calvin follows, I catch sight of my sister leaning toward our direction in order to get a glimpse of who has arrived. "Hey, Garden," I call out as we approach her. I see her confused look at the stranger following me. "This is my new friend, Calvin." Garden, unaccustomed to visitors, gets up and nods warily at him.

Calvin, to his credit, acts completely normal when he sees my sister, who has taken off her prosthetic leg. I have found it is a good barometer of tact and decency, noting how people react to Garden when they see her disability. He just gives a friendly wave to her.

She looks him up and down, and then turns to me. "Another one?" she says drily. "You've been busy."

Calvin arches his eyebrow and turns to me with a delighted grin. "Wow, River, your sister is so sassy!"

After I open a bottle of wine, Calvin and I sit at the kitchen table. My sister puts her prosthetic back on and excuses herself to go to her bedroom. "Was nice to meet ya, Garden," Calvin calls after her.

He turns to me when she's out of earshot. "So about your sister—"

I gulp down the wine a bit too fast. "Birth defect," I say, coughing. "She was born with only her left leg. My earliest memories are going to the hospital to see her."

Calvin nods solemnly. "That's good to know...but I was actually gonna say instead that I feel like I've met her before. It's not like I've seen her face or whatever, but it's almost like...her energy is familiar. Do you ever get a weird feeling like that?"

"I have more than weird feelings. I'm just kinda weird overall, Calvin," I say, chuckling. "At least that's what I've been told my whole life. I was way more awkward when I was a teen. I know I'm better now—"

"Yeah, cuz you got hot!" Calvin pinches me on the cheek like an auntie. *Handsome guy!* he says in what is probably the only advanced Mandarin he knows. "Tale as old as time! Weird kid got hot. It isn't rocket science. I don't think you realize how much people stare at you. I was fending off thirsty hoes all night last night."

In the dim light of the kitchen, no longer entranced by dazzling lights and mind-altering drugs, I finally get a good, calm, sustained look at Calvin. He honestly does look like the lead member of a K-Pop band, with floppy bangs and long eyelashes. He truly is the hot one between us, even if he does look a little tired. And he is easy to talk to. I refill both our glasses, more generously this time.

Calvin takes a wet slurp of wine. He brushes his wavy hair out of his eyes, looking at me reflectively. "Actually, I was thinking on the drive here that I've had your cock in my mouth and we just had this crazy night together, but I barely know you."

I rarely giggle but he is really amusing me. "We aren't breaking any stereotypes, are we, Calvin? I don't think we even got past hello before you were unzipping my pants."

"Listen, it's LA." He shrugs with a shit-eating grin. "Most boys here ruin the moment if you let them talk too much. No, I don't want to know your moon sign and, yeah, bitch, I know that is so Taurus of me!"

This time I actually snort red wine and it stings, but it feels good to laugh. Calvin leans over and gives me a quick rub on the thigh. "Besides, I was just using you to warm up for Peril."

"So romantic," I groan.

"So what's your deal anyway?" Calvin asks as he leans in toward me. "Let me guess. Strict immigrant parents from Asia, closeted, high-achieving academically..." He gestures to a framed photograph of my mom and her husband next to the coffeemaker. "The Mr. Rogers–looking white pastor stepdad is throwing me a little, though."

"Hey, at least it's a not a stereotype!" I laugh. "He's all right, I guess. I think we've spoken like ten sentences to each other, ever."

"Where's your biological dad, if you don't mind me asking?" Calvin peers over the rim of his glass.

"He died when I was a senior in high school. My mom started seeing Donald while my dad was sick," I say quietly. "Now she's off in Africa somewhere spreading the gospel with the good pastor. At least I think so. She doesn't really check in with Garden and me that much. I actually haven't seen her in a long time."

Calvin winces. "Fuck. Christians, am I right? I'm really sorry about your dad."

"It's all right. It was almost five years ago now. I think what still affects me the most about it was that my dad deserved more life than that. He was a good person. I mean, he was in his early forties when he got cancer and died. Is that really all he gets?"

Calvin sighs heavily, patting me on the shoulder. "River, I think we are nearing that point where we decide whether we descend into wine madness and tears, or we change the subject." He holds up his glass. "But to be clear, in both scenarios we continue to drink Pastor Donald's excellent wine."

I scoot my glass toward him. "Fill 'er up, buttercup."

Calvin beams at me like a Cheshire cat with pink-stained teeth. "Next subject, then. Let's talk about boys."

I realize at that moment I've been absentmindedly fiddling with Joey's bracelet during this entire conversation. I quickly stop. "Fine, enough about me, though. Tell me about you, Calvin. Let's talk about your boys. I mean, look at you, you must have people chasing you everywhere."

"Eh, whatever." Calvin shrugs modestly. "I was engaged a while back...to a really close friend. We sort of grew up running around West Hollywood together while I was at college and we surprised ourselves by falling in love, and I eventually asked him to marry me." He drains his glass. "But it didn't work out."

"Sorry to hear that. What hap—"

"Anyway, I'm not big on dating these days," Calvin continues. "I'd rather party. And get into trouble with cuties like yourself."

I laugh as we clink glasses. I suddenly feel a tinge of emotion toward him. For a moment neither of us says anything, though I keep catching myself looking down at his plummy lips. The red wine has made me feel a little oozy and happy.

"You know, you and your sister have the same eyes," Calvin says, staring deeply into me. "What do you even call that color?"

"It's just a light brown," I murmur, feeling a bit shy.

Calvin shakes his head to disagree, but smiles. "Whatever it is, it's beautiful."

Calvin reaches over and places his hand on my wrist and begins to lean toward me. I close my eyes, not sure what is about to happen. I can feel his lips linger near mine.

But then I feel his finger brush against Joey's bracelet. I open my eyes as he pulls back, both of us looking down at it.

"Hey, doesn't that belong to Winston's money boy?" He

touches the larger misshapen green jade in the center. It catches the dim light of my kitchen and winks at both of us.

I jerk back as Joey's inscrutable face suddenly flashes in my mind. "Yeah, but don't call him that."

"Hey, I was out of line this morning. Sex work is honest work," Calvin says, also leaning away from me. "No disrespect meant. What happened anyway after you ditched me at the pool at Winston Chow's house?"

"Actually," I reply, "I wandered upstairs and I entered this huge room where there were all these statues of men having intense sex."

Calvin's eyes widen. "Whoa! Rich people are so weird. Did you take a pic?"

I shake my head. "No, but I wish I had because… I don't know how to put this, but they all had the same face. They all looked a lot like me."

Calvin stares at me for a second and I wonder if I've freaked him out. But then he just bursts out laughing. "River, you were just trippin' on really excellent drugs. We both were."

I snort. "I guess you're right. I think I'm done with party drugs for a while. They don't mix very well with my anxiety."

Calvin swats me playfully. "C'mon, I'm relying on you to be my new wingman. Don't register for AA yet."

"He gave me this bracelet after he dropped me off home this morning. But I think he lied to me. He said he was leaving for Asia tonight. But I just saw on the news that Winston has some swanky event tomorrow. I wonder if they are still together."

Calvin perks up. "Right, that gala with the funny name! Everyone is talking about it. I have a few clients that are going."

It strikes me just now that I don't know Calvin's job. "Clients?"

Calvin smiles. "You probably wouldn't have guessed I work in corporate PR. I rep some pretty legit white collar criminals." He raises his glass and we clink cheers, grinning at each other.

"You are full of surprises, Calvin," I reply as I refill our glasses.

"So why do you think Joey lied to you? Do you think maybe he just left for Asia by himself?"

I bite my lip. "I don't think so. Maybe he was just trying to shake me off. I mean, why would he want to be with me?"

Without warning, Calvin bonks me on the side of my head, not hard, though it startles me, and some wine spills out of my glass onto the table. "Stop talking like that, River! You are a queer Asian person! There are more of us in the world than there are Western Europeans. Be confident and proud!"

"That's very empowering," I reply, rubbing my skull, "but Winston is queer and Asian, too, and he's a literal billionaire."

"Yet, Joey was glommed onto *you* all night at Peril. Not Winston."

"That's true," I say. "They did get into a fight on the ride over dropping me home."

Calvin's eyes widen. "Whoa, rich people problems. What did they say?"

"Winston said something weird about my face, and Joey defended me," I recount.

"Okay, Joey gets a point already."

"And then Winston made a remark about how he discovered Joey giving blowjobs in a dirty restroom."

Calvin recoils in disgust. "Whoa, fuck you, Winston!" More wine slops out of his glass onto the table as he gesticulates. "That is a Real Housewives of Circuit Parties level of trashy. What a dick!"

Amused, I grab a napkin and sop up the spilled wine. "Yes, Winston sucks, but he is pretty frickin' hot."

Calvin nods vigorously. "Oh, totally. That muscle daddy makes me want to throw on an apron and fry up some eggs." He holds up a finger. "But... I saw the way Joey looked at you."

"Oh, really? And how did he look at me?"

Calvin sighs romantically at the memory. "Like you were the most important person in the world." He pauses for a second, then takes out his phone and starts texting rapidly.

"What are you doing?" I ask, leaning over to see what he's typing.

Calvin keeps clacking away at his phone as he replies. "I am telling my assistant to finagle me two tickets to Winston's gala. We are going there and you are going to confront Joey and tell him how you feel."

I'm a bit tipsy now and can only giggle at his enthusiasm. "Calvin, how have you only managed to get us into ridiculous situations?"

"What else are friends for?" Calvin asks with a seductive smirk. His phone buzzes and he reads the screen. "Nice! She thinks she can get us tickets."

I'm shaking my head and still laughing. "Are we sure this is a good idea?"

"River, we don't do good ideas. We do great ones." Calvin tips the rest of his wine down his throat, then places a hand on my shoulder dramatically. "Tomorrow evening you have another date with me...and destiny."

HE SHICAN
1740

Dr. Qi Yewang and I stared aghast at Jiulang's grandmother as she struggled against her invisible bonds, capable of making only the most muted of protests. She shot us an intense stare. *Do something*, her eyes seemed to demand.

Yewang glanced over at me nervously. *I will go get Huang Jiulang*, I said, reading his mind, and quickly walked out of my inn in search of the boy.

But upon exiting, I found Jiulang standing peacefully outside, next to Dama at her trough. The boy and the indigo horse were looking at one another as he stroked her muzzle, whispering to her. Dama was peering back into his eyes with a strange familiarity that surprised me.

Jiulang? I asked almost timidly, wondering what mysterious connection I was interrupting.

He responded without looking at me, as Dama nuzzled him affectionately. *Forgive me, Master He. I've always had an affinity for animals, particularly blue ones.*

It seems as though she has an affinity for you, too, I replied quietly, *as she is normally spooked by strangers.*

Once upon a time, Jiulang spoke dreamily as if to himself, *she led two wayward strangers back together when they both needed each other the most.* He kissed her on her forehead as he spoke to her. *Will you do it again?*

I had raised Dama since she was a newborn foal back in my hometown village, so his comment made no sense to me. But I thought it better to focus on the task at hand. *Jiulang, your grandmother—* I began.

Jiulang snapped out of his reverie. *Yes, of course.* He bent down to pick up a bundle of firewood at his feet, and promptly walked back into my inn. I followed.

Back inside he went over to where his grandmother and Yewang were sitting, kneeling beside her. *What are your first impressions, Dr. Qi?* he asked as he gently brushed a stray hair off her forehead. Her eyes became once again unfocused and cloudy, as though her consciousness had gone into hiding. It sent shivers down my spine.

Yewang cleared his throat. I could tell he was unsure what to say. *Well…first of all, what do you think ails her? How is she when she is healthy?*

Jiulang walked over to my kitchen to make tea. Already he moved around my inn as though he had lived here his whole life. *To be honest, Grandmother has never been that well, sadly.*

Yewang glanced over at me uncomfortably. *And she seems to not speak?*

Jiulang placed two teacups on the table and poured the hot water onto the leaves inside. *Did I not mention? Alas, Grandmother is a mute. Always has been.*

No, I said quietly. *You failed to mention that.*

Jiulang did not reply. He just sat back down at the table, smiling sweetly at us. *Drink it before it gets cold,* he chided gently, motioning at the tea. Obediently as children, both Yewang and I cupped our tea in our palms. And yes, as I looked into the amber liquid, the suspended tea leaves began to stir to life. Slowly at first, they orbited around the porcelain rim, their speed picking up with each revolution.

Yewang, I said in a scared whisper, even though Jiulang could easily hear me. *Look.*

The doctor was staring at his tea as well, his eyes furrowed in disbelief. Then, with much effort and strenuous force, he flung his cup away from him, as though it weighed a hundred pounds. It shattered on my floor into a dozen pieces. When he spoke, his jaw was locked shut as he hissed through clenched teeth. *You are a powerful spirit, Huang Jiulang.*

Jiulang reached out and folded Yewang's hand into his. *You need not be frightened, Dr. Qi,* he said gently. *Everything is going as planned.*

And the room began to spin around us.

As though he were released from a hold, Yewang slumped in his chair. *Yewang,* I cried, grabbing on to him. I was terrified. *Please stop!* I begged the boy.

All throughout this episode, Jiulang had remained placid, unassuming even. *You think it is I who glamours you?* he responded. *You are sorely mistaken.*

Yewang and I followed his line of vision as he turned toward his grandmother. Her vacant eyes had turned jet-black as she ever so slightly swayed back and forth with deadly intention.

Dr. Qi, thank you for being so dependably brilliant, he said as he bowed his head to Yewang, *so that you would come here today to help me with my grandmother. She and I do not stray far from the woods, otherwise I would have gone to Tiaoxi myself to beseech you.*

The movement of the room actually began to knock over chairs. From my kitchen I heard bowls smashing to the floor. Yewang's bag of instruments fell off the table, its contents spilling everywhere.

You knew, I realized, staring entranced at Jiulang. *You knew that if I asked Yewang about the Primordial Bolus, he would come here himself to investigate.*

Yewang was staring helplessly at his precious tools. Jiulang leaned over and took the doctor's face in his hands. *We have no need for your human gadgets. I do not seek you for medical counsel. I have come in search of magics.*

I am no magician, Yewang spat, still refusing to look into Jiulang's amber eyes.

Dr. Qi, Jiulang pressed on, *I know that you come from a bloodline of shamans from the Far South, those who can call upon the spirits and who have aided my folk in our times of need. I ask for your help to formulate the Primordial Bolus, so that you may free my grandmother from her suffering. I have gathered the ingredients already. All I need is your help.*

My head was aching from the dizzying rotations of the room, which was spinning into a blur around us. I began to feel ill. But Yewang remained resolute, looking at me and then back toward Jiulang. Finally, he shook his head. *No, Spirit. I will not.*

There was a deafening crack, and the room jolted to a halt so abruptly that Yewang and I had to hold on to the table to steady ourselves. I could feel the pall of something powerful and sinister lifted from upon us. I turned to look at Jiulang's grandmother. Her eyes had returned to normal and she seemed as though tamed.

Or perhaps relieved, I wondered to myself.

Release us, Yewang demanded, as though emboldened. *Let us go. We will leave and not speak of this again.*

For the first time, Jiulang was angry. His cheeks flushed and his eyes flashed as he stood. *Do not mistake my deference for weakness, Doctor. You see, I could have chosen anyone to bring you to me. But I chose Master He. Let me show you why.*

Leave him be! Yewang cried, but already Jiulang was reaching across the table at me, his arm outstretched. And with his open palm, he smacked me hard upon the forehead.

Shican! I heard Yewang shout.

Instantly, I am airborne, propelled backward with the force of a herd of wild animals.

I hear Yewang shout in protest, but already he sounds far away. I shoot away from the two other men, expecting to smash against the wall to my certain death, but instead, I keep falling and falling backward, as the world around me evaporates into nothingness.

I think: Has Jiulang killed me with a single blow? And then I wonder if the dead can think.

In the nothingness, I feel myself cartwheeling in a free fall. Somewhere, I can barely hear the distorted voices of Yewang and Jiulang, but I cannot understand them.

Then, far in the distance, I see a blur of colorful lights. Closer and closer I barrel toward the lights, which first I think is a city at night, but as I reach closer I realize it is a gathering of people. My speed begins to accelerate toward them. I shield myself, bracing for impact.

With a thud, I land in the midst of a grand party, men drinking and reveling together. It is as though I have fallen into someone else's body, unable to control it. As I adjust to my surroundings, I am astounded to discover by the clothes and the faces around me that I am in a palace of an ancient time, perhaps even thousands of years ago.

A hush suddenly falls over the crowd and I wonder if I have been discovered. But the body I am in turns and I watch in wonder as a familiar young man, dressed in the dazzling robes of a king, enters the room. On either side of him strut two shimmering blue peacocks.

Everyone in the room bows their heads to the ground, but I can still see him as he nears. I can hardly dare to believe it, but I can see it plainly now when the king turns to face me.

The young king is Jiulang.

Shican!

With a jolt I came to, gasping as though I had been holding my breath. I was back on the floor of my inn and I could feel Yewang behind me, his arms wrapped around me protectively. Above us stood Jiulang. It was striking to see that same porcelain face, from humble country boy to king and back. He was expressionless.

Yewang, I responded, coughing. I patted his arm. *I am all right. I am all right.*

Yewang stood, pulling me up with him. He dragged me away from Jiulang.

The boy had an odd tone when he spoke. *So we agree on the terms, Dr. Qi?*

Yewang pulled a chair to us and sat me down in it. He crouched to face me, inspecting my eyes and feeling the pulse in my neck. *Yes, Spirit,* he said darkly. *We have an agreement. I will make you your Primordial Bolus.*

Jiulang smiled mysteriously. *A favor for a favor,* he purred.

What transaction had I missed? I took Yewang's hand. *What did you agree? Why did you agree?*

Yewang pulled away from me. *Be quiet, Shican.*

He went over to Jiulang's grandmother and helped her to her feet. *Let me lay you down,* he said. The two of them went over to the stairs and walked up to her room.

He agreed to help me because I know the truth about him, Jiulang said to me quietly once Yewang was out of sight. He cocked his head and spoke as though thinking aloud. *How funny it is that you two found each other in this life.*

Why are you doing this? Feeling the strength returning to my limbs, I forced myself to stand up and walked over to him. *Please, just let Yewang go!* I demanded as I grabbed him by the shoulders, knowing full well he could strike me again.

But instead, the boy placed a hand gently upon my cheek. As he spoke, his breath was cold as winter's extreme.

You have been searching your whole life for this moment, Shican. Just let it happen.

DONG XIAN
4 BCE

The very next day after my not-so-chance encounters with the Emperor and that damned Commander Jujun, I came back to my chambers at midday to receive yet another. Fu's eunuch, Shi Li, stood waiting at my door. If he felt the same awkwardness as me, he didn't show it, remaining as stoic as ever.

Arching at his feet, Miaomi was also outside, disturbed by my intruder. The normally serene blue cat was poised to strike, and she hissed at us in warning.

Shi Li led me to a remote part of the Palace grounds I'd never been to, a hidden scenic pond that had so many padded blossoms that one could barely see the surface of the water. Their fragrance wafted through the air, and in the humid heat of approaching summer, the sweet smell was almost aggressive.

Sitting under the cool shade in a glen of trees, the Grand Empress Dowager Fu waved me over, flashing that silver smirk of hers good-naturedly. She was adorned with an elaborate headpiece made of gold leaf-petaled flowers and dangling pink pearls. As I sat down, I could see her more clearly in the true light of day, and noticed that what I thought was flawless skin was actually strategically layered powder. At the corners of her eyes, there were cracks betraying her age, and I wondered how she actually looked beneath this porcelain mask.

Behind her were two beautiful ladies-in-waiting, both around my age and dressed in pink to match Fu's pearls. The ladies were sharing a pipe, blowing that gray smoke into the breeze. I watched, expecting the smoke to dissipate, but it stayed solid, like miniature storm clouds, as they floated away and disappeared into the trees.

Fu spoke in a gravelly singsong as ruby-red tea was placed in front of me. *I heard that Liu Xin went about yesterday as though ferried by clouds, lauding the mysterious young man he chanced upon in the gardens.* Once again she referred to the Emperor by his birth name Liu Xin, which I had since learned was sacrilegious. But she said it in a way that was cavalier and dominant.

Am I to understand that he isn't to know of my special relationship with you, my lady? I asked. After Commander Jujun's threats, I had a foreboding feeling that continuing to withhold this secret from him would spell disaster for all of us, especially me.

She rolled her eyes, bored by this mundane talk about the mechanics of machinations. *Dong Xian, even before my grandson became Emperor, every waking moment of his life has been a carefully choreographed dance. Why not allow the boy some serendipity, some fantasy?*

This flighty talk of fantasy was peculiar coming from the perverse woman who in our very previous meeting had drugged me into plowing her eunuch. *Apologies, my lady. I am very glad to hear His Radiance enjoyed my company.*

As though it were a reward for my good work, the pipe had found its way over to me and was placed to my lips by a lady-in-waiting. Inside its bowl the coal was still burning hot, and I could see the contents sparkle at me, laced with that mysterious metallic dust.

I placed my lips around the pipe and inhaled. Instantly, I

could feel that thick smoke course through me, as the world grew fuzzy and warm. The effects of this drug were different, though, in the direct sunlight. It made me feel giddy, with all the joys of drunken mirth without the nausea. I hadn't a care in the world. My body was humming.

As the Grand Empress Dowager and her ladies observed, Shi Li reappeared and obediently got on his knees in front of me. When he parted my robes, my influence was already awakening. I closed my eyes as the eunuch's thick lips wrapped around it.

Impressive, Grandmother, I heard one of the ladies-in-waiting murmur approvingly to Fu.

Yes, Grandmother, cooed the other's pretty voice. *You were not exaggerating. This one is a fine specimen indeed.*

As for me, I needed no words as I was mindlessly enjoying the revolutions of Shi Li's tongue around my tender meat, grunting softly as his hands slid under me to knead my cheeks. I opened my eyes to watch his head glide up and down upon mine, his smooth hairless face beginning to glisten in the sun with his blessed sweaty effort. I felt my pouch start to reliably tighten.

Do not release your seed, young Dong! Fu's abrupt voice pierced through my ecstasy. Exasperated, I turned to her as her eunuch continued his job. She had leaned forward, her arm still outstretched toward me in her command. *Despite appearances, this is not a garden party. You must control yourself.*

I moaned with both lust and anguish. *Please, my lady, but why?* As though purposely torturing me, Shi Li only feasted upon me with more conviction and I could feel my influence straining to be spent.

The Emperor's grandmother sat back as I writhed and panted. *Child, my people are from the birthplace of the Han, from the land that is within the Yellow River. It is here where the ancient pleasures are still Remembered, and passed down for generations between those who are loved by an Emperor.*

My groin began to involuntarily buck into the air. I tried to think about my own grandmother in order to delay my arrival.

We are brewing your energy, Dong Xian, Fu chided, as though I were a fool for not knowing. *Now that you have caught the Emperor's eye, every action and inaction you take is solely for his pleasure. This simple exercise is how you keep your life force charged at the ready for the Son of Heaven at any given moment...but it is all for naught if you release your seed!*

Shi Li sadistically switched the direction of his tongue, and my whole body spasmed. *My lady, I feel as though I have been set up to fail this exercise,* I whimpered. *I will not be able to contain myself much longer.*

Fu was looking down at Shi Li with a peculiar affection in her eyes. *I have taught Shi Li well for this very reason,* she said.

As she finished speaking, I felt something cold and flat in Shi Li's mouth as it was pushed up against my skin. I looked down as well and Shi Li opened his mouth wide to show me. Sitting on his tongue was a razor-thin blade, looking lethally sharp. It glinted as it caught the sun behind me. Before I could react, the eunuch closed his warm mouth around my still rigid influence!

My first instinct was to leap away from him, but I could feel the needle-sharp edge of the blade tucked snugly underneath the ridge of my head. Tearing away from him would slice me open. So I sat there immobilized, cold sweat beading on my chest.

With his long tongue, Shi Li began to maneuver the cold metal round and round my throbbing member at increasing speeds, displaying skill that was both precise and merciful. Yet, despite his adeptness, I was still distressed, especially whenever I felt the slick blade bump against one of my raised veins, less than a hair's width from nicking the hypersensitive flesh.

As traumatic as this exercise was, it was also working. I remained fully erect—and brewing—but my anxiety around getting cut overpowered my need to release, lest I injure us both! I slowed my breaths so I could stay as still as possible for Shi Li's task and just concentrated on the feeling of that lethal blade as it scraped over my skin.

There now, you see? Fu looked proud, and the ladies behind her both nodded in agreement like a pair of vipers. *So tell me, child, how did the two of you end it? Pray tell, what happens next for the Emperor and Dong Xian?*

I was trying to control my breathing and replied stiltedly. *He asked for a regular audience with me so I might recite poetry for him.*

She smiled delightedly. *I see you manage to surprise, young Dong. Who would have anticipated you would have such a command of the classics? And how clever you were to parlay your skills into more encounters with Liu Xin.*

Still sucking, Shi Li had withdrawn one of his hands from my buttock and was now using it to gently massage my sorely aching pouch, churning my life force within. I shuddered at the sensations but continued speaking. *I worry about one factor, my lady. You see, I met that soldier. The one I asked you about the first time we met.*

Fu's smile vanished. *I see. You met Jujun.*

I nodded. *He was none too pleased about my budding friendship with the Emperor.*

Her eyes were now flashing with anger. *That inbred bastard has been meddling since the day Liu Xin was born. His return to the Endless Palace at my grandson's ill-advised behest could be the downfall of us all. Beware of Jujun, young Dong. He may look like a blunt object, but he is as sharp as the blade in Shi Li's mouth.*

I felt my heat rising, too, as even the mere thought of Jujun enraged me. His smug face appeared in my mind, still laughing at me. *Yes, my lady, he threatened to expose the two of us to the Emperor if I did not retreat. I fear that he will fulfill that threat unless I back down from gaining your grandson's favor.*

Fu was grinding her gleaming teeth, deep in grim thought. She finally said, *It is a race to the finish, then. Dong Xian, you must land your courtship of the Emperor with precision and speed, because I in turn shall now accelerate what I must do.*

I immediately regretted telling her. *But my lady, I only just met the Emperor!*

Fu let out an exasperated sigh. *Some men might have beauty, but none have a woman's cunning,* she hissed at her ladies, who rolled disappointed eyes at me. She turned back to glare at me. *Dong Xian, this is your moment! Seduce the Emperor, or be bested by his Commander. And I warn you now, not even I can protect you from Jujun's brutality if he decides he can dispose of you without recourse.*

This was concerning news. The pipe had made its way back to me once again and I gratefully took another labored hit. Fu's face lit up. *Unless...*

My heart was fluttering rapidly now. *Unless...?*

She spoke as if daydreaming a lifelong wish. *Unless we send Shi Li to visit Jujun's chambers while he is sleeping.*

As I exhaled another plume of silver smoke, I had a vision of Commander Jujun in his bed—out of his heavy armor, vulnerable in deep slumber, his naked body outlined under a thin blanket. My mind's eye trailed up the impressive hills of his built musculature as Fu's voice continued to narrate.

All Shi Li would need is a knife and the Commander's exposed neck. Now I was envisioning Jujun's thick, swarthy throat, studded with his coarse beard. I could see the sharp tip of Shi Li's knife encroaching upon it, toward a pronounced vein running down his neck that was pulsating to the same beat of my heart.

Just a stab in the dark, Fu whispered, her voice now echoing around me, *and you will be released!*

As I focused in more on Jujun's throbbing vein, hearing the blood coursing within, suddenly I felt as though the ground gave way beneath me. My eyes snapped open as I realized what was happening. I was arriving, and there was no way I could stop it!

With a roar of sweet gratification, I was knocked back by a climax as searingly sharp as the blade that had produced it.

Fortunately for me, Shi Li had unlocked his lips around my influence and withdrawn the blade safely at the very last moment. He held it between his teeth as he sat back away from me. Unfortunately for him, he had expertly brewed my life force to the very brimming limits. Scalding strands of milky pearls erupted out of me to splash upon the eunuch's face, glistening in the sunlight. I could only twitch about and yelp in guilty relief as the tides rippled out of me.

As my passionate throes abated, I turned timidly to the Grand Empress Dowager to apologize, but I witnessed something fantastical. Maybe it was her hypnotic drug, maybe it was the intensity of my release, or maybe it was something else altogether—but when I looked in the direction of Fu and her ladies-in-waiting, I saw instead three wild beasts!

The silver-haired monster that stood in Fu's place had what appeared to be writhing tails behind it, hundreds of them!

I blinked in alarm, and in that instant the beasts disappeared, replaced again by Fu and her ladies. Fu wore an expression of profound annoyance. I must have imagined what had just transpired, I thought, and I put it out of my mind.

Many apologies, Your Imperial Majesty, I said meekly as I refastened my robes. Dripping in my seed, Shi Li stood up emotionlessly, wiping himself down with a piece of cloth. He then spat out a mouthful of blood. My accidental release had one casualty, it turned out. I wasn't sure if I should apologize to him, too.

What a shame, but quite a show! one of Fu's ladies giggled.

A few days later I was awoken early by a loud rapping on my door. When I opened it, I was surprised to see who it was. *Father? What are you doing here?*

It was true that my father and I both worked at the Court, but as one of the senior administrators, he made it a point not to be seen with me, lest someone not recognize me as his son and he be seen as socializing with a lowly clerk. He was not the most paternal type, but he was a pragmatic and careful bureaucrat—

and he fathered like one, too. In two years he had only visited my quarters one other time—the day I was moved in.

He strode in stiffly. *Third Son, the Emperor's grandmother means to throw a banquet in my honor in a month's time. You are to come with me to represent our clan.*

I'd been yawning off the dregs of sleep until he said that. Instantly, I was wide-awake in the face of Fu's accelerated intrigues. For a moment I did not know how to respond.

Then I blurted out, *Father, what sort of fruit would you like her to serve?*

He gave me a look of bewilderment.

RIVER
PRESENT DAY

As we drive up Mount Hollywood toward the Reign Incarnate Gala, I turn to Calvin one last time. "Don't forget. We bail the moment things go south. What's the safe word?"

Calvin is dressed to pinprick perfection in a velvet plum tuxedo with his wavy hair slicked back, looking every bit the K-drama heartthrob. He gives me a look of mock confusion. "More lube?" He laughs as I roll my eyes.

Climbing out of our Lyft, I look up at the Griffith Observatory, swathed in red banners and sitting atop the hills looking like a Lunar New Year gift. The entire grounds are lit aglow by spotlights in the early evening. Lion dancers and drummers revel in front of the iconic building, ringing in the holiday and welcoming the many guests arriving in splashy cars.

At the base of the stairs leading up to the Observatory, Calvin stops me to adjust the white bow tie he had lent me. He steps back to take me in, and then proudly claps me on the shoulders. "You clean up well, River. It's like you were poured into this suit."

We begin to ascend the stairs together. "The last time I wore this suit was to my dad's funeral."

Calvin groans. "Remind me to teach you how to hold the moment without killing it. By the way, I forgot to mention that it turns out my assistant couldn't find us tickets."

I nearly trip on my patent leather shoes. "You mean we aren't on the list?"

We are nearly at the top of the stairs and Calvin is striding casually toward the doorwoman, who is holding a clipboard. Next to her stands a bouncer the size of a house. "Honey," he purrs to me breezily, "when you look as good as we do tonight, you're always on the list."

We approach the incredibly chic woman, who looks to me like she snorts razor blades for breakfast. "Names?" she sneers, without even looking up at us. Calvin clears his throat but she still doesn't lift her head. "Names!" This time she snaps the word in half, clearly not one to be fucked with. Calvin and I look at each other, and I can see he's already out of ideas.

"Peaches," I blurt aloud.

She finally looks up at me incredulously as I say the safe word. Calvin face-palms himself as she looks back down at her clipboard. "Your name is Peaches?" she growls as her eyes scan her list. Behind her, the bouncer cracks his knuckles menacingly.

She looks back up, and I am seriously about to grab Calvin and bolt down the stairs. But then her face changes while she does a double-take at me. She suddenly becomes flustered, as though she's seen a ghost. "Oh...are you...?" she stutters, before she finally moves aside and gestures into the Griffith Observatory. "Welcome to the Reign Incarnate Gala."

As Calvin and I walk into the Gala, he has a jaunty swagger in his step, as though we hadn't just had a close brush with being thrown down a flight of hard stone steps. "I told you we looked good," he exults as he scans the crowd of predominantly Asian glitterati, dripping in diamonds and gold. Kicky remixes of old Cantopop songs I recognize from my childhood play over the speakers.

"Calvin, I don't think she let us in because of how we looked. Did you catch the way she stared at me, like she recognized me? Do you think she mistook me for someone else?" The possibilities unsettle me.

Calvin grabs a couple hors d'oeuvres off the tray of a caterer walking by us, popping one into his mouth. "Look at this sexy dumpling," he says with his mouth full, holding it up for us to inspect. The gold-tinted steaming morsel has the umami fragrance of black truffle and pork fat, and looks like dim sum redesigned by Jeff Koons. Calvin eats the other one as well, licking his fingers contentedly. "I'm gonna pop my tuck if I eat any more of these."

The Gala is already pretty crowded, and though some of the more luminary faces I can recognize, including a dapper gentleman who looks awfully like the Crown Prince of Japan, I don't see Winston or Joey anywhere. Another server walks past us and Calvin swipes two bubbly cocktails that appear to be garnished with edible birds' nests. He hands one to me, but I take them both from him and set them down on a table. "No drinking tonight, Calvin. We have to stay clear-headed."

Calvin makes a strangled sound of protest but I quickly walk toward the central staircase, looking for a higher vantage point. He follows me, throwing his hands up in defeat. In my pocket, I feel my phone buzzing and I pull it out. It is Garden calling.

"This time," she had said to me as I left home for the Gala, "if I call you, pick up. I have a weird feeling about all of this." I had promised her I would.

I answer the phone as Calvin and I reach the top of the stairs, and lean against the railing. But as I try to take advantage of our new view, the lights suddenly dim into a warm reddish tone, making it hard to see.

"River, how is it over there?" Garden asks, and I hear her typing away at her keyboard.

"Chinese New Year meets *Eyes Wide Shut* vibes," I reply quietly. "It seems like every rich and famous Asian person is here, G."

"Not just the famous ones. There's been a lot of chatter on-line," Garden says, "that this Reign Incarnate Gala has links to Asian triads and crime syndicates. You need to be careful there."

Maybe I should've taken that drink. "What on earth? Why?"

I can hear her exasperation over the phone. "Who do you think has been hiding those artifacts from the public all these years? They weren't just floating around in space. They were being harbored by powerful criminals."

I look around me at the other attendees dressed to the nines and wonder what a mob boss looks like. "Okay, I hear you, G."

"I get that you want to look for that guy, but this feels more and more dangerous. You should grab Calvin and come back home. Don't forget what I told you yesterday, Riv."

We hang up and I turn to talk to Calvin—and he's gone missing. I spin around looking for him, and he's nowhere to be seen. Because, of course.

I walk along the railing of the second floor, texting Calvin and wondering what to do next. Then I suddenly feel a strong grip on my shoulder and I am yanked back behind a giant marble column, hidden from view. I find myself face-to-face with the same house-sized bouncer from the front entrance. He leans down at me and bares his teeth, as if he is about to eat me. But then he steps aside, revealing the man behind him.

"Winston!" I say, trying to sound casual. "Great party. Everything okay?"

Winston Chow finally looks like a true billionaire, in a pristine crimson tuxedo and a Blancpain on his wrist, but it is the look on his face that makes my blood run cold. Out of sight from the crowd, I begin to grow scared. He walks up to me, and I almost shield myself reflexively, but slam my hands in my pockets instead.

"River," he says, his voice dripping with disdain, "we can't seem to get enough of each other. You certainly have a talent for turning up to my events uninvited."

I try to chuckle. "Funny story, my friend is the PR agent for a bunch of the guests here, and we got tickets. I didn't even know it was your event until I arrived! What a crazy coincidence, huh?"

Winston does not even pretend to be amused. Instead, he reaches out with gloved hands and lifts my chin with his fingers, scrutinizing my face closely. I pull away from him, increasingly panicked. Behind Winston, the bouncer shields us from view of the main party. I am trapped.

It is hard to describe the expression on Winston's face. He looks enraged, but there also seems to be hurt in his eyes. He takes in a deep breath, as if steadying himself. When he speaks, his breath smells like iron. "I don't know what you and Joey are up to, whether you are trying to embarrass me or swindle me, but I am warning you now that I am a very creative enemy with infinite avenues of expressing my discontent."

I am backed up against the column, wondering how I can escape. "I promise, Winston, I have no idea what you are talking about! I only just met Joey at Peril yesterday."

"That's a lie!" Winston spits out in fury. "I had my suspicions when we first met at my house, but seeing you again now, I cannot deny it. I want you to stay away from Joey. Do you understand me?" He presses his fist into my chest, pushing hard into my rib cage. I can feel him pushing the air out of my lungs.

"The truth is," he snarls, "Joey belongs to me."

I watch as Winston nods over his shoulder at his bouncer. The bouncer reaches into his jacket and pulls out an old-school butterfly knife.

"There is a specific point on your body that runs just below the nipple line that, if punctured, is not lethal," Winston says as he moves to the side to let his bouncer approach me. "But if incised just right, it never fully heals and causes a lifetime of excruciating chronic pain."

I fight back tears as the bouncer steps toward me, his blade glinting as it catches the light overhead. Winston nods at his man. "Let's see if we can find it."

With a sudden motion, Winston clamps his hand over my mouth and pins me against the column. I close my eyes as I feel the encroaching knife, and then I hear a familiar voice cry out.

"Peaches!"

Winston, the bouncer and I turn to see Calvin rushing up the stairs calling out our safe word, holding a half-empty cocktail glass. The two men instantly break away from me, allowing Calvin access as he rushes to me, breathless and sweaty. "Peaches," he says again, triumphantly.

Winston looks at Calvin nonplussed. "Peaches?" he asks. The bouncer shoots daggers at Calvin and me, clearly exasperated to be dealing with this shit again.

Calvin talks loudly, and other Gala guests turn to look in our direction. I realize he's keeping us both safe. "Yes…peaches. I am hella allergic and I was just told there is peach fuzz in this drink." He does his best to look indignant.

Winston squints at us both. "And…?"

Calvin then actually hands his drink to Winston Chow, who is too surprised to refuse it. "And my friend here has my EpiPen in his car, so we need to skedaddle ahora." He starts to cough violently. "I can already feel my throat closing up!" he wheezes. Now everyone around us is staring. Calvin, you are brilliant.

Calvin grabs me and pulls me away from Winston as he continues to cough and gag. "Snaps for the open bar, but you should label your drinks better. The immunocompromised community thanks you." He leads me down the steps, but not before calling back to Winston. "Big fan, by the way! If I make it out of here alive and you're looking for a new PR rep..."

I look back apprehensively at Winston and his bouncer, but both men are already slinking away out of sight. "Calvin, they were literally about to shank me. We need to get out of here. Garden just called and—"

Calvin turns to me at the base of the stairs. "We can go, but you need to see something first. Trust me."

He starts guiding me in a direction away from the front entrance, as I resist. "No! Winston almost just turned me into shish kabob. We need to leave right now!"

He is pushing me toward another section of the Griffith Observatory, where there is a well-lit museum that normally features famous asteroids. As we enter, I see that the museum has been converted into a gallery showroom, with various paintings and sculptures on display.

I turn to Calvin, perplexed. "Why are we here?"

Calvin doesn't say anything, but instead looks around at the art on the walls and on the floor. I follow his gaze and then it strikes me.

The paintings and sculptures are varied and diverse, but they all feature the same subject. It is unmistakable who it is.

They all feature me.

Indeed, everywhere I look in the room, I see my likeness staring back.

I stumble a bit, and Calvin holds on to me, though he is also speechless. Then, in the far corner of the room, surrounded by guests and media alike, I see the artist himself fielding questions from the reporters and enthusiasts. The artist suddenly seems to feel my eyes upon him. He looks up and we lock eyes.

The artist is Joey.

HE SHICAN
1740

After he put Jiulang's grandmother back in her room, Dr. Qi Yewang announced that he was going back to his horse to get something. He said it to no one in particular, just in the direction of the space between Jiulang and me, his voice tired and his brow furrowed. He then left, shutting the door firmly behind him.

Not knowing what else to do, I stood up and began to clean the mess in my inn. Plates and cups had fallen from cupboards, shattering everywhere. For a while, Jiulang watched me work with those unreadable eyes of his before he finally spoke. *Master He, you must think me an evil creature.*

I shook my head as I swept with my broom. *I do not. I only wonder what predicament you are in to resort to such desperate measures. And I feel bad to have brought Yewang into it.* I paused to look back at him. *What are you, Huang Jiulang?* I asked.

Jiulang rose, gliding toward me. *You ask me that so accusingly, as though you have not been searching for me your whole life. What else would you seek when you walk the woods at night, Master He?*

His face was now just a few inches from mine. I swallowed, unsettled. *I seek nothing. Spirits only come to you when—*

When we want to be found, Jiulang interrupted, his voice echoing. He took my arm in a cold grip and led me to the sitting area, pulling me beside him as we sat down on my bench. *You have many questions. What do you wish to know, mortal?*

I know that the Primordial Bolus is meant to destroy. I hesitated as Jiulang raised his eyebrows, but still I pressed on. *Is that why your grandmother seems to fear it? She seemed like she was relieved when Yewang refused to help you at first.*

The boy looked up the stairs in the direction of his grandmother's room, then turned back to me. *She is not just my grandmother, Master He. She is also my captor.*

I was incredulous. *Jiulang, the woman is half-comatose!*

Jiulang clasped both my hands and his skin was suddenly warm and full of life. *You saw how powerful she still is, glamouring you and Dr. Qi even in that weakened state. Please, you must believe me.* I felt my own heat rise.

With a grunt I shoved him away. *You bewitch me again.*

Jiulang sat hunched over from the force of my push. He flicked his eyes back at me like a wounded cat. *Nay, Master He. I know what you saw earlier, when I pushed you into the timeless space. An ancient palace, a debaucherous party and a king who shares my face. I know you realize there is more at play here than a simple request.*

He was right, but I said nothing.

Jiulang sat back, folding his legs under him on the bench. *Dr. Qi must sever the bond between that woman and me. She and I are bound by magics that only he can unravel.*

I thought for a moment before I replied. *If you want Yewang's help, you need to tell him the truth about this woman. He deserves to know what he is actually doing.*

I will tell Dr. Qi the truth, the boy agreed, *as long as you encourage him to help me. Yewang will need your support as he summons powerful forces not of this world. If you reassure him, he will be calm and he will be able to perform the severance.*

I have one more question, then, I said.

Ask.

A favor for a favor, I recalled. *That is what you said to Yewang after he agreed to help you. What favor did you promise him?*

He reached over and held my chin with the assuredness of someone much older than his years. He smiled. *Beyond requesting that you remain unharmed, he also asked me to help him forget you.*

I was stunned by Yewang's request. *Is that a power you possess? To manipulate memory?*

Those are simple magics, Jiulang said, shrugging. *Memories are already so immaterial that it only takes a nudge for them to dissipate away, like waking dreams. Half the battle is already won because Yewang actually desires to forget you. He loves you, after all. Even if you cannot truly return the feeling.*

I looked down at my lap, unable to respond.

Yes, the pain of loving someone who does not love you in return is perhaps the most mortal of emotions. The boy leaned back, dangling his legs over the bench. *Like the sun itself has decided not to shine upon you anymore.*

As though in response, the door opened again and fading sunlight splashed into the inn. Yewang walked in, holding two squirming bags. I stood, backing away in alarm. Yewang unceremoniously dropped the bags on the ground, and I could hear a curious, furious thrashing inside. *I found your ingredients outside*, he said to Jiulang, still emotionless. *We can begin at sunset.*

Jiulang stood, gliding over to Yewang. He hooked an arm around the doctor's shoulder, who flinched but remained steady. *We are all friends now*, the boy said. *Let us not be cross. We are about to accomplish great things. I am about to free my grandmother from her perpetual sorrows. Dr. Qi, you are about to bend the laws of reality with the magics of your birthright.*

Yewang shook his head, finally appearing darkly amused by his predicament. *And what of our friend, He Shican?*

Jiulang smiled as I walked past them. *Master He? He is about to cook us all supper.*

And sure enough, the moment he finished his sentence, I was already in the kitchen reaching for my pots.

Later, as we sat around a largely untouched meal of preserved fish porridge and stewed bamboo, I felt a hand upon my thigh. Yewang, Jiulang and I were sitting in a circle around my table, and the boy had already told Dr. Qi about his actual plans for the Primordial Bolus and the woman he claimed was his grand-mother. I had done my best to be encouraging. Looking entirely detached, Yewang had nodded, saying nothing.

But then he placed his hand on my thigh.

As discreetly as possible, I glanced down as Yewang used his finger to trace something. First, he drew a horizontal line, then hooked it downward. And then he lifted his finger and added a whisker to the line that curved away from the hook.

He was drawing a character. It was the word *knife*.

I blinked my recognition, hoping that Jiulang did not notice anything. As this happened, Jiulang was looking back and forth between Yewang and me with that same disaffected demeanor of his. *Dr. Qi,* he was saying, *you and Master He seem to have a very special relationship.*

You seem to be especially obsessed with it, Yewang replied coldly, unable to conceal his contempt.

I stayed with Dr. Qi for a while, I interjected quickly, *as he was kind enough to provide shelter for me back when I lived in Tiaoxi.*

Do you provide shelter for many of your patients, Dr. Qi? Jiulang continued to probe, as though relishing our mutual discomfort. He smiled beguilingly at Yewang. *Is this a perk that I might enjoy if I were to engage your services for myself?*

He Shican was not a patient, Yewang snapped. He gritted his teeth, fuming at the boy's invasive questioning. As for me, I did not understand this antagonization. The true nature of the previous relationship between Yewang and me was clear to everyone sitting at my table. Why did Jiulang seem so intent on shaming Yewang, whose help he needed?

Yewang stood up suddenly, clearly done with this conversation. *The sun is setting*, Yewang announced coolly. *We should begin.*

Jiulang seemed ever so slightly wary, the smile remaining frozen on his face. *So eager now, Dr. Qi.*

I began to clear the table. Jiulang remained sitting, still staring at Yewang. Yewang shifted his feet, then walked over to the now-motionless bags he had dropped on the ground earlier. *I would like to get home at a reasonable hour*, he said.

Jiulang chuckled, standing up finally. *A reasonable hour. What a mundane concept.* He picked up the candle on the table. *The rest of the ingredients are already in the room.*

As the boy and the doctor began to head toward the stairs leading up to Jiulang's room, I swiftly carried the bowls to my kitchen. I turned around to see Jiulang and Yewang disappear up the stairs. Noting what Yewang had drawn on my thigh, I opened the drawer and pulled out my sharpest knife, concealing it in my tunic. Then I rushed to the stairs.

They were nearly to her door when I caught up to them, feeling the cool metal of the knife pressed against my skin.

The boy knocked gently on the door. *Grandmother? We are coming in.*

Inside, there was not a sound. Jiulang pushed the door open, and we all walked in. We looked around. The room was empty.

I stuck my head back out the door into the hallway, as though expecting she had somehow slipped past us unseen. Jiulang rushed to look under the bed, while Yewang opened the window and looked outside at the ground below.

Equally unsuccessful and all confused, the three of us turned back to each other.

Suddenly, we heard a scratching sound from above us.

At the same time, we all looked up.

DONG XIAN
4 BCE

The next month was a whirlwind as I met continually with the Emperor to recite the Three Hundred Songs for him. During this time, the leaves of our courtyard's massive tree grew thick overhead, graciously blocking the sun as its heat intensified by the week. As Uncle stood by and fanned us with a large palm branch, we drank yellow wine in the quiet garden. The Emperor marveled at my memory, as I was able to recall each poem that he requested by its numerological order.

How about the fifth ode of Zhou & South in the Airs of the States? the Emperor would ask.

It brought me great joy to watch his face light up each time I reliably recited the requested poem back to him.

A peach was gifted to me,
And I in return gifted you a beautiful jade.
This jade was not a payment,
But a promise that our friendship might be everlasting.

These conditions appeared to be exceedingly idyllic and invitingly romantic for courting an Emperor, but there was a bruising blemish in the perfection. All of my meetings with the Emperor were attended as well by his bodyguard, the contemptuous Commander Jujun.

The soldier would stand at the far end of the courtyard, behind his younger cousin, to glower at me with furious eyes the entire time, souring the wine in my mouth. If I ever tried to even lean closer to the Emperor, Jujun would grip his hand around his sword threateningly, quickly extinguishing any passion I might hope to ignite. Thus, our sessions may have been productive in terms of poetry, but all the romance remained trapped within the old rhymes, unable to be brought to life between us.

As for the Emperor himself, he was an enigma. I could sense that he enjoyed my company and he was becoming more accustomed to me—but surely he knew my reluctance to engage with him on a deeper level was being stymied by his cousin. At least, that is what I hoped; I could not afford to message indifference to him.

As for me, I felt like a show pony destined for the slaughterhouse, doing my best to perform my tricks while a steadily increasing panic plagued me. The date of Fu's banquet ticked closer by the day, and I was sure that if I couldn't secure the Emperor's favor before whatever she had planned, I would be ruined.

One thing that did progress was my ever-growing hatred for Commander Jujun. As I lay in my bed each night, I could not wipe from my mind the image of his detestable face laughing at my plight. He did not know of my struggles and my sacrifices to get to this point, but even if he did, I was sure he'd simply relish his torture of me more.

He had me trapped, and we both knew it. The tension of my perilous circumstances was unbearable, and I began to yearn to be released, even if it meant my doom. If the Commander was thus intent on exposing me to the Emperor, what was stopping him?

But an imperial order is an imperial order, and I dutifully marched to meet the Emperor each time I was summoned, to the beat of a funeral drum in my head.

The only moments of happiness in my life during these weeks were ironically from the source of my angst, as I cherished my afternoons with the Emperor, finding him to be a calming presence who was generous in his attentions to me. As I recited the odes to him, he would stare at me dreamily with those expressive amber eyes. No one had ever looked at me the way he did—as though he knew what I truly was, and he didn't fault me for it.

At least that was what I hoped. It was all that might save me.

Then a miracle happened. It happened a little more than a week before Fu's banquet, when I arrived to our usual courtyard to discover the Emperor was unguarded, save for Uncle, who stood by quietly as always. Commander Jujun, it was explained to me, had an unexpected matter to address elsewhere and would not be joining us today.

I sang silent praises to Heaven as I sat with the Emperor, who also seemed cheerful and uplifted by our hard-earned intimacy. After I poured us both liberal servings of yellow wine, he grinned at me.

How about a lighthearted ode to start, for once? he pondered, leaning back in his seat. *My heart does feel exceptionally light today and I dare fathom at least one of these poets was a cheeky man.*

I knew exactly which poem would fit his request, and I made a point to lean in toward him as I sang it.

Plop fall the plums! But seven remain.
Let the gentleman who wishes to court me
Come while it is still lucky!

Plop fall the plums! But three remain.
Let the gentleman who wishes to court me
Come before it is too late!

Plop fall the plums! Now none remain.
Let the gentleman who has come to court me
Speak now while there is still time!

The Emperor laughed that bell-like laughter of his, truly amused. *That one is indeed lighthearted, though there is a hesitation from the gentleman that suggests he has yet to make up his mind.*

Or, I replied, *the gentleman is unsure if his affections will be returned, because the truest feelings often remain unsaid.*

I could've sworn the Emperor blushed at this. He turned away slightly and took a sip of his wine, but his lacquered cup could not hide his smile.

I envisioned my battering ram at his door. *What I don't quite understand, though,* I pondered, *are all the plums and peaches. Why are the Three Hundred Songs dominated by these two fruits? Were these poets also fruit farmers?*

The Emperor laughed loudly this time, throwing his head back, but then quickly clamped his hands over his mouth.

Why do you cover your mouth, Son of Heaven?

He was shaking his head as he continued to chuckle. *Because it is uncouth to display one's emotions so openly. As uncouth as, say, the answer to your questions about plums and peaches!*

I feigned confusion. *But what might be uncouth about plums and peaches?*

He sighed, exasperated but bemused. *I think it is the symbolism about their shapes, Dong Xian.*

I dropped my mouth open. *How dare you accuse Grandfather Confucius of these salacious fruit selections!*

His eyes widened and we both burst into fits of laughter, though behind him I could see Uncle groan and shake his head at us.

The Emperor had his left hand on the table between us. I placed my hand next to his. *With seriousness, though, my Emperor,*

I hope you know that I would cherish it if you displayed all of your emotions to me openly.

He arched an eyebrow. *Be careful what you desire. I have many emotions.*

Son of Heaven, I feel one emotion very strongly these days. Led by my unassuming pinky, my hand slowly encroached toward his.

What is this emotion, Dong Xian?

Wonder.

Startled, he turned to me. *What do you wonder of?*

I wonder if my Emperor desires only poems from me. I looked back at him. *If that is the case, then the gentleman's fear is confirmed that his affections are not returned, and he will curse plums until the day he dies.*

The Emperor didn't laugh this time but looked quietly reflective. We were both looking down at our hands on the table, side by side with a tiny width of space between them. Somehow, that thin space felt as wide as the Yellow River.

He sounded sad when he finally replied. *If I show emotions too openly toward a person, it might put him in danger.*

With that, I wrapped my hand over his, and we looked into each other's eyes.

I am not afraid, my Emperor.

He rotated his hand so it could fold into mine and we held each other like that for a while, looking up at the afternoon sky, listening to the twittering of hidden birds. Once again, I was surprised to find myself so at peace with him in this moment, despite the chaos that my life had become. Whenever I was with him, I felt like I belonged.

I didn't realize I was crying until I felt the tears roll down my cheeks. I cleared my throat and quickly tried to compose myself without him seeing, but I heard him laugh gently.

I wouldn't have guessed you were a crier, Dong Xian, he teased, giving my hand an extra squeeze.

I shrugged, a bit embarrassed. *I don't recall the last time that happened.*

I am sure you cried when you fell off the horse, said the Emperor.

What horse? I blurted without thinking.

Instantly, my blood froze. How could I have forgotten?

The Emperor frowned. *The horse riding accident that broke your legs. How you ended up memorizing the Three Hundred Songs?*

Here was the moment for me to recover quickly from this slipup. But when I tried to salvage my lie, I could not bring myself to speak. I was looking at the Emperor, so manipulated by everyone around him that he could not even safely show emotions. I could not lie to him anymore.

I looked down at our clasped hands. *Your Radiance, I confess I never fell off a horse. I had difficulty speaking when I was a child. I taught myself how to speak properly by reciting the Three Hundred Songs over and over again. I did this every night for four years. That is how I memorized them.*

My heart sank as he pulled his hand from mine. *Why did you not tell me this when I first asked you?* he demanded, his voice suddenly terse.

I glanced up at him, but he was looking away in the distance, his amber eyes flashing in the sun. He was angry.

I bowed my head toward him. *Apologies, Son of Heaven. I was ashamed and I lied. I was shunned by my father for this speech ailment.*

The Emperor put his face against his hand, looking confounded. *But why would you lie about something like that, Dong Xian? It is admirable that you worked diligently to improve yourself— why are you only focused on your initial shame?* He looked back at me, genuine hurt on his face. *Now it is my turn to wonder. I wonder if you remember that among my first words to you, I told you that I was not feeling well. If I can be honest about that to you, why can't you return the favor?*

I felt like I had tripped over a mountain. *If it pleases Your Radiance—*

He threw up his hands. *Don't talk like that. I hate it.*

I took a breath. *Please, Son of Heaven, please understand that I am nobody. To compare you and me—*

You are missing the point, Dong Xian, he snapped, talking faster and faster. *I learned very early in my life that people hide their weaknesses when they are trying to best you. Why did you deceive me? What other designs are you hiding, citizen, that you cannot be truthful to your Emperor about something so clearly seminal to who you are as a person?*

It was as though my childhood stutter had returned. My words would not form.

Speak! the Emperor commanded. *What other lies have you told me?*

I knew that I had already failed and that this would be the last time I ever saw him. Trying not to think about the awful fate awaiting me, I decided that I would tell him the entirety of my alliance with his grandmother. He deserved that much.

Son of Heaven, I—

A deep gruff voice interrupted me from behind us. *Son of Heaven, is everything all right?*

Both the Emperor and I turned around to see Commander Jujun standing there at the courtyard entrance, backlit by the reddish skies of the early evening. I never thought I would be so conflicted upon seeing him—desperately grateful for the interruption but then fearful of what might happen next.

The Emperor stood abruptly. *Your timing is impeccable, cousin. We are done here.*

With Uncle following him out in a low scurrying bow, the Emperor strode out of the courtyard, brushing past Jujun. He never looked back once.

Commander Jujun, however, did look back at me before he exited. He grinned at me like a wolf would a cornered lamb.

I sat motionless in that courtyard for a long time. Then, out of the corner of my eye, I saw a familiar streak of blue fur. I turned to realize I wasn't alone. Staring at me intently from under the big tree was Miaomi. I was startled to encounter her here, because I had never seen the blue cat anywhere else in the Endless Palace, other than when she came by my quarters to be fed.

Cautiously, I approached her, but she slinked around to the other side of the tree's massive trunk. I followed her, only to find that she had inexplicably vanished, perhaps up out of sight into the thickly overgrown branches. Even she had abandoned me.

Days passed and I did not hear from the Emperor. I did not expect to. His cousin Jujun had most surely revealed my betrayal to him, so the only message I awaited was a summoning by the executioner. I had less than a week left until Fu's banquet, but I wasn't sure if I'd live to see it.

I thought about confessing everything to my father and begging protection, but the man had gone missing since barging into my chambers with news of his precious banquet. When I tried to reach out to the old philosopher Yang Xiong for guidance, there was no reply, either. I'd been completely forsaken.

The day before the banquet, a package from my father was delivered on my doorstep. Wrapped within were fine robes of the deepest shades of blue, emblazoned with the seal of the Dong Clan. As I tried them on, I could not help but feel bittersweet. Had I known as that stuttering boy in a forgotten library that I would one day attempt to woo the Emperor? And if I had known of the dangers surrounding me now, would I still have chosen the Endless Palace?

I heard mewing and looked up. Standing at my doorway was Miaomi, licking her paws innocently. I was delighted to see her again, as I hadn't since her peculiar appearance in the courtyard. I scrambled to fetch her some scraps of food.

But when I presented the blue cat with treats, she paid them no heed. Instead, she stared wide-eyed at me with an intention I had never seen from her before, nor from any animal for that matter. Then she tiptoed out of my quarters.

For some reason, I knew to go after her.

My legs moved as if on their own as I wordlessly followed Miaomi's silent steps through the grounds of the Endless Palace. I noticed she was leading me back to the scene of my crime; the path was familiar, and sure enough soon we were approaching the hidden courtyard.

But it was empty, not even our usual table and chairs were there. The cat went back around the massive tree, and this time I made sure to track her closely. There was a large rock resting on the side of the tree, nestled between its exposed roots. Miaomi leaped upon this rock and scratched at a crack where it met the tree.

I peered closely at where she was scratching and I felt an unexpected current of musty air blowing upon my face, as though a wind was coming from within the tree itself. Intrigued, I pulled at the rock. An unseen mechanism was triggered, and the boulder popped forward, as if released from a latch! Without much effort at all, I pushed aside the rock, shielding myself from a sudden gust of dank air. I peered at what I had uncovered.

Beneath the fake rock was an opening into the ground, revealing a long row of stairs that disappeared into blackness.

Assured as ever, Miaomi hopped down into the hole. Without stopping to think, I descended the stairs after her, as the boulder slammed shut behind us. After a few paces there was a light ahead. I saw it was a lit torch in an indent in the wall. Someone had been here recently.

All around us was stone. I wondered if this was a dungeon. I grabbed the torch and ventured deeper.

The tunnel was small and I had to stoop a bit. I followed Miaomi as we came to the end of the stairs. There was an opening there and I peeked my head in cautiously to reveal a much more spacious passageway that stretched on in all directions.

We were in an underground tunnel, deep beneath the Endless Palace.

For a while, I trailed Miaomi as my torch flickered, startling me each time its crackles disturbed the otherwise eerie quietude of this crypt. The cat suddenly made a hard left and I saw that she had brought us to a wooden door in the stone wall. It was slightly ajar. There was warm light from within spilling out at me. Extinguishing my torch, I pressed my ear to the door.

I must have pressed too hard, because the door gave way and I stumbled into a luxuriously appointed room. Looking around, I saw that it was an office, as intimate in size as my own chambers, but it felt undeniably regal, with fine red silks draped over intricately polished pieces of furniture. Each was glistening under the glow of the torches hung on the walls all around. At the center of the room was a magnificent desk sculpted out of gold-veined black marble.

Casually, Miaomi strutted over to a miniature dais in the corner, and leaped onto the dark blue cushion upon it, customized to perfectly match her fur. She yawned cozily and then glanced over at me as I stared at her, stunned to see her in her own bed.

So this is where you live? I asked her, incredulous. At this point I would have been no more surprised if she had opened her mouth to respond to me in speech.

Shaking my head at her admiringly, I turned my attentions to the opulence around me. Then a green twinkle caught my attention. There was what appeared to be a small emerald box on top of the black marble desk.

My heart pounding, I slowly approached to get a better look, leaning over the desk to inspect it closely. It was a single piece of perfectly carved jade, and on top of it was an orgy of many dragons, tangled together in one swirling, squirming mass. The details were exquisite, as though they had been chiseled with embroidery needles, and I could not tell how many dragons there were.

Unable to resist, I picked it up, instantly feeling the ridges underneath. I turned the jade over to reveal the impression of the seal on the bottom, reading the fine calligraphy. I recognized the characters instantly, hearing them in Commander Jujun's voice, envisioning the same message he had sliced into the dirt the first time we met.

As is Heaven's Will, a long and prosperous life.

I had never seen this jade treasure before, but I knew exactly what it was. Every man, woman and child in the world knew of this legendary stamp.

It was the Heirloom Seal of the Realm.

二十

RIVER
PRESENT DAY

The moment Joey and I lock eyes from across the Griffith Observatory museum, he begins to walk toward me, brushing past the throng of his admirers. Everyone in the room looks to see where he's headed, and I quickly shield my face, painfully aware that every sculpture and painting in the room shares it.

I feel a tap on my shoulder and turn to Calvin, who discreetly hands me his aviator sunglasses. I slip them on over my glasses as Joey nears, hoping they are enough to disguise me. "Good luck. I'll be at the bar because I need a fucking drink," Calvin whispers as he scoots away. "Sue me."

Joey gets close to me, but I pull back and instead walk over to one of the portraits that bear my face. This one is a life-size hyper-realistic painting of me, stripped nearly naked except for columns of ancient Chinese characters written down my body in bright primary colors, as I smoke an opium pipe while looking skyward. I look at the date on the description next to it. He painted it...five years ago.

Five years? How did he know me back then?

"River, what are you doing here?" He doesn't ask it with any obvious emotion other than surprise, but I'm triggered. He adjusts the sharp suit he is wearing, looking uncomfortable in it.

"What am I doing here? What are you doing here? You said you were leaving for Asia yesterday!" I don't mean to raise my voice but people are already looking our way. "And what the hell is all this?" I gesture around us, my focus now landing on a sculpture of my likeness a few feet away, this one absurdist as it sports real peacock feathers as tails.

Joey looks at me, still unreadable. "You weren't supposed to see this," he says quietly.

I can feel the edges of a panic attack scraping against my brain. "This is...crazy. These pieces are years old, but we only met yesterday. Who are you, Joey? What's going on?"

Joey takes me gently by the arm and I let him lead me out of the gallery, though not before catching a final look at the painting next to the door. It is of both of us, Joey sitting next to me in a dark forest, surrounded by dozens of iridescent foxes.

"The statues at Winston's house," I say, the dots continuing to connect in my head. "The exclusive artist he was talking about. Why he asked me about my face... It is all you."

We find an isolated corner of the Gala. Joey leans against the wall, rests an arm beside my head, looking troubled. He seems to be thinking fast.

"Don't think," I snap. "Just talk. Why have you been creating art with...my face for years? Have you been following me this whole time? Or was yesterday truly the first time we met?"

Joey groans, placing his hand on his forehead. "River, I can explain everything but it isn't safe for you to be here. Let me get you out of here."

I raise my hands, trying to create space between us. "No, you need to tell me now, Joey."

Suddenly, a bell chime sounds over the loudspeakers throughout the Observatory. As though activated by the sound, all the attendees begin to walk out of the central hall. Joey nods at me, though he still looks conflicted. "Let's follow everyone. You should see it for yourself."

We come out of the building to see that the attendees are all filing up the external staircases that lead to the rooftop. There is a strange energy in the air, an electric anticipation that is palpable. The sun has set, the sky painted in darkening pinks and tangerines. Joey leads me up the metal stairs.

Upon reaching the top of the Griffith Observatory, I see that its normally sparse and industrial rooftop has been transformed into what looks like a dynastic throne room from an ancient Eastern land. A crowd has formed around the middle stage area, where I see a line of nine square columns, each draped with a red covering. Clearly, something is about to begin.

Joey and I watch as Winston Chow emerges to approach the microphone, all smiles and unflappable as ever. He looks down at his palm, on which a hologram appears, ostensibly notes for a speech. Winston clears his throat and Joey leans next to me on the wall, as we both watch the stage. I take off Calvin's sunglasses.

"Friends," Winston announces grandly, his voice amplified and echoing throughout the Griffith Observatory. "Welcome to…the Reign Incarnate Gala."

As the crowd applauds, I clock Calvin at the rooftop bar to the left of the stage, flirting with a handsome mixologist. He sees me, too, and gives a thumbs-up, raising his glass just a tad too high.

"Why do I call this historic gathering the Reign Incarnate?" Winston proclaims, as another hologram materializes behind him, creating a screen showing video of Winston at excavation sites with researchers, studying artifacts with archaeologists in labs, shaking hands with important men dressed in black.

Then the screen changes to display images of dazzling jewels, royal headpieces, armor, vases and other grand relics of Asian antiquity. "'Reign,'" Winston continues, "because it is a word that harkens back the imperial glory of ancient China, when Emperors were worshipped and adorned like living gods...with riches beyond imagination. But due to war and treason, many of these riches are lost, existing today only in myth."

The hologram screen disappears, and the entire Observatory dims even more. Then, each of the nine square columns is lit with a spotlight from above. I can feel the crowd brimming with anticipation.

I suddenly realize that I am no longer standing next to Joey. I have been slowly walking toward the stage this whole time. I look down at my feet and they are moving of their own free will.

Something on the stage is pulling me closer, closer.

I turn back to Joey, expecting him to be following me, but he, too, has his eyes transfixed at the stage. He stands immobile, his mouth just slightly open, as if in awe.

"And what of 'Incarnate'?" Winston snarls out the word with relish as I turn back toward the stage. He motions to the columns before him. "Thanks to the anonymous benefactors who are lending them to us for tonight only, I have the honor of presenting to you legendary treasures of the Middle Kingdom, once thought lost to time and plunder. But now they are incarnate, in the flesh before you... Reign Incarnate!"

A hush falls over the crowd as the red holograms over each of the nine columns deactivate, revealing a row of warmly lit objects atop gold display cases. An eruption of flashes from phones and cameras floods the room like a spontaneous swarm of fireflies. I am now pushing past people, inching my way closer.

The objects in the display cases vary in size, though the largest is an ornate bronze cauldron about the size of a shoebox. The other objects are expectedly gold and opulent trinkets, except for a calligraphy brush that bookends the far left side. But what I am drawn to is the center column, upon which there appears to be a small green cube.

The audience near the edge of the stage is thick and unmoving, but I force my way through it rudely. I can't explain it, but that green cube is pulling me toward it with a magnetic force. A corner of it twinkles, winking at me. As I near it, I realize that this bottom corner of it has been capped with gold, as if a piece of it had broken off and had been repaired.

The seal is adorned with an intricate swarm of dragons carved into the jade. Maybe it is just a trick of the lighting, but the dragons seem to be moving, writhing, beckoning me to them.

I am now so close that I can read the inscription below it.

傳國璽

THE HEIRLOOM SEAL OF THE REALM

Then I feel eyes upon me and look past the center column to see Winston's infuriated face as he stands behind it. He has spotted me. But I turn my gaze back to the Heirloom Seal, and suddenly—

I am no longer in the Griffith Observatory, as the world around me dissolves.

I find myself hurtling through space at a speed that feels faster than light.

What is this? A hallucination? Residual drugs left in my system? Whatever it is, I don't feel any fear.

Then just as suddenly as I took off, I land in a dark room in someone else's body.

The room is humble and not American. The architecture is old-fashioned Eastern woodwork.

Beside me, I see a man in a solemn black tunic, hunched over a hearth of burning embers.

As he lifts his head, I see that he shares Winston Chow's face.

Seemingly out of nowhere, he raises a massive snake in each hand, both of their fangs exposed and dripping with venom. The snakes strike at each other as the man who resembles Winston chants in strange tongues.

The room around us is spinning. The body I am in looks around, and I see that another man, who looks like Joey, kneels across from me. His eyes widen at me.

In front of us, the snakes begin to glow...

There is a loud crack, and instantly I am back on top of the Griffith Observatory under the evening sky. Blinking, I steady myself. What the fuck was that?

There is another loud crack, and I realize I am not the only person who hears it. The entire audience is looking around with murmurs of worry and anxious stirring. On stage, Winston breaks his eye contact with me to look around as well. Whatever is happening, it's not part of the show. He is quickly ushered off the stage by his bodyguard and vanishes into the crowd.

I feel a hand on my shoulder and turn to see Joey as he begins to pull me back. *We need to get out of here*, he whispers in my ear, his voice urgent. *Right now.*

We are pushing our way through the crowd when I hear screams and shouts behind us. Still being pulled by Joey, I turn to watch a spectacular sight. Dangling from armored drones like futuristic apes, a group of masked figures in full riot gear descend from the sky. One of them is firing a machine gun into the air. Instant mayhem and widespread panic engulfs the Reign Incarnate Gala as the attendees try to escape off the roof.

Calvin pushes toward us through the madness of the crowd with one hand while filming the commotion on his phone with his other. "What the fuck!" he yells.

"Follow me," Joey yells back, and we push against the crowd that is clamoring to go down the main stairs. He leads us to a partially hidden fire escape attached to the side of the building, which has a fireman's pole to slide down to the ground level. "You first," he says to Calvin.

Calvin looks down the pole at the forty-foot drop to the ground. "I knew those pole-dancing classes would come in handy one day," he says as he grabs ahold of it and begins to slide down.

I turn back to see a squad of police helicopters in the distance approaching the Observatory rooftop. The masked figures are now on the stage, circling the nine treasures. They smash open the display cases.

And yes, one of them plunders the Heirloom Seal, its gold corner winking goodbye to me one last time before it is concealed in a black pouch.

Just as quickly as they appeared, the heist team grabs ahold of their hovering drones and prepare to lift off with their new loot. There is a sudden explosion as one of the drones bursts into flames. On fire, its passenger drops back onto the rooftop, flailing helpless as they are consumed. Clearly, the police helicopters have gotten close enough to open fire.

Joey pushes me toward the escape. "Go first," he says to me. "I need to stay here."

"What?" I exclaim, grabbing him by the arm. "No, Joey, you are coming with me! You could get killed here!"

Joey clasps his hands around mine. *Death is an old friend of mine. I do not fear it. But if I leave with you right now, Winston will know, and that puts you in danger.*

I hear a torrent of gunfire behind us. *You still never answered any of my questions,* I say to him.

He pulls a pen out of his pocket and writes something on my

wrist, underneath the jade bracelet. I glance at it and see it is an address somewhere on the east side of LA. *I will be here until tomorrow*, he replies. *Meet me at this location tonight.*

With that, he embraces me. We hold each other tight for a moment, and my heart surges with that feeling again. Then he turns me around and gently presses me against the fire escape. When I look back, he is already disappearing around a corner.

Flying overhead, the remaining airborne robbers have managed to elude the helicopters and zip away into the night as quick as bats. As I slide down to the ground, I wonder who they are and what will become of that mysterious jade stamp.

Calvin is waiting for me at the base of the escape. "Where's Joey?" he asks as we begin running away from the building.

There is another loud boom and we turn around to see the helicopters still circling the building as smoke fills the air. Something is on fire.

Calvin trips over his feet and lands hard on the ground, twisting his ankle. He cries out in pain as I help him back up, slinging his arm over my shoulder and pulling him along with me.

"Just keep running!" I say as we join a stampede of terrified people. Everywhere around us we hear sirens and pandemonium. I look back one last time to see one of the iconic Observatory domes aflame.

"Just keep running, Calvin! Just keep running!"

I hope that Joey is safe.

二十二

HE SHICAN
1740

At the same time, Dr. Qi Yewang, Jiulang, and I all looked up.

Hanging from the rafters was a ferocious silver-haired beast with black fangs and hundreds of writhing tails. It pounced onto Yewang, wailing a high-pitched hellish scream that knocked the wind out of me.

But I recovered quickly and leaped upon the monster, trying to pull it off Yewang, who was yelling underneath. Horrified, I watched as the beast's head rotated fully around toward me like a demonic owl. With a hacking cough, it spat caustic mucus upon me. The bile burned my eyes as I pummeled its snout with my fists.

Neither Yewang nor I was any match for it. With a swipe of its numerous tails, the beast threw me off. It opened its mouth and lunged for the doctor's neck. I covered my eyes.

And then all was silent.

I looked up again to see Jiulang holding his hand above his head, where a mysterious green light emanated from his fingertips. The beast was gone, and now all that was left was Jiulang's grandmother, her garments tattered and her hair crazed. She was slumped on top of Yewang, who shook her off him hurriedly and backed away toward the door. He was traumatized but not seriously hurt.

Twitching like a wounded insect, the woman drooled onto the floor.

Jiulang lowered his hand, and I finally noticed there was a jagged green jade stone between his fingers that had been the source of the light. It had faded by now, and Jiulang quickly slipped it into his pocket as he stooped down next to his grandmother.

Do not fight, he said to her firmly, though I could hear a melancholy in his tone. *It is finally our time.*

Jiulang nodded at Yewang, who crept forward. He was shaking from anxiety, but knowing him, I understood that Yewang was finally truly convinced to help Jiulang. He had witnessed the perverse monstrosity of whatever this woman was, and now he would not leave until he figured out how to vanquish it.

From underneath the bed, Jiulang pulled out a medium-size bronze ding and placed it in front of the woman. From inside it he pulled out a leather pouch and handed it to Yewang, who had knelt down beside him.

Opening the pouch, Yewang poured into the ding a few measures of dead herbs, wilted and lifeless, mixed in with what appeared to be crushed scorpions, spiders, and millipedes.

When it appeared to be empty, he inspected it closely, apparently seeing something else inside. He cupped his palm and poured something into it that twinkled in the candlelight. Intrigued, I leaned over to see what it was.

It was a small heap of metallic dust. We all stared at it.

What is that? I whispered. The way it shimmered at me gave me chills.

Jiulang looked at me as though I should know. *It is powdered gods, Master He.*

Yewang tilted his palm at different angles so he could peer

closer upon the oddity. Then he wordlessly poured it into the
ding. He motioned for the candle, which had been sitting on
the floor. Jiulang reached over and handed it to him. Yewang
held the flame just a finger's width away from the ding, when
he paused. *I have not called upon spirits in a long time.*

Jiulang reached over and placed his hand on the candle as well.
Once you call upon them, spirits never leave you, Dr. Qi.

Together, the boy and the doctor touched the tip of the flame
to the mixture in the ding.

Instantly, it was set ablaze, but the fire was black and engulfed
us in an eerie light. I watched as Yewang opened his two bags
from earlier, and from them he pulled out two massive vipers.
I recoiled as they hissed and thrashed in the air, spitting poison
at each other.

Holding them high above his head, Yewang chanted in a dia-
lect I had never heard before. As if in response, the ding began
to billow out thick purple smoke. I was amazed how adept
Yewang was at performing this bizarre ritual. He possessed a
preternatural ability at these occult magics.

The serpents snapped at each other in the air, blood and
fury in their slitted eyes. Yewang turned his head toward them
and began to chant louder in a trance, as if provoking them. It
worked, and one of them finally lashed out, leaving its fang imbedded into the other snake's eye. The wounded creature hissed
in torment, but then sprang from Yewang's clutch and pounced
on its adversary. Both of them tumbled to the floor in a convulsing tangle as Yewang continued to chant.

The smoke in the room made it hard to see, but lit by the
flames, the snakes cast a shadow behind them of their brawl. I
watched in awe as they fought savagely, tearing at each other,
choking each other in twists of their bodies, striking at the speed
of lightning.

Finally, one bested the other. I gasped in shock as we watched
the victor unhinge its jaw and swallow the other snake whole

within a minute. Yewang fearlessly grabbed the surviving viper and held its head toward the smoking ding. The victor looked me directly in the eye with its one remaining eye—its dead foe's fang was still imbedded in its other eye.

With both thumbs, Yewang pressed against the back of the snake's jaw. The snake opened its mouth and gagged. Its venom dripped into the fire. Yewang placed it back down, where it slithered away.

All three of us peered over at the ding apprehensively. But nothing happened for a while. The smoke began to sputter, and the tension in the room seemed to abate. Yewang looked down at it, suddenly lucid again. He stopped chanting.

What happened? The sound of my own voice made me jump.

Yewang did not reply. Instead, the woman began to laugh. Though still immobilized, she laughed so hard that her body shook on the floor. Her laughter sounded like the barking of wolves.

It should have worked, Yewang said, picking up the ding carefully to inspect the sad smoking heap.

It is not yet finished, Jiulang said lowly, his eyes downcast. *There is one ingredient left in the Primordial Bolus.*

The woman ceased laughing.

Yewang scratched his head. *What are we missing?*

Jiulang tilted his face up, and looked back and forth at each of us for a long moment. He finally spoke.

Betrayal.

Jiulang held out a hand toward me. I felt my concealed knife pulled out of the seams of my tunic by an unseen force. Its razor-sharp edge grazed against my stomach as it flew out of my robe to land perfectly into Jiulang's outstretch palm. In that same second, the boy slashed toward me with the blade. I watched as it sliced the air under my chin.

I did not feel anything except the warm liquid pouring onto my chest.

I looked down, and blood was spurting out of me in a ruby-red waterfall.

Yewang screamed. It was a furious, bestial bellow of betrayal. And in his hands, the ding began to emit a brilliant white light.

Dropping the ding, Yewang sprang to my side. He clamped his hand to my throat.

Gurgling on the bitter river pouring out of me, I drenched both of us in red.

DONG XIAN
4 BCE

As I held the Heirloom Seal of the Realm in the hidden office underneath the Endless Palace, its luminous jade reflected a hypnotic green glow back into my eyes. I was captivated to be in the presence of such a hallowed object, having heard great war stories about it since I was a child. This sacred treasure was the physical manifestation of the very soul of our Empire!

Then I heard a creak. I looked up and saw the Emperor and his head eunuch Uncle gaping back at me from through the open door. With a gasp I quickly placed the Heirloom Seal back on the desk and stood back with my hands up in surrender.

Faster than the wind, Uncle leaped across the room with astounding agility. Before I could react, he was behind me with a dagger to my throat. *Who brought you here?* he growled into my ear.

He had his blade pressed so tightly against my throat that it drew a drop of blood. *P-please!* I stammered. *I can explain!* But I knew my explanation, even if true, was unbelievable. Uncle pressed harder and I could feel him tearing deeper into my tissue.

The Emperor had been staring at me with his penetrating amber eyes the entire time. He was wearing a simple gown of red, his long hair down past his shoulders. He finally held up a hand and Uncle released me immediately. *Leave us be, Uncle.*

With that, Uncle mercifully withdrew his dagger and retreated out of the office, shutting the door softly behind him. I backed away from the desk as the Emperor strode forth to stand behind it.

I instantly got down on my knees before him. *Son of Heaven, I did not think I would see you again!*

How did you find my office? I heard him ask, his voice dangerously soft.

I turned my head to look over at the Emperor's cat on her little blue throne next to his desk. She was sleeping peacefully, without a care in the world. *Forgive me, Emperor, but I followed what I thought to be a stray cat into this place. I had no idea there was an underground to the Endless Palace. Forgive me my trespass—it was not intentional.*

The Emperor did not respond at first, and I feared the worst. But finally, he just nodded, saying simply, *I did not think I would see you again, either, Dong Xian of Yunyang.*

He sat down at his desk. *They call these underground tunnels the Shadow. Centuries ago they were designed by Gaozu of Han himself as a hidden network of pathways connecting places of importance to the Emperor. You are not the first civilian to accidentally stumble upon the Shadow, and you certainly will not be the last.*

I could hardly dare to believe his leniency. *Your Radiance, I thank you for seeing this as the chance encounter it is. I only hope my presence here if surprising is also pleasing to my Emperor.*

You may rise, Dong Xian.

Obediently, I stood up, though keeping my face downcast.

The Emperor leaned back in his seat. *Since I have you, I would like to request one last poem of you, Dong Xian.*

I winced. *If it is truly to be my last, I hope the Son of Heaven desires a lengthy one.*

He was unsmiling. *It is one of the Lesser Court Hymns from the Decade of Xiao Min. It begins with, "What other men have in their minds..."*

I knew it exactly, and we recited it together.

> *What other men have in their minds,*
> *I can measure by reflection.*
> *Swiftly runs the crafty hare,*
> *But it will be caught by the hound.*

I let the words ring in my mind as he stood again, picking up the Heirloom Seal with his left hand. He walked around to my side of his desk and held it up between us, its emerald brilliance catching the torchlights. *I saw you admiring my stamp.* He motioned it toward me. Gingerly, I received it from him.

Have you ever heard the story about its origins? he asked.

No, Son of Heaven.

He leaned back against his table as he spoke. *This jade seal you hold was once part of an uncut stone that a peasant found in the hills. The peasant understood the magnificence of what he had discovered and knew that the only one worthy to possess such a treasure was the king himself. So the peasant took the long journey into the kingdom.*

When the peasant was brought before his king, he proudly presented the uncut stone. But the king had an adviser who claimed that this peasant was a fool and his stone was exactly what it looked like—an ordinary rock! For wasting the court's time, the king had the peasant's left foot cut off and sent him away.

But the peasant was persistent, and he waited outside the kingdom, standing on his remaining foot, until the king would grant him audience. And once again, he brought the uncut stone to present to the king, hoping that his devotion would demonstrate his trustworthiness.

But the same adviser decried the ordinary rock, claiming that the peasant was insane and was now harassing the king. To discourage him from ever coming back, the king had the peasant's right foot cut off and sent him away.

Now crippled and humiliated, the peasant sat outside the gates of the kingdom, clutching his uncut stone, bemoaning his sad circumstances. But the peasant was not sad for himself. He was sad that he could not convince the king that his gift was worthy! The peasant sat there for days, weeks and months, in the heat, rain, then snow...until the king's guards took pity upon him and arranged for the king to pass by him one day.

The king recognized the peasant upon sight and was stunned by his dedication. He approached the wretched man and asked him why, even if the uncut stone truly was precious jade, why the peasant would want to gift it to the king after he had been so cruelly treated?

"Perhaps I am foolish, perhaps I am even mad!" replied the peasant. "But that is why Heaven chose me to find this jade, because no matter how much my king denies me, I will not stop until he sees that my heart is true and my treasure is real.

"My king, are you done denying me?" The peasant wept. "Are you done?"

"Yes," the king replied. "I am done."

The king finally received the uncut stone from the peasant and invited him into the kingdom as his most cherished friend. And their ordinary rock was chiseled down to reveal the most precious and perfect of jade. The very jade you now hold in your hands, Dong Xian.

As the Emperor finished his strange tale, the Heirloom Seal felt even weightier in my hands. I ran my fingers along its tangle of dragons, lost in thought. *I thank my Emperor for this story,* I said slowly. I handed the jade back to him and he placed the fabled stamp back down on his black marble desk.

Do you know why I tell you this story, Dong Xian? The Emperor stared back at me, his amber eyes glowing under furrowed brows.

I did not know, but thought quickly. *It sounds to be a story of devotion toward one's ruler?*

He scoffed. *That is what a sycophantic historian would say. Perhaps on its surface this feels like another fawning parable about a discerning king. But carve a little deeper and it is revealed. This story is a story about madness.*

I was taken aback. *Why would my Emperor wish to share a story of madness with me?*

With this, he stood and took a step toward me. Instinctively, I carefully took a step back. *How have you fared this past week, Dong Xian?*

I have felt broken, Son of Heaven. I could only answer honestly.

And why is that?

Because I have lost my Emperor's favor.

He nodded. *These past days have been painful for me as well. For the first time since we met, I fell ill again.*

I bowed my head. *That was surely my fault, and I am so ashamed, Your Radiance. It was a stupid lie.*

He took another step toward me, and I moved back again. He spoke lowly. *And how shall you repent your mistake to your Emperor?*

Tell me, Son of Heaven, and I will do it!

I had pushed up against a chair that was set in the middle of his office. The Emperor was now just a pace away from me. *What if I have your leg cut off?* he whispered.

My Emperor! My blood ran cold. I fell back upon the chair, looking at him. The air in the room had grown hot and suffocating.

He was unrelenting. *Why does that alarm you? Did you not say that my story was a story about devotion to your ruler? Are you not devoted to me, Dong Xian?*

My legs were shaking. *I am, Son of Heaven. But please—spare me my leg!*

He scoffed again. *Yes, of course you would want to spare your leg.*

Because to cut one's leg off, even to appease a king—that would be madness! The Emperor then sank down onto my lap, straddling his legs on either side of me, pinning me to the chair.

He ground himself against me, brushing against my influence under my robes. *And now you know my dilemma, Dong Xian. It is the curse of every Emperor.*

He lifted my chin so that he could peer into me with those flashing eyes of his. *Because,* he continued, *only a madman could truly love a king!*

The Emperor leaned down and kissed me as I wrapped my arms around him, guiding him upon my lap.

Here was the moment that I had dreamed and lusted so many times. His body quivered above mine. His eyes were burning into me. I could smell his desire. Finally, the Heavens had parted for my entry!

But something was wrong.

He felt it next. He pulled away from me, breaking our kiss, his face expressionless.

I shifted uncomfortably beneath him. I could not do it.

The Emperor was mine to have...but I had lost all my influence.

The air went cold again as he slid off me. He turned and walked back to his desk emotionlessly. As he sat back down, he waved me off without looking at me.

Just go, Dong Xian.

Without bowing farewell, I left the Emperor. I exited the room, where Uncle stood just outside waiting to lead me out of the Shadow.

As I walked back to my quarters, I should have felt afraid, but I had run out of fear at that point. I felt nothing—I had no feelings left anymore. I had finally been broken. I moved slowly through the rest of my daily duties, as if in a daze.

However, time did not slow for me. Instead, it inevitably

plummeted forward, like a felled tree, toward my uncertain fate. I was still sitting in bed, having never taken off my formal robes, when my father arrived at my quarters the next day to bring me to the grandest hall in the Endless Palace.

The Grand Empress Dowager Fu's banquet was about to begin.

I had been to banquets at the Endless Palace before, but the one that the Grand Empress Dowager Fu orchestrated for my father was of an entirely different prestige.

In the grandiose Hall of the White Tiger, enough tables to seat hundreds were loaded with an overabundance of foods, some of which I realized were meant only for royal events. Sea turtle soup served in their own massive shells, roasted cranes, whole camel hump, stuffed ox—I could smell the feast even before I entered. The scale and magnitude of the banquet was thrilling; it even knocked me out of my doldrums.

My father seemed nervous, which surprised me. He was jittery and anxious in a way I'd never seen him; he was always king back home in Yunyang, but here he seemed overwhelmed. Still, I was happy for him. He had labored hard his whole life and deserved the recognition. But I did wonder how he would react if he were to find out this had all been part of a ploy so that his youngest son might seduce the Emperor. I shook my head. It all was so surreal.

Arriving to the banquet, all eyes were trained on us, something I'm sure my father wasn't accustomed to. True, our family was distinguished and well regarded, but that was because of our purported austerity. Extravagant parties were not commonly associated with our level of bureaucrat. Indeed, I could read the faces of my father's colleagues, no doubt wondering how Dong Gong had suddenly attained such divine attention.

Now stand close to me, Third Son, and don't say anything to any-

one beyond pleasantries, my father muttered to me. I looked over at him and was reminded how little we knew each other. He still thought me a stuttering tyke, when I had matured into a man whose tongue was commander.

Yes, Father.

Dong Gong, our guest of honor, a familiar guttural voice purred behind us. The Grand Empress Dowager Fu wore the formal gown of a sitting empress, with gleaming gold pins protruding from her mass of raven hair like victory pikes on a battlefield.

My father bowed deeply. *Your Imperial Majesty, I am eternally your servant. I was told that you personally arranged this beauteous banquet, and while I am an unworthy and troublesome dog, tonight I am both lifted up and vanquished by your infinite grace.*

Even I could not help but wince at my father's clumsy attempt at wordplay. He had abandoned me as a child and left me to be raised by poetry books, but perhaps that had been a secret blessing.

Fu was smiling and nodding at my father in a way that I could tell she already hated him. *Now, Dong Gong, this is a casual party. Let's save such lofty words for your tax collectors.* She turned to me and nodded. *Dong Xian, thank you for helping me choose the fruit.* My mouth dropped open as she left us to take her place at the head table.

As much as I wanted to, I couldn't look at my father because I had a strange panicky desire to burst into fits of laughter, and I was afraid that seeing his face would surely push me over the edge. But I was certain that he was flabbergasted the Emperor's grandmother not only knew me personally, but also apparently planned his banquet with my assistance! I quickened my pace so he could not see my broad smile.

Yellow wine and barley beer were poured for all, and the atmosphere was loud and merry. That is, except for my father. I saw him as conflicted—madly curious about his lesser son's familiarity with the formidable Fu, yet also saving face by not asking me directly about it.

Third Son, look at that tall man over there, he whispered at one point, as he lit a pipe for us. He prodded me to look over at one of the far tables. *That is Jujun, Commander of the Armed Forces and cousin to the Emperor.*

Trying not to audibly groan in front of my father, I looked where he was pointing and witnessed Commander Jujun, who was sitting at what was likely the military officials' table, as the men around him were similarly stacked into impressive army uniforms. They were reveling the loudest, goading each other to drink and eat more in that manly way of soldiers.

Is he a friend of yours? I asked my father, feigning ignorance but also curious to hear his assessment.

My father shook his head as he handed me his pipe. *That man is a friend to no one. He was abandoned by the Imperial Family and forged in war instead—he does not know friendship. But it is peculiar that he is here tonight at a banquet thrown by the Grand Empress Dowager.*

As I smoked from the pipe, I watched Jujun down his goblet of wine with gusto and spank the backside of a maid as she walked by. He must have felt my eyes on him, because he suddenly met my gaze with steely set eyes. I quickly turned back to my father.

It is peculiar because he and the Emperor's grandmother are sworn enemies, are they not, Father? I was licking at my lips as I said this, because the tobacco from the pipe had a curious taste of rotten fruit, though I was too distracted to contemplate its familiarity.

My father shook his head. *He does not know enmity, either. Jujun is not as blunt as he looks. He will do whatever it is to survive as someone with a probable claim to the Dragon Throne, which is historically a death sentence. That is why I heard that when Fu reached out with a tenuous truce a month ago, he accepted and the two of them have aligned—for now.*

I was glad my father was still looking in Jujun's direction because I could not hide the shock on my face. If Jujun and Fu were actually working together, then why had he tortured me so? I seethed under my breath. I'd had enough of that sadist!

Oblivious to my inner turmoil, my father was still politicking aloud to himself as he puffed at his pipe. *Still, a public appearance from him as a guest of Fu's is a bit heavy-handed for a man who keeps his allegiances this well guarded.* My father's mind seemed to be galloping. *Unless…?*

As if to answer him, a hush suddenly fell over the crowd, and I felt a strange chill wash over me. I turned to see everyone kowtowing as the Emperor entered the room, wearing a brilliantly blue silk robe that was embroidered with nine gold dragons that swooped and flew as he moved.

Splendidly, he was flanked by a strutting pair of trained peacocks, their tails fanned open in shimmering rainbows of emerald and blue. This was a surprise appearance, fully intended for dramatic flair. I remembered what Fu had said to me at the pond. *Every waking moment of his life has been a carefully choreographed dance.*

The crowd of stunned drunk officials comically slurred the customary greeting. *O Radiant and Holy Son of Heaven, we are eternally your servants!* Next to me, I felt like my father might explode from excitement.

Dramatic though his entrance was, the Emperor himself looked detached and lifeless, apparently having been ushered to yet another Court event that interested him little. But as he walked over to his seat at the front table, he saw me.

How could one look contain infinite emotions?

I, too, was on my knees in kowtow, but unlike everyone else, I had lifted my head to watch him. I could not help but admire his tall height and his deliberate gait. He paused when our eyes met. Then a small smile formed across his lips.

I grinned back, my heart singing back to life. Perhaps, I thought, I still have a chance.

Fu had risen to her feet as the Emperor sat down beside her, and his peacocks flew to roost in the rafts of the ceiling above. She raised her cup. *To our Eternal Emperor, we praise you for your presence!*

All raised their goblets, and out of the corner of my eye, I saw that Commander Jujun had done the same, as everyone joined in a chorus, *We praise you, our Eternal Emperor!*

The Emperor and Jujun nodded to each other. Fu and the Emperor never made eye contact, despite sitting next to each other. Their proximity was offset by the chilliness between them, undermining her pretty words.

Once we all drank, Fu continued. *We come here today to honor one of our most loyal and distinguished officials, the honorable Dong Gong.* The entire crowd turned to face our direction.

My father stood straighter on cue, and I could see he was trembling, a simple man suddenly thrust into the blinding lime-light. I suddenly had an unfilial thought about how common he looked amongst all this grandeur, and felt slightly guilty. This was the man whose attention I'd craved throughout my childhood to no avail, and now all I wanted was to shrink away from him.

Fu addressed my father, but her eyes trailed to me as she spoke. *Dong Gong, for the hundred years of devoted service that you, your father, your father's father and indeed your entire clan have given to the Dynasty of the Han, the Court bestows upon you the hereditary title of Royal Marquess.*

I nearly spat out my wine and my father seemed like he might faint. The room went silent at this profound promotion.

With a single sentence uttered by the Grand Empress Dowager, my father and I were now nobility.

She sat down as casually as if she'd announced the weather.

But it was the Emperor I was looking at, because he seemed to just realize what was happening. He looked at my father, then at me and then at his grandmother. When our eyes met again, his were full of a hopeless sadness.

Finally, he knew the truth.

RIVER
PRESENT DAY

"What the fuck, River?" Garden yells the moment she opens our front door. "What happened at the Griffith Observatory?"

Pushing past her gruffly, Calvin and I pile into my house, his arm slung across my shoulders as I help him limp to the living room where I drop him onto the sofa in a heap. Exhausted but my mind racing, I sink down next to him, my face in my hands. The TV is still on from when Garden was watching it, as the stunned news reporter details what Calvin and I had just experienced.

"Shoes off, both of you!" Garden exclaims as she turns off the TV. "What sort of Asians are you?"

Calvin kicks off his shoes, yelping in pain when he accidentally knocks his foot against his twisted ankle. He curses in Korean, grabbing his poor leg. "It feels like my foot is gonna fall off!"

"Oh calm down, Calvin," Garden retorts, sitting down in her usual armchair. "There will be only one disabled person here tonight, don't worry."

Realizing his faux pas, Calvin meekly relents, "Sorry, Garden."

"Take it easy on us, G," I say, holding a hand up in surrender. "We've had a hell of a night."

In the distance, we can hear the wailing of emergency-response vehicles. Garden motions around us, still frantic. "You can hear the sirens from here. All of LA is on alert!"

"I hope the damage to the Griffith Observatory is minimal," says Calvin, wincing as he massages his foot. "It will be hard for the community to live it down if LA's most iconic building is destroyed during a Lunar New Year event."

"Fuck the Griffith Observatory!" I shout in an outburst that is a few notches higher than I intended. But the adrenaline is still rushing in me and I am confused and angry...and conflictedly worried about Joey. I stand up and start pacing.

"That building happens to be a historic treasure of our city," Calvin retorts, fishing in his pocket and pulling out what appears to be a joint in a glass tube. "Have some respect for the Griff O."

"No one calls it that," Garden replies, rolling her eyes. "Need a light?"

Calvin grins at my sister. "Hell fucking yes, I do, G." He turns to me. "If it wasn't official before, River, it is now. Your little sister got all the cool." He accepts the lighter that Garden rummages out of our coffee table's junk drawer and lights the joint.

I lean against the wall, though my feet are still fidgeting. "I'm...sort of freaking out right now, you two. I've seen a lot of weird shit the last forty-eight hours. I might be having a psychotic break."

"The solution to that is literally burning between my fingers this very second," Calvin stammers as he holds in his breath. He then lets out a massive plume of smoke. "Sit the fuck down, you self-important queer, and take a hit of this."

With an exasperated sigh, Garden snatches the joint from him. "Do not give him weed. He gets paranoid and annoying. River, just sit down and take it easy, okay?" She takes a toke, though, and passes it back.

"I do not get paranoid and annoying," I grumble, a bit unconvincingly, but I sit down next to Calvin.

"No, that definitely tracks for you," he chuckles.

"Are neither of you listening to me? I feel like I'm going crazy!" I shout.

Garden stands, crossing over to the other side of the sofa to sit next to me, so that I'm sandwiched between them. "Okay, big brother, tell us everything that's on your mind."

"I'll make us some tea," Calvin says as he limps to the kitchen. "I remember seeing some Yogi here last time."

Feeling a bit better, I rub my eyes, my glasses falling off my face onto my lap. "It started right after that gay rave—"

"They're called circuit parties, babe," Calvin calls from the kitchen.

"Right after that circuit party, when I was upstairs at Winston Chow's house in the Hills. There were all these statues that looked like me, and then it turns out that Joey sculpted them, along with a whole gallery's worth of art that also all looks like me."

"Sounds kinda romantic," Garden says quietly, a funny look on her face.

"Or deranged," Calvin calls loudly.

"Listen, I haven't even gotten there yet. How did he know my face? He has to have known me or at least known of me for a while. Some of those art pieces were years old."

"Sounds like your textbook stalker." Calvin shrugs as he returns with steaming mugs of tea.

I wrap my hands around my mug, its warmth soothing me. "C'mon, Calvin," I say gently, "you know it's more than that.

This is not just some random guy. You told me earlier that he was famous. What is he famous for?"

Calvin sighs. "I don't know, but it's my Mainlander friends who all say he is famous. He's been famous there since he was a kid, I think. Some sort of internet personality."

"That's less romantic," Garden mumbles to herself.

"And now he's Winston Chow's money boy?" I ask, incredulous. "That doesn't add up."

"Oh, sweet Jesus!" Calvin cries out, nearly spilling scalding hot tea on me. "Winston Chow is a fucking billionaire playboy. Everyone plus their grandma would gladly be his butt boy, including the people in this room!"

Garden takes out her phone and clicks away at it. "Do either of you know Joey's last name? Or his Chinese name?"

Calvin and I look at each other and shake our heads.

"I'm just image searching 'Winston Chow and Joey,'" she says, as she scrolls her finger up and down on the screen. She shakes her head. "Nothing, just a ton of photos of Winston and people named Joseph or Joe, but I don't see your Joey anywhere."

Calvin lights up his joint again and takes a long drag. "So I know I'm not being very subtle about it, but I think we should just quit while we're still ahead and alive. I can now say I've lived through an international art heist, so I think I just need to lay low and drink excessively for a few weeks."

I turn to him, placing my hands on his shoulders and looking him square in the eye. I give him a soft shake. "Calvin, please work together with me to figure this out. You are a brilliant strategist, and you know the most random useful stuff. I can't do this without you."

Calvin shakes his head, laughing in retreat. "All right, all right, enough. You are a terrible liar, but I'll help." He turns to Garden. "It doesn't matter what you search online when it comes to Winston Chow. He owns a stake in nearly every global media group so he can edit his online presence however he wants."

"So he's purposely keeping Joey secret." I lean over to look at Garden's phone. "Because why bother to only scrub photos of Joey and him?"

"Exactly," Calvin says, nodding, "and you know those thirsty hoes have their pictures taken at every rice queen festival in the world. There should be hundreds of pictures of them."

"Or Winston's just another closeted Asian businessman," Garden says with a shrug.

"Why would he date someone famous like Joey if he cares what people think? It just doesn't make sense," I say.

"I agree with River. There is something very trippy about Joey." Calvin pauses to cough. "And he can also still be a stalker."

"So what else, big brother?" Garden walks to the bay windows behind the living room sofas. She opens one, letting in the cool air. "It isn't just Joey, right?"

"No…" I say, feeling uneasy about telling them. "So you know that old stamp that was taken in the heist? It has a long, epic name."

"The Heirloom Seal of the Realm," Garden and Calvin both instantly say in unison. Then my sister says its name in Mandarin, for good measure.

I lean back, surprised. "That was impressive."

"I'm pretty sure we both just Wiki'd it when we first heard about it on the news, River." Calvin rolls his eyes at me. "You know, like normal people would."

"Yeah, I totally fell into a Wikipedia hole about it, too," Garden laughs. "It's pretty interesting."

"You know, it's so weird," I say, "because ever since I first heard of it, I can't explain it… It's like I actually do know that old stamp so well, but I'm missing the memories I'm supposed to have of it." I realize I am looking down at my hands. My palms are joined along their pinkies, forming a bowl as though I am cradling a small object.

"That is bonkers, but I've been having a lot of strange feelings like that, too, recently." Calvin sounds a bit mystified for the first time.

Garden takes the joint from him and crushes it into her empty mug. "You two have been doing drugs for days. And not weed. Real drugs. I can tell. Both of you need go to sleep and stop worrying about weird feelings."

"You don't feel anything, G?" I ask her. "You haven't had any visions or dreams or anything like that?"

She thinks hard for a few seconds. Then she shakes her head at me. "No, none." She's telling the truth. "But what did you see?"

"Right before the heist happened, Winston Chow revealed the Heirloom Seal of the Realm. And the moment I saw it, I was transported to another place. It wasn't just a vision. I was actually there."

Calvin and Garden are now both staring at me intently.

"Go on," Calvin says.

I frown, trying to recall. "To be honest, I don't remember much. I remember...snakes, and that it felt like a long time ago. Like old Asian architecture and candles. But what I do remember is that Joey and Winston were both there, too. Joey looked scared and Winston was chanting some Chinese voodoo-sounding shit."

"You mean like a past life?" Calvin says.

Garden snorts. "Are you for real?"

"Excuse me, this is a 'yes and' environment, G," Calvin replies, "and billions of people around the world believe in reincarnation. Why is it so crazy to think we might be able to tap into other lifetimes?"

"My mom left my dying dad for a pastor," Garden says curtly. "Sorry if I am not into religion."

"We are dealing with some ancient, pre-Jesus, OG supernatural shit of the East!" Calvin replies. "Don't insult it by calling it religion! It's our magical birthright!"

"Did you just seriously refer to it as 'magical birthright'?" Garden throws up her hands. "I don't believe in any of that stuff, sorry."

"What did you two learn about that old stamp?" I interrupt. "Maybe it is some sort of psychological trigger for me."

"So it was crafted out of a very special jade stone," Garden says, brightening up at the change of subject. "And it was handed from emperor to emperor as the physical manifestation of the Heavenly Mandate. When challengers to the throne tried to replace an emperor, they would also have to snatch away the Heirloom Seal, otherwise they don't have Heaven's blessing. That was the claim that Chinese emperors all had—that they were living gods, so therefore they should rule the country. They were even called 'Son of God,' or something like that." She stared pointedly at Calvin.

Off Garden's look, Calvin admits, "Fine, some of it is a little like Christianity. But you're missing the most important part." He stands up, very hyped by the story and gesturing enthusiastically while limping. "More than a thousand years ago, the Heirloom Seal vanished. It was passed down from the Qin Dynasty all the way to the Tang Dynasty, but then one day, poof! Disappeared into thin air. No one knows what happened to it. It is one of the greatest mysteries in Asian history."

"And I guess it is missing again now," Garden muses. "Snagged right in front of your faces." She shakes her head. "Being Asian is so dramatic."

"Well, my vision, or whatever it was, it definitely was not about emperors," I reply. "I don't think anyone in that old tavern was royalty."

"You said that the person who looked like Winston was chanting some sort of spell?" Calvin pushes aside some magazines on the coffee table and sits down on it to face me. "Probably some form of shamanism."

"Right, shamanism," I say, nodding. "I didn't know the correct term."

"Well, hear me out and advanced apologies to Garden," Calvin continues. "Perhaps in a previous life, Past Joey and Past You attended some sort of ceremony that was conducted by a shaman Past Winston. It makes sense that you would flash back to that particular moment because Past Winston is doing magic. Ripping a tear into the fabric of space-time."

As he speaks, an odd tingling begins to hum in my head. Wincing, I rub at my scalp, thinking I might need ibuprofen. "If you're right about that, then it makes me wonder what brought those three people together back then, and what it has to do with me today."

"Maybe the point was to summon you," says Calvin. "Or maybe they were doing a completely unrelated spell but it still pulled back the veil to allow you to peek in after you were triggered by seeing the Heirloom Seal."

Garden is looking at me, her eyes widening as Calvin finishes talking. "Riv, are you okay?" she asks.

Suddenly, I am trembling all over. My teeth start grinding together as beads of sweat begin to roll down my face. Calvin's careful recounting of my vision has somehow reignited it in my mind once again. It becomes clearer and clearer, a true memory that isn't mine but is now somehow claiming me. I can actually feel it blooming to life in my brain, anchoring itself into my subconscious.

But more alarming than the pain is what I see. What I remember.

"Oh, my God!" Garden gasps, as Calvin reaches over and

clamps his hands over my arms, trying to secure me as I begin seizing. "What's happening, River?"

"What do you see, River?" Calvin shouts. "What are you remembering?"

"Blood!" I begin to sob. "So much blood!"

HE SHICAN
1740

The blood poured out of me in a ruby-red waterfall, drenching Yewang as he clamped frantic hands over my neck. But still, my blood spurted through the gaps of his fingers, unable to be dammed.

Jiulang stood back and watched us both collapse to the floor, his porcelain face expressionless. He dropped the knife with a clatter.

No, no, no! Yewang cried, as my blood sprayed through his fingers onto his face. He turned to Jiulang, enraged. *Huang Jiulang, you demon! We had an agreement!*

Jiulang spoke quietly. *You should know better about agreements with spiritfolk, Yewang. Our agreement was never about the agreement.*

He picked up the luminous ding from where Yewang had dropped it. It was leaning on its curved side, rolling slightly back and forth, but its brilliant contents had not spilled. He peered inside. *It was about the last ingredient of the Primordial Bolus.*

My body had crumpled from the loss of fluid. Only clear liquid was coming out of me now. I could feel my last breaths approaching as I quivered in a puddle of my own blood.

Jiulang's amber eyes turned into golden suns as they caught the light. He tilted his head back, looking directly into me.

I needed the betrayal.

With that, he held out an open palm toward me. I felt a strong vibration emanate from him into me. With a flourish of his wrist, he twisted his hand and balled it up resolutely into a fist. Stunned, Yewang and I watched as the blood pool we were in began to drip upward into an expanding red bubble, hovering a few inches above the floor. Even the blood on Yewang's fingers lifted from his skin to float away.

When all my blood was suspended in the air, Jiulang flicked his fist toward me. In an instant, the blood bubble shaped itself into a funnel and reentered my body through the slash in my throat, inflating me back to life. Then I felt the tissue in my neck seal back up, the force of it pulling my chin back down!

Gasping, I clutched at my throat, finding it completely healed, with no wound nor scab. I was completely unharmed.

Yewang grasped at my throat, too, in disbelief. Upon seeing I was all right, he burst into tears and held me in his arms. He turned to Jiulang, with the sound of awe in his voice. *Huang Jiulang, you are no mere fox spirit*, he cried. *What are you truly?*

Jiulang was staring into the ding, but he was listening. *I, too, have shared your astonishment at my abilities this evening. Some of them I did not even know I had!* He then looked back and forth at us, and cocked his head. *Perhaps it is the power of our reunion*, he mused.

What do you mean? Yewang asked. *Whose reunion?*

But Jiulang ignored him. He was looking at me again. *Shican*, he said, *I also lied to you earlier. That was not my favor to Yewang. He is not trying to forget you.*

Confused by this, I turned to Yewang. He did not look back at me.

Jiulang walked toward the woman on the ground, who had remained motionless throughout the entire blood ordeal. Her face was turned away from us, her black hair now streaked with sparkling gray. He stood over her and raised the radiant ding above his head.

The room was now brighter than day.

Slowly and carefully, Jiulang began to tip the ding forward over her body. I could just barely see the strange solid itself peeking over the brim of the ding...but then Jiulang paused. He lowered the ding again.

He was looking down at the woman, but for the first time ever he seemed his young age. He seemed almost human to me. He was sad.

Farewell at last, Grandmother, he finally said to her.

He began to pour the dazzling contents of the ding onto her. But no more than a few seconds after he started pouring, he was shrieking in pain like a wounded pup. He fell to the floor on his knees, releasing the ding, which tumbled away.

It had happened so furiously fast that I had missed it, but I witnessed the aftermath. The woman's arm had turned back to the talon-clawed beast paw of her true form, and all five of her razor black fingernails were imbedded in Jiulang's exposed calf, puncturing through both sides.

Wailing in agony, Jiulang tore away from his grandmother. His flesh simply burst open as her talons ribboned out of his leg. Jiulang fell upon his rear and scrambled backward away from her, clutching what was left of his shredded calf. Almost immediately, his limb began to miraculously heal itself, but it was clear his top priority was getting as far away from her as possible.

We all watched as the strange substance began to pool over Jiulang's grandmother.

The Primordial Bolus was not liquid, substance, or gas, but rather it was an expanding packet of brilliant light, white as untainted snow, that began to consume the woman alive. She wailed and scratched at the air as it rapidly spread through her body, like the invert of a shadow, until only one hundred tails remained, thrashing and flailing in all directions.

Finally, the light ate her whole. And in a blinding flash, it disappeared. It had happened so quickly. The night fell silent.

Still holding each other, Yewang and I could only gasp for air as we caught our breaths. I looked over at Jiulang, expecting to see him sated and victorious.

But what I saw I did not expect. Jiulang was curled up on the ground where he had stood. The power had left him. What remained was a broken boy.

I pulled away from Yewang and crept over to Jiulang, taking him into my arms. He felt thin and frail, his pale skin almost translucent.

Jiulang, are you all right? I asked, frightened.

He began to weep unceasingly. And I cried with him, our bodies still trembling as we held each other. I knew not why we wept.

It was like we shared an ancient pain that I could not remember.

Shican, move aside.

I looked up to see Yewang standing over us. He had picked up the ding and was reaching into it. Before I could stop him, Yewang pulled out a remaining ball of the incandescent light and threw it directly upon Jiulang's face.

With a howl straight from the hells, Jiulang leaped up. He clawed frantically at his face as the Primordial Bolus melted through it like molten metal.

DONG XIAN
4 BCE

In the Endless Palace, the grandest hall is called the Hall of the White Tiger. It is named as such because legend has it that our first Emperor of the Han, Gaozu, had an encounter with a white tiger when he was a child. Gaozu of Han had been born a peasant, though one doesn't say that out loud in polite society, and one day he was tending the fields when a white tiger emerged from the tall grasses. The beast licked its chops as it pondered which part of Gaozu to devour first.

Young Gaozu was terrified for his life, and in desperation he pleaded with the tiger to spare him. To his amazement, the beast responded, revealing itself to be a tiger spirit. *And why should I spare your life*, the white tiger growled, *when I am a divine spirit who is hungry and you are but an inconsequential waif?*

Thinking quickly, young Gaozu replied, *Because I am the son of a dragon and destined for greatness!* He knew there was only one creature more fearsome than the tiger, and that was the dragon.

But the white tiger was not swayed. *If every mortal who claimed to be born of a dragon was truly that, half the countryside would be flying scaly freaks!*

Be that as it may, for me it is true, Tiger Spirit, and if you attack me, my dragon father will surely avenge me and destroy you. Gaozu may have been a peasant, but as I'd been told by our tax collectors, there's no one scrappier or more resourceful than a peasant child.

The white tiger pondered for a moment and decided to humor the boy. *All right, then. If this dragon father of yours is so formidable, call upon him to claim you and I shall spare you. Dragons are quite speedy. What say we give him to the count of thirty?*

Young Gaozu knew he was done for. Closing his eyes, he bowed his head and made a silent plea to Heaven for his death to be quick and painless. He waited for the sharp jaws of the tiger spirit. But after a minute, there was nothing.

Gaozu peeked to see the great white tiger fleeing for its life like a frightened kitten, already far across the field and scampering into the horizon. Astounded, the boy immediately looked upward to the sky, where—and he swore this for the rest of his life—he saw the tail of a dragon disappear into the clouds.

Perhaps this all may have been figments of a daydreaming peasant boy. But that same boy grew up to defeat the powerful Dynasty of the Qin and become Emperor of his own. To celebrate the infinite rule of his new Dynasty of the Han, he built the Endless Palace, including its grandest hall.

This is why the Hall of the White Tiger is often used to bestow high honors upon those who have pleased the Dragon Throne. Gaozu's legend is a reminder that some of us are truly destined for greatness.

Dong Gong, the Court bestows upon you the hereditary title of Royal Marquess, the Grand Empress Dowager Fu proclaimed. There was an instant hush over the crowd of revelers in the Hall of the White Tiger, not even the accidental clink of a cup. Behind her was a massive wood carving of a tiger fighting a dragon.

With those simple words, uttered so casually by Fu, I was no longer a lowly Court clerk. I was now the blue-blooded son of a nobleman. But the swelling of excitement within me was quickly dampened when I saw the crestfallen look on the Emperor's face as he sat next to his grandmother.

I realized that perhaps Fu had overplayed her hand with all this pomp and circumstance; now that the Emperor knew I was her puppet, would he deny me? My heart began to race. No doubt Fu would still blame me if I failed to secure the Emperor's favor. At the pond, she had made me an ominous promise of bad tidings should her efforts go to waste.

My father's colleagues all stood and cheered as they came up to congratulate him. I took the chance to move away from everyone, too scared to look back at the Emperor, searching for a quick exit so I could gather my thoughts.

But I felt a determined tug on my sleeve, and I looked back to see something I had never seen—my father's eyes as they looked right into mine. *Dong Xian*, he said, *my colleagues would like to meet you.* Bewildered, I went back to his side as his fellow senior officials congratulated both of us. Many lacquered cups full of wine were pushed my way by the elders as I heard my father speaking highly...of me? They were generic fatherly compliments, but it was also a deluge of affection that had been withheld from me all my life, suddenly heaped upon me.

I couldn't help it; I was beaming as I stood next to my father. No longer was I the nameless Third Son.

At some point I looked back in the direction of the head table where the Emperor had been sitting, but he was no longer there. His grandmother Fu was whispering to a large man in a eunuch cap. I squinted my eyes to confirm that...yes, sure enough, it was her henchman, Shi Li. They both stopped speaking at the same time and turned their heads to look over at me like a couple of disturbed owls. I quickly looked away, following my father as we took our seats at the banquet table.

As platters of roasted swan were brought out of the kitchens, a troupe of brightly dressed women came out to dance. I looked at the luxurious foods before me on the table, the rich aromas of animal fat and rare spices delighting my nose, but my stomach was in knots. Everything seemed to be happening so fast.

My father and I were now seated, his colleagues still gathered around us as they piled the food onto their plates and gulped down cup after cup of yellow wine.

So, Dong Gong, what endears you so to the Emperor's grandmother? one of the colleagues asked, with a bit of a facetious grin. *What do I have to do to get my own banquet that is attended by the Son of Heaven himself?* But there was an edge in his voice that told me he believed this promotion was not quite deserved on my father's own merits.

I was also surprised to hear such frank talk, especially when the subjects were sitting in the very room. It was a fascinating glimpse for me into a higher tier. My father scoffed, shrugging it off with mock offense. *Come now, Master Zhu, must everything be intrigue? I have sat next to you enduring your farts for two decades— is that not enough reason for a promotion?*

The whole table laughed uproariously as my father and Master Zhu raised their glasses in good jest. Master Zhu then turned to me, taking me in. He was a clever-looking man, a little younger than my father, with a sharply pointed face made even sharper by a bristly goatee. *And you, young lord, what have you inherited from your accomplished father?*

My father put a hand on my shoulder and I tried not to instinctively flinch. This man was still new to me, as friendly as he was. Before I could answer, he spoke. *My son inherited nothing from me,* he replied, *and that will be to his great fortune.*

Unsure of what he meant, I turned to look over at him. He nodded at me, as though I was supposed to understand him. But as he had been his whole life, my father was still unknowable to me.

The other men at the table seemed to ponder this riddle for a moment as well, until Master Zhu started laughing. *Old Dong,* he crowed as he refilled my father's cup, *there are easier ways to say that you are ugly while he is as pretty as his mother!*

The men all burst into laughter, raising their cups and drinking more. I took the opportunity to glance back over to the throne table. The Emperor was still gone. I quietly excused myself from my father's table.

As I passed a large silk screen on the far left side of the hall, I was suddenly grabbed by a huge pair of gruff hands. My yelp of surprise was drowned out by the party as I popped out of sight.

In a matter of seconds, I was shoved face-first against the hard wall. I could feel my eyebrow split open upon impact, stinging blood invading my eye. I knew it immediately. This was an assassination. Terrified, I held up my hands. *Truce!* I said. *Let's talk.*

I'd been told that you yield easily, boy, but this is just pitiful.

Recognizing the deep, gruff voice, I let out one long, shuddering sigh, then inhaled all the courage Gaozu of Han could ever bless upon me. I turned around, looking him squarely in the eyes. *Commander.* I nodded my greeting. *I respectfully disagree. I think a dog who attacks from the back is more deserving of pity.*

His armor clinking along with him as he laughed, Commander Jujun leaned over me onto the wall, resting a hairy hand next to my head. Though his eyes were sharp as ever, and his words crisp and clear, I could smell the alcohol emanating out of him. He was so drunk his breath made me heady. *How little you know my cousin*, he jeered, *beyond dusty poetry and old lady schemes. I'm doing you a favor here!*

I have lasted this long without your favors, Commander, and I am fine to continue that way, I said through gritted teeth. He had pulled us into a dimly lit hallway; we were unseen and alone. I thought to myself that if I made it out of this interaction alive, I would be carrying a blade from now on.

Jujun pulled out a handkerchief and handed it to me. I dabbed at the blood running down my cheek. *A little blood suits you. The Emperor likes his men tough and rugged.* Jujun puffed out his broad chest dramatically as he ran his thumb over the shiny scar on his right cheek. *I would know—I supply him with the finest men in my army for all his desires.* He grinned, then made a lewd gesture with his tongue at me as he gloated. *Hundreds of men, the most beautiful, most heroic, most talented men in the Empire.*

I could only glare at him. I was suddenly engulfed with an unfamiliar feeling, my ears burning hot and my throat constricting. How dare any other man touch my Emperor? It was a betrayal that made me dizzy, because this Emperor that Jujun was describing was not the man I thought I knew.

Most of all, I hated Jujun for telling me. Hated him!

But I controlled myself, and all I said was, *He is the Emperor. We all live and die at his pleasure. He can and should have anyone he wants.* I pressed his cloth against his chest and pushed his body away from me, a substantial task. *I worry less about his bedmates and more about the duties of his throne. Perhaps you should focus on the same, Commander, instead of traitorous gossip more fit for eunuchs and concubines.*

Jujun narrowed his eyes at me, his smile turning into a snarl. He slammed his fist against the wall, right next to my head. It made a loud sound but I took heed not to flinch. *Don't test the limits of my amusement, boy. It doesn't matter how many fake promotions that hag cunt Fu bestows upon your family. If you want to survive even one night as the Emperor's favorite, never forget that you need my protection.*

Yes, Commander, but for how long? I replied, keeping my voice calm and steady while my mind was furiously working. I was not going to reveal that I knew of his new alliance with Fu, at least not yet. *If I am such a threat, why didn't you kill me when you had the chance just now?* Seemingly caught off guard, he opened his mouth to reply but I continued, interrupting him. *You know as much as I do that we need each other. You have returned to dangerous times in the Endless Palace. The Emperor is weak and his grand-*

mother hates you. But you have your cousin's trust, and I have hers. If we are both to survive, we should be friends.

Jujun was silent for a moment. I could feel the tension seep out of him, and I felt a surge of confidence.

I reached up and carefully released his fist from the wall, bringing it down to his side. *Nay, not just survive, Commander—if we are to succeed, we should be friends,* I said, looking into his eyes. I gave his wrist a squeeze before letting go.

Finally, he spoke, softly. *And what does friendship mean to you, Dong Xian?*

It means that we work together from now on. Triumphantly, I moved to leave in the direction of the grand hall, but not before saying as I turned my cheek, *And it means that if you ever touch me like that again, Jujun, you will regret it.*

Like a flash of lightning, his fist was around my neck. Unable to yell, I clawed at his hands as I choked for air. Jujun lifted me as easily as a bag of feathers. I felt the cartilage in my neck pop. He brought his lips right to my ear, his words boiling hot.

The reason I didn't kill you just now is because... I felt his teeth graze across the tip of my ear. *I don't usually lay with men outside of battle. But there is something about you, boy, that makes me want to fuck you until you are screaming.*

With that, he released me. I fell to the floor, coughing and clutching my neck.

Welcome to the family, Dong Xian, he growled as he strode past me, returning to the party.

RIVER
PRESENT DAY

After my strange seizure subsides, Garden and Calvin sit with me on the living room sofa for hours into the night as Calvin ices his sore ankle. Eventually, he and I change out of our suits and I lend him pajamas. A little before midnight, Garden goes upstairs to get ready for bed, but Calvin remains by my side, smoking his joints and scrolling through his phone.

His steady exhales of billowing weed smoke swirl around me as I lean against him, making me heady and dizzy, but it does also calm me down a bit. I drift in and out of a waking consciousness, comforted by Calvin's muffled heartbeat.

I wake when I can no longer feel him. I sit up on the sofa and look around; he's not with me anymore. But I hear the murmur of a conversation in another part of the house.

Tiptoeing toward it, I approach the staircase but I stop before turning the corner once I can hear my sister and Calvin exchanging hushed words. I stand there, hidden from their view, listening.

"—a bad feeling about all this," Garden is saying. "You are new in his life. He was never like this before. He has been behaving so recklessly."

Calvin replies, trying to be reassuring. "Listen, when I first came out, I had a slut phase, too. It's not a big deal."

Garden's voice turns icy. "Don't call my big brother a slut. You're the one, aren't you, Calvin, that has taken him down this even steeper road? You've been giving him those hard drugs, haven't you?"

"Hey, now," Calvin counters defensively. "River is a grown-ass person capable of making his own decisions, and by the way, I hope you can tell that I am one of the good ones. I know I just met him, but I care about him a lot."

Garden sighs. "Yes... I can tell. But what works for you won't necessarily work for Riv. Besides, did your 'coming-out slut phase' involve art heists and evil billionaires?"

"I mean, it was pretty epic in its own right, but I see what you mean," Calvin relents. "There is something strange at work here, and I don't understand it."

"Who is this Joey?" Garden wonders with a sad desperation wavering her voice. "And what is this psychological grip he has over my brother?"

Prompted by the mention of Joey, I glance down at his jade bracelet as it clinks against my wrist. But then I do a quick double take. The address that Joey had scrawled onto my skin at the top of the Griffith Observatory—it's gone!

I snap wide-awake instantly, bringing my wrist closer to my face to inspect it closely. There is a trace of the pen ink left but it is unreadable. Someone scrubbed it off while I was asleep.

"What the fuck?" I say aloud before I can stop myself.

I hear the scampering of feet down steps as Garden and Calvin appear in front of me in the hallway.

"River...you're up!" Calvin exclaims awkwardly. "Um...how long have you been standing there?"

"Don't bother," Garden says to him, rolling her eyes. "Clearly, he heard everything."

I raise my wrist at them. "There was something written here. What happened to it?"

"We figured it was an address that Joey gave you, so we erased it while you were sleeping, Riv," she announces matter-of-factly.

"'We'?" Calvin protests, but quiets down as my sister glares at him.

"You need to stop enabling him, Calvin," Garden seethes. "We both agreed it's for the best. Joey is bad news, and all of us know it." Usually when she's in this state, I let her win, but for some reason, I am filled with fury.

"No one is enabling me!" I raise my voice at her. "And Calvin is right. I am a grown person capable of making my own decisions, and I'm not going to base my life around what you want, Garden…just because of your crippling abandonment issues!"

Calvin grimaces as Garden glowers back at me, her wide eyes filled with pain. Without a word, she turns around to head upstairs.

"Goddammit!" I curse at myself, instantly regretful. I bury my face in my hands.

I feel Calvin tug me on the shoulder. "Hey there…" he says quietly. "Let's go for a walk."

The moon above us is full and red as Calvin and I pace back and forth in the cul-de-sac in front of my house. Calvin has lit another joint and takes long pulls of it, his face unreadable. His limp is better now, but still he lets me walk ahead of him; I am jittery and upset, unsure of what to do next. For a while, the only sounds are our shoes shuffling on the pavement and the occasional chirp of a cricket.

"Hear me out," Calvin finally says, putting up his hands. "If that really is an address Joey gave you, I think your sister is right. You shouldn't go to him."

"Calvin, that was not your decision to make!" For the life of me, I cannot recall even a single digit of the address. The chaos at the Gala is all a blur now. The only thing I know is that Joey will be gone by the morning.

Calvin lets out a frustrated gasp, flicking his finished joint into a bush. "And why isn't it? I'm a part of all of this because of you! You didn't see yourself earlier, when you were scream-ing about blood like you'd been possessed! We are tapping into something very dark and traumatic here, and it's like I keep say-ing, we need to quit while we are still alive!"

"You can leave, then, Calvin." I walk away from him, unable to look at him anymore.

"Because he died," I hear Calvin murmur, almost to himself.

I spin around. "Who died?"

"Yesterday I told you that I was engaged once. He died be-fore we got married."

I feel my anger drain out of me. "Oh, Calvin... Your fiancé died? I thought you told me that it just didn't work out."

He glances down. "Well, technically it didn't." He looks pale and more vulnerable than I'd ever seen him. "He was murdered. It's a long story for another day, but...he was also drawn to dan-gerous things. There was someone else he loved."

"Damn," I reply quietly. "And who was that someone else?"

Calvin looks at me with a small smile. "We all have that someone else—he has many faces. A dangerous love that pulls us to the brink, that slips us over the edge. All we can do is try to save each other from him...or from becoming him."

I put my hand on his shoulder. "You're scared that I will be hurt, too. But, Calvin, I'm not your fiancé."

He looks up at me, his eyes wide and honest. "But you mean the same to me as he did."

"Calvin..." I don't know what to say.

"I know, I know." He pats his hand on top of mine. "Our vibe is unrequited love, River. I knew that from the first moment I saw you, standing at my doorway, nervous as shit about another random hookup. I should have just let you go home after that, but—you reminded me of him." His eyes get shiny and my heart aches. I pull him to me and we hug.

"So you met a mysterious hot-and-cold boy who keeps disappearing on you?" Calvin chuckles, his chin on my shoulder. He pulls away from me, his hands remaining at my sides. "Welcome to being gay! But you can break the cycle, you know. You don't need to be caught in a web of mind games and blood seizures. Take it from me as someone who has seen this happen way too many times. Sometimes the right person is right in front of you."

Calvin then stands up straight. His beautiful face turns fully serious, something I don't think I've ever seen before. He looks refined, confident and sexy. He takes my face into his hands, pulls me to him and we kiss.

A real kiss.

I close my eyes and I feel his kiss.

In Calvin's kiss, I feel his soft, cocoa-butter lips. I feel the love he has for me. I feel that hidden sadness that I finally understand.

But what I don't feel is that feeling, that truth I feel when I am with Joey.

My heart heavy, I break the kiss. I can't look him in the eye. "Calvin, I really do have so much love for you..."

Calvin composes himself. "I'm gonna get going." He reaches into his pocket and takes out a piece of paper, handing it to me. I look down at it and it is Joey's address, safely written down by Calvin.

When I look up, Calvin is walking toward his car parked in front of my house. I rush to his side. "Calvin, you don't need to leave. It's so late and there's plenty of space—"

I can hear the tension in his voice. "Why would I stay here when you are about to leave?" He looks back at me. "Because now that I've given you his address, you're going straight to Joey, aren't you?"

I cannot lie.

Calvin's chest is heaving now, but still he speaks softly. "I hope you like chasing a disappearing man. Because no matter how many times you manage to catch him, a disappearing man is all he'll ever be to you."

I shake my head in dismay at his words. "Let's talk about this tomorrow…"

He unlocks his car with a beep and opens the door. "No, I think I'm done here. I don't want to be in a love story unless I'm the co-lead. I think that's fair." He takes my hand and shakes it like we've concluded a business meeting. "Best of luck, River. I hope you find whatever it is you are looking for."

Before I can respond, he gets into his car and drives off. I watch him go.

Feeling empty and alone, I look down at the scrap of paper with Joey's address. The address is somewhere in East LA.

It is nearly 2:00 a.m. as I pull out of my garage in my old Acura. The city seems quieter, as a lot of the commotion from the heist at Winston's Gala has apparently died down. I drive along Sunset Boulevard through the city, past the iconic buildings of LA, but I barely notice them. Only when I am passing within view of Mount Hollywood do I look up, hoping to see the Griffith Observatory. But it is too dark.

At least that means they've put out the flames.

Joey's street is off Sunset a few miles after it makes its southbound turn into Silver Lake, past a bridge draped with trees. It is a small street of artsy houses overgrown with queen palms. I park in front of the one that matches the address, but I am dismayed to see that it looks dilapidated and abandoned.

There is a sign on the front door, taped onto the wooden planks nailed across it. I approach it in the darkness and read it. "Deliveries to back of house."

Cautiously, I walk to the side of the dark house, stepping on the overgrown lawn and using my phone flashlight to light the way. A cat scurries in front of me as I enter the backyard, scaring the shit out of me. The backyard looks just as barren as the house, but there is a source of light coming from what looks like an old garden shed.

I am a bit spooked, but I walk up to the door of the shed and press my ear to it. It's quiet inside.

I take a deep breath, then I knock.

HE SHICAN
1740

Jiulang shrieked in agony, and the entire inn shook. The Primordial Bolus was consuming him like it had his grandmother, its bright light advancing down his head like an avalanche. With his hands he tore at the light.

Yewang and I watched, aghast, as Jiulang's remaining body transformed into the shadow of a large fox, though still it was dwarfed by its massive bouquet of expansive tails that flowed in all directions around it. The light had eaten past its head and was working its way down its long neck, but the shadow fox was nimble and was shimmying back and forth, trying to maneuver its way out of the light.

Jiulang's resistance was met with an equally tenacious response. As though offended that the fox would not accept its fate, the Primordial Bolus began to emit catastrophic shock waves, blasting apart entire walls of my inn. The window in the room shattered, and the candle toppled over, setting the bed aflame. The roof above us simply burst apart, sending wood and tile flying in all directions, exposing the red moon above us.

It could not best Jiulang, though.

With a final motion, the shadow fox pulled itself entirely out of the white light, which shrank back down into the same small ball of light that Yewang had thrown into Jiulang's face. It floated in the air for a moment before the fox opened its mouth and swallowed it whole.

It was silent again, for another moment. Yewang and I did not dare breathe as the shadow turned its head toward us.

There was an explosion.

One moment I was on the floor of that room, and the next I was flying high through the air. I landed outside on the grass in front of my horse trough, hearing the bones crunch in my leg and the horses whinny as they fled. I turned around, and what was left of my inn was afire.

I stared as it burned in an unholy inferno, until I felt someone lift me up.

We have to go! Yewang yelled. I looked up at him. He had a deep cut on his forehead that painted his face half red. He grunted as he steadied himself under my weight, walking a few paces into the woods.

But Jiulang—I protested, reaching out toward my inn.

With no warning other than an enraged growl, Yewang threw me onto the ground. I cried out more in shock than pain and shielded myself as he held up a fist as if to strike me. *Still, you pine for the demon! After he slashed your throat, destroyed your home!*

He took a breath, calming himself. *You are truly mad, He Shican.*

There was something about the way he said that last sentence that gave me pause. *Qi Yewang, what was the favor?* I asked. *A favor for a favor. What did the fox spirit promise you?*

Enough of this nonsense! Yewang snapped as he approached again as if to pick me up. *The fox spirit may still live! We have to get out of here!*

I violently recoiled away from him. *I am not moving from this position until you answer me, Yewang, and if you refuse, I will crawl back into my burning inn.*

Yewang seemed different to me now. There was a clinical coldness in his eyes that I had never seen before. *He promised me he would not harm you,* he said quietly.

I know that much but there is something else. I reached up and pulled down on his sleeve until he looked toward me again. *Yewang, why did that boy call me your patient?*

My eyes followed him as he slowly sank down onto the ground beside me. *Yewang?*

He would not look at me. The doctor stared straight ahead as he spoke quietly, each word like the first raindrops of an approaching storm.

When they first brought you to me, you had been roaming for days through the streets of Tiaoxi naked, raving mad, ranting about silver teeth and dead beasts. Your inn had been shuttered, and you had no family to help you. So the concerned citizens of Tiaoxi asked me to take you into my care.

He continued. *There happened to be a little girl in my clinic that day—perhaps a daughter of one of those concerned citizens, I do not recall—but you were calmed by her innocence, therefore I let you believe she was my daughter. It helped you trust me.*

I felt numb as our truth finally came out. *So…there is no little Mei?*

Yewang nodded, now looking down. *I have no daughter. I conjured that little girl's likeness whenever I needed her in order to calm you.*

Yewang, I said, realizing the truth as I spoke, *you are no ordinary doctor. You are also a powerful magician. I was marveling at your powers as you created the Primordial Bolus, thinking they were natural gifts. But now I see that they are well-practiced as well. It has been you all along who bewitched me!*

He finally turned to me. *My magics cured you! When it comes to madness of the mind, science can only go so far.* He reached out to clasp my hands. *I did it to save you. I celebrate that I called upon spirits for your sake.*

I pulled away from him and stood up. I had grasped onto a fallen branch when I had been sitting, and I leaned on it as a cane. Yewang rose as well, that stony look still in his eyes.

If your magics are so worthy of celebration, I demanded, *then why did you erase my memories of them? Why is it that when I think back upon our shared history, I remember you as my lover...not as my doctor?*

Yewang had no response.

I spat bloody mucus onto the ground. *You did more with your magics than treat my madness. You also manipulated my mind. Did I truly fall in love with you, Yewang, or was that part of your so-called treatment as well?*

At this accusation, he finally looked at me, his eyes flashing with anger. *All the magics in the world could not get you to look at me the way you look at that damned fox spirit!*

And that was your agreement with Jiulang? A rage was rising in me, too. *He knew the truth about what you had done to me, and you made him agree not to tell me!*

No, Yewang snapped, *that was not the favor he granted.*

Whatever it was, somehow, I doubt it was selfless, I snarled back. *To all the Middle Kingdom, you are the celebrated Dr. Qi, but I know now that you are a dangerous fraudster. I understand now why, when I try to remember our relationship, there are so many black holes in my mind. Am I the first patient you bewitched into your bed? Or is this common practice for you?*

You were the one and only! Yewang said this as if I should have been honored by it. *I do not know why I did what I did. But you became so precious to me, He Shican, and as I summoned magics to treat your madness, I could not stop myself from using them further. I know it was wrong, but I had fallen in love with you! Shican, you are the companion I have been yearning for my whole life. I was unable to resist your kindness and your beauty, and did not want you to leave me once you were better.*

So it is my fault, then, I seethed, *that you betrayed me, that you took advantage of me at my most vulnerable. And all this time you told me to fear the fox spirit, when—Qi Yewang, it is you who is the demon to be feared!*

With a wrathful bellow, Yewang leaped upon me. Backlit by the burning wreckage of my inn, we struck each other with increasingly chaotic blows. But hindered by my broken limb, I fell to the ground, the pain like embers pressed against my flesh. The doctor mounted me, pinning me down with his legs.

Shican, you cannot hide from me out here in the woods forever! With surprising strength, he held me down as I struggled against him. *You were happy with me. Let me make you happy again.* He tried to press his half-bloodied face against mine but I turned my cheek.

Do not forget, Yewang, I snarled at him, *that despite your deception and your dark magics, I still managed to leave you! What makes you think I would return to you now, now that I know the evil of your true nature?*

Yes, you grew a resistance to my magics, Yewang said. *That is why I asked for the favor from the fox spirit.*

Stunned, I began to pummel him with my fists. *You asked the fox spirit to grant you dominion over me again? Damn you, Yewang!*

But then Yewang held up his palm at me, and instantly I was immobilized. My arms fell to my sides like lifeless sticks. I could not even blink. The surroundings began to grow hazy around us, as though a fog was rolling in.

A favor for a favor, Yewang whispered at me, his voice beginning to echo in my head. *Indeed, I feel a new power inside me. I had wondered if the fox spirit would truly grant me these stronger magics, but now as you and I are reunited, I feel as though nothing between us ever changed.*

I could feel his groin upon mine, thickening. He began untying my robes, his hand creeping between my numb thighs to push them apart. In this moment I wished that Jiulang had let me die.

The fox spirit is gone, Yewang chided, as though reading my mind. Behind him I watched what was left of my inn crash down into a fiery heap. *But you and I are together again. You have returned to me at last, Shican.*

He spread open my tunic, exposing my naked body, stiff as a corpse. *Do not be frightened*, he said, as he took my hand and brought it to his lips.

He Shican, the truth is…you belong to me.

Yewang began to tenderly kiss each of my fingers, in the same way I had remembered him kissing them countless times before. But finally, I understood that this gesture was actually his spell. Indeed, with each of his kisses on each of my fingers, I felt my mind relinquishing all control to him.

DONG XIAN

4 BCE

Clutching at my bruised throat, I bolted out of the Hall of the White Tiger, slamming shut the raucous revelry of my father's banquet behind me. I took a second to breathe in the night air, slowing down the beats of my heart, trying in vain to extinguish Commander Jujun from my mind.

Outside, the air was muggy and buzzing with summer insects, insistent cicadas chirping in an unending high note, drowning out the dull roar from inside of merry men. I blinked as my eyes adjusted to the darkness.

I had to find the Emperor, wherever he was. It'd been nearly an hour since I saw him seated at the throne table, but I wasn't sure where he'd gone.

I heard chuckling behind me. I turned to see a man collapsed in a drunken heap next to the grand door of the Hall. He was clutching a full goblet of wine like it was a bird trying to escape, giggling to himself as he watched me. He let out a wet belch.

I cautiously approached and then recognized those long white eyebrows. It was Old Yang, the court philosopher! I hadn't seen nor directly heard from my teacher since my fateful summoning by Fu to the Unicorn Pavilion all those months ago. But I shouldn't have been surprised to see him here, as he was a friend of my father's.

Why, though, was he outside by himself in this sorry state?

Teacher Yang. I rushed to his side, never having seen him so disheveled. *Let me help you up and take you back to your quarters.*

He laughed louder and swatted at me. *Curiouser and curiouser, indeed! Young man, you care so much about saving your old mentor's face, but I have led you woefully astray and placed you in danger's way.*

I quieted and sat down next to him. *Sir, indeed I had been wondering what role you've played in my recent endeavors.*

The philosopher became serious, swaying to the humming of the cicadas. *Just three years ago I promised the former Emperor Cheng that Fu's sensitive and intellectual grandson would be a worthy successor to the Dragon Throne, that this boy would return the Han to greatness through benevolence and virtue. But we all knew there was one obstacle.*

I nodded slowly. *Fu herself. Her scope of power seems endless.*

He leaned forward so he could turn to look me in the eye. His unruly eyebrows drooped over his face and he brushed them out of the way. *But that promise, young man, was made to the Emperor Cheng, may he reign in Heaven forever, and we must do our part to fulfill it. The Dynasty is at stake. Corruption and greed strangle the state. We must protect the Han before it consumes itself.*

That is why you shook hands with Fu to promote me, I realized aloud. *You want me to play both sides.*

The philosopher nodded. *Dong Xian, if you win the Emperor's favor, you may be the only person who can guide him to reclaim the true power of the Dragon Throne. This is the power that is rightfully his, not hers. Do you understand me? The fate of the Empire rests on your shoulders.*

I stood and began pacing. *So much confuses me, Teacher Yang. Why go through the efforts of setting up a chance encounter in a garden between the Emperor and me, then follow it with a blatant promotion of my entire clan?*

The massive doors to the Hall of the White Tiger burst open suddenly, and a pair of drunken revelers stumbled out. I quickly moved out of their way as they walked off into the night, paying us no heed. I sat back down next to the philosopher.

Yang laid a comforting hand on my shoulder. *It is the same reason why everyone has aligned behind you, young man, whether they want to or not. It is because everyone knows.*

What do they know?

That your ascension is inevitable.

I wasn't sure if I believed him. He pulled a long metal pipe out of his robes and lit it. I watched as a plume of smoke snaked into the night sky. He let out a satisfied sigh. *You know, there is another part of that story of Fu and the bear.*

He handed me his pipe, and seeing that it was regular tobacco leaves inside its bowl, I inhaled the sticky, sweet brown smoke, only coughing a little. *You mean the origin of her rivalry with the Princess Feng Yuan?*

The very one. There is a detail in it that is never said aloud, mostly because Fu has smited out nearly every person who knew it. As drunk as he was, he had the wherewithal to speak only with hushed tones.

What was it, Teacher?

Fu and Feng Yuan were not just rivals. They were lovers.

I started coughing out of shock. *Surely you jest, Teacher.*

The old philosopher smiled darkly at the memory. *It was something to behold. Men like us can play with swords, numbers and words, but Fu and Feng Yuan only ever had their beauty, relentless wills to survive…and each other. But then we all realized there was something else within Fu—much deeper, much darker altogether. I am sure you have learned by now that when it comes to the Grand Empress Dowager, nothing is what it seems.*

He reached back into his robes but didn't seem to take anything out. His thumb and forefinger were pinched together. Then I saw him sprinkle a sparkling powder into his pipe.

I reflexively recoiled as I recognized the strange particles from my encounters with Fu. Yang Xiong dragged on the pipe as the shiny dust crackled and burned white-hot. He offered me the pipe. I shook my head. I could see his eyes begin to cloud over, as though a tempest was brewing inside his head.

When he spoke again, his voice sounded different, almost as though he was chanting an incantation. *Do not forget, Dong Xian, that night in your father's guesthouse. As much as the waves may toss you, it was you who first dived into the sea.*

I bowed my head. *What do I do next, Teacher?*

The Emperor awaits you in your quarters tonight. He took another hit of his pipe.

I started in surprise, but steadied myself. I took a breath and nodded. I stood and helped Yang Xiong to his feet. He placed his hand upon my forehead, as if feeling for thoughts. *Honor the promise to the dead Emperor Cheng, young man.*

He tilted his head skyward, his eyes now glowing. *This rain feels good. Perhaps it will wash us clean.*

I looked up at an empty, cloudless sky. There was no rain.

After I located the philosopher's attendant inside the Hall and sent Old Yang off, I checked on my father, who was still celebrating with his colleagues. He was rip-roaring drunk. Clearly, I hadn't been missed.

But sitting next to the Emperor's empty seat, the Grand Empress Dowager Fu acknowledged me with a tilt of her head and an expectant gleam in her eyes. I bowed my head to her. *Go,* she mouthed over the din of the party, her metallic teeth glittering in the candlelight.

Without saying goodbye to anyone, I left the Hall of the White Tiger.

I made my way back to my quarters, realizing that this may be the last night of an era for me. Still, the night was warm and quiet, and the full moon seemed to light my path in a display of celestial approval. The past few weeks had been a whirlwind, but for this moment the air was stagnant and steady. Even the cicadas had gone silent.

But as I neared my quarters, an unexpected gale picked up and it began to rain. I looked up as clouds materialized out of thin air and encroached upon the moon. In the far distance I could hear thunder rumbling like the growling stomach of an insatiable god. I quickened my pace as dense droplets fell upon me. Soon I was running through the grounds of the Endless Palace in a torrential downpour.

When I finally got to my quarters, I paused and rested my ear against the door as rainwater dripped and snaked down my legs. And even though I couldn't hear anything over the raging storm, I could feel his presence inside. The Emperor was waiting for me in my chambers. Behind me, the night sky lit up with a bolt of lightning. I took a deep breath.

I pushed open the door.

RIVER
PRESENT DAY

The door opens and Joey stands there before me. He is wearing a paint-splattered tank top that generously outlines every cut and crease on his sculpted body beneath. He is wide-awake and looks relieved to see me.

"Thank you for coming," he says, moving aside.

I peek in, at first apprehensively. But as my eyes adjust to the dim light inside, I see that this sketchy-looking backyard shed is actually an artist's studio. There are buckets of paint and blocks of clay in one corner, unfinished canvasses stacked against the wall, and a dingy blow-up mattress on the floor. There is a rack with a few pieces of casual clothing next to a cracked old mirror. A far cry from Winston's mansion in the Hills.

Joey shuts the door behind us. That's when I notice that he has a nasty gash about two inches long on the side of his shoulder, the lacerated skin gaping open.

"Joey! You've been hurt!" I motion at it, pulling his arm to me to inspect it more closely.

Unbothered, he glances at it. "Just a scratch," he says, shrugging.

"We should take you to the hospital," I conclude. "This needs stitches."

He shakes his head. "I have a thing against doctors," he replies. "Fell in love with a bad one once."

I frown at him. "You know, I'm actually studying to become a doctor."

He smiles at me. "Well, I'd be all right with you treating me."

Actually, I have taken emergency medical classes and I've sutured dummies before in lab, but that sort of practice is a last resort. However, Joey is not to be dissuaded, and once he shows me that he does have a sewing kit—for his mixed media art pieces—I thoroughly wash his wound with soap and water, and then sterilize the needle and thread in his electric kettle.

He sits down on a wooden crate and gestures to another one next to it. I sit beside him. Holding the needle between the blades of a pair of scissors, I pause right above the edge of his wound. "You ready?" I ask, feeling like I am the more nervous of us.

Joey is looking at me in that soulful way of his, enough that it makes me blush a little. "Ready," he says and nods.

Carefully, I thread the needle through the sides of his wound, pulling the severed skin back together. Joey ever so slightly winces a couple of times when I pierce his flesh, but I work quickly, and soon enough I've stitched him up.

He looks down as I tie a neat surgeon's knot and snip off the extra thread. "You are good at that," he says softly. "You'll be a great doctor someday."

I stand. "I think there's a first-aid kit in my car. I'll go grab some antibacterial ointment."

But he pulls me back down. "No rush. Stay with me first." We take a careful look at each other. He lets out a long sigh. I look at an unfinished painting on an easel, and it bears my profile.

"You have a lot of questions," he then says, rubbing his brow.

"I will try to answer them, but some things are impossible to understand."

"Who are you?" I ask, leaning toward him. "Does that have an answer?"

He suddenly chuckles quietly. "Sometimes I don't even know." He picks up a dirty paintbrush and rolls its bristles between his fingers. "Well, what little I've told you is true. I'm from China. I work with Winston Chow and that's how I ended up in LA."

"'Work with'?" I repeat. "Is it actually true that you are his money boy? I think he's obsessed with you."

Joey's face doesn't change. "I know where my talents lie. Winston is powerful and wealthy, with endless influence and resources. I need him to accomplish my mission." He paused.

"This isn't going to work," I retort, "if your answers only lead to more questions."

Joey suddenly takes me by the hand, and instantly that feeling emanates from his palm into mine. He looks me in the eye. "You have landed in the middle of something that I have devoted an entire lifetime to. Everything culminated tonight at Winston's Gala."

It strikes me just now that Joey had warned me before anything had happened at the Reign Incarnate Gala. *We need to get out of here*, he had said. *Right now.* Only after he said that did those masked figures appear out of the sky.

"You knew," I gasp, the truth dawning in my mind. "You knew those people would appear and steal those artifacts."

"It was the perfect setup," Joey continued, "to have the respected billionaire Winston Chow host a gathering where the secret holders of China's lost treasures could anonymously showcase them to the world for one night. With this backdrop, Winston created a scheme to be carried out in plain sight. He staged a heist and stole the treasures for himself. And it looks like he got away with it."

My mouth has dropped open in shock. "Do you…" I ask, "Do you work for a government or something?"

Joey smiles. "I work for no one, not even Winston. I work for myself."

I get up and start pacing back and forth in the studio. "But why would Winston help you? He has everything to lose!"

Joey stands as well. "He does not know he is helping me. It is a shared mission we have, unknown to him. Because we both want one of the treasures in particular. It is a desire he has that transcends logic and reason. You know of which treasure I speak. You, too, felt it back there. I saw your face as you walked toward it."

Indeed, a flash of the memory blooms in my brain. The center column in front of Winston at the Gala. That little green cube, winking at me with its gold-capped corner.

"The Heirloom Seal of the Realm," I utter, and its name is like an incantation that fills the studio with energy. "I was drawn to it even before I could see it."

Joey nods. "Carved more than two millennia ago from a single block of sacred jade, presented to each Emperor as his official stamp. The symbol of the Dragon Throne, the Seal went missing during the Ten Kingdoms period a thousand years ago. Over history, many imposters and counterfeits attempted to pass themselves off as the Heirloom Seal, but none of them possessed its signature defect."

I look down at Joey's green bracelet, realizing I've been mindlessly rolling its jagged center stone between my fingers. Joey is looking at it, too. "No," I whisper. "You can't be serious."

Joey reaches over to my wrist and touches the center stone of his bracelet. "At the end of Emperor Ai's reign, his grandmother threw the Heirloom Seal at the feet of his traitorous successor, cursing the betrayal. When it struck the ground, this corner piece of it broke off. That is why the Seal was repaired with gold."

"Okay," I say, looking him directly in the eye, "suppose I believe all of this. That you are involved in this crazy heist with Winston Chow and that the stone on this bracelet really is the missing piece of the Heirloom Seal. But there is something else, isn't there? There is another layer here that you still aren't telling me."

Joey looks away from me into the cracked mirror next to his bed, where our many fractured reflections stare back at us. "Yes, there is something else at work here. Something ancient, something powerful, that binds us together. But if I told you, you would not understand. Not yet anyway."

I reach toward him, taking his chin between my fingertips to gently turn him back to me. "Try me, Joey."

His eyes staring deeply into mine, Joey's face softens. He nods, relenting, and then lets out a long sigh, as if releasing a heavy burden.

What if I told you, he begins, *that the feeling we call love...is actually the feeling of metaphysical recognition, when your soul remembers someone from a previous life?*

Joey slides his hand into mine, the green jade bracelet clinking between our wrists, as he continues. *How would that change the way you look at each stranger, knowing they could be the epic romance across all of your lifetimes?*

All of your lifetimes? I repeat, remembering what Calvin had said about past lives. *But Joey, you are talking about a specific life... aren't you?*

Between our palms, the green jade stone seems to grow warmer. I don't know if it is in my imagination, but once again it feels like it is vibrating, like a bee trying to escape our clutch. Joey tightens his grip around mine, as if affirming me.

That emperor you spoke of just now... I continue apprehensively. *Who betrayed him?*

Joey looks down, releasing my hand. *He was betrayed by those he trusted the most, and it changed the course of history.*

And you... As I put everything together, panic begins to creep over me. *You are now after this Heirloom Seal, because of what? Something that happened thousands of years ago? Joey, you could be arrested if they find out you had something to do with Winston's heist. What you've done is dangerous. They could lock you up forever!*

Joey laughs, shaking his head in dismay. *You think being arrested is something I fear? I have lived nearly one hundred lifetimes. I have wandered every corner of this earth. I have witnessed civilizations rise and fall. I have marveled at the miraculous advents and dazzling destruction of human progress. You think I fear anything? I am a soul who remembers.* He looks up at me, his eyes intense and black. *I fear nothing that might get in the way of my mission to reclaim the Heirloom Seal. I have searched too long, and now, in this lifetime, it is finally within my reach.*

My heart breaks a little as I realize finally that Joey may be unwell. "No, Joey." I shake my head. "You need to stop this now." I reach out to him. "Let me help you. I think you need to talk to someone, and I know a psychiatrist—"

His face drops and he turns away from me, grabbing a bag from the floor. He begins snatching clothes and personal effects from around the studio and stuffing them into the bag, clearly ready to leave. *This is why I did not want to tell you. I shouldn't have even stayed with you on the bleachers at Peril that night. I should've just walked away. I knew you would not understand.*

"Joey, please," I say as I try to pull at his arm, but he shakes me off.

I've wasted enough time here, he growls as he zips his bag shut. *I need to follow Winston before he disappears with the Seal and it is too late. Already he must be wondering where I am.*

I am truly upset. I grab him by both hands, forcing him to stop moving. "Joey, wait!" He stiffens and pauses, standing still. But he refuses to look at me.

"Joey, how do you expect me to react to all of this?" I exclaim. "What am I supposed to believe, that you are the reincarnation of some ancient Chinese emperor trying to avenge his throne?" Even as I'm saying it, I shake my head at how preposterous it all sounds.

Joey inhales a sharp intake of breath. His eyes widen at me.

"What?" I ask him. "Why are you looking at me like that?"

Joey sighs. "No, River," he finally replies softly. "I am not that emperor."

"What do you mean?"

Joey closes his eyes.

"River... You are the emperor."

Joey kneels in front of me on both knees, his hands stretched out before him, bowing his head deeply. He proceeds to speak an ancient Chinese-sounding language that I do not recognize, but for some reason I understand.

O Radiant and Holy Son of Heaven, I am eternally your servant! He lifts his head to look back up at me.

I feel as though I might explode into a billion pieces.

My Emperor! Tears glisten in Joey's eyes.

My Emperor. My Emperor.

My Liu Xin.

HE SHICAN
1740-1741

As Yewang tenderly kissed each of my fingers, I could feel my mind slip away from me. No longer struggling against him, I felt the movement return to my naked body as it began to obediently receive his advances.

You are mine again, at last, Yewang whispered as he untied his clothes at his waist. He licked his lips, his face still half-painted with his own blood. A thin trail of saliva spilled out of the corner of his mouth and dripped onto my cheek. He positioned himself over me, readying himself to reap the spoils of his newfound powers.

I closed my eyes, focusing on the sound of the dying fire behind us.

But for a moment nothing happened. Then I felt a sudden rush of wind above me.

It was followed by Yewang's screams.

I opened my eyes, and Yewang was no longer on top of me. Startled, I sat up, looking around. I gasped aloud when I saw it.

No longer a shadow, a sleek fox with amber fur and nine

enormous tails materialized before me. It was set aglow as the moon redirected its beams in order to better shine upon Huang Jiulang in his true glory.

Still screaming, Yewang was high above us, sailing back and forth in the air at dizzying speeds. Once my eyes adjusted to the sight, I saw that he was being flung wildly about by one of Jiulang's fantastical tails, which had him gripped by an unlucky leg. Placid and silent as a frozen lake, the fox spirit looked calmly back at me.

I stood up with the help of my makeshift cane to watch as three more of Jiulang's tails shot up to Yewang, each coiling itself around one of the wretched man's remaining limbs. The tails stretched him outward in all four directions so that he was fanned open above us like a kite, his face pointed toward the stars above. His screams intensified as the tails tightened their grip, pulling his body taut.

In horror, I realized the gruesome fate awaiting Yewang. I covered my eyes just in time to avoid seeing it, but I heard it happen. It was the sound of a man being torn open and apart, as each of Jiulang's tails quartered Yewang like a boiled chicken at supper. There was another flurry of wind sounds, as the tails flung their pieces of him far away into the woods beyond.

The only mercy was that the screaming had finally stopped. I opened my eyes and Jiulang was suddenly right in front of me, somehow at once both a fox and a boy, his long whiskers grazing my cheeks, his pink lips just barely parted.

I backed away, knowing I could not outrun him.

And why would you run? asked Jiulang. *What do you fear? Do you not believe he deserved that fate? Do you not Remember what he did to us?* Around us his massive amber tails were suspended and flowing in all directions, as though we were underwater.

He told me I was the only one he ever bewitched, I said, noting that there was blood on Jiulang's tails, staining them the color of raw gold.

Jiulang narrowed his eyes at my response, looking disturbed. *So you do not Remember?*

I blanched, unsure what he meant but feeling apologetic. *There are whole months of my life that I do not remember anymore. Yewang punctured so many holes into my mind that I can no longer tell if I am dreaming or awake.*

The fox spirit let out a long sigh, as if defeated. His supernatural aura faded away, and he presented in full human form once again. The night grew darker with him.

I bid you farewell in this life, He Shican, Jiulang said simply. The boy gave me a small nod, and then turned to go.

I was aghast. *What? No, wait!* A bit rougher than I intended, I pulled on his shoulder to stop him. Jiulang hesitated, but did not turn back to me.

You cannot just leave, I gasped. *You cannot just appear one day and destroy my life, and then just leave!* Together we looked at the smoldering heap that had been my inn.

You knew what I am, he replied. *You invited me into your home. You know what happens between fox spirits and men. What surprises you so?*

Unable to stand any longer, I collapsed to the ground. I wrapped my arms around his legs. He tried to walk away but I held on. *Then take me with you, Huang Jiulang!* I begged.

Jiulang looked down at me. *You have nothing left for me to take.*

And with that he vanished, leaving me behind, my hands grasping only at the empty darkness of my surroundings.

Jiulang! I screamed into the night, struggling back to my feet. *Jiulang!* Hobbling as fast as I could on my walking stick, I limped into the woods, calling out his name. *Jiulang! Come back!*

I heard a twig snap and looked in that direction. It was my trusty old horse Dama emerging from the shadows, returning to me after first fleeing from the fire. Gratefully, I mounted her and we galloped through the trees. With every leap she took, my broken leg throbbed upon impact, but I ignored the pain. *Jiulang! Jiulang!* I called into the wilderness.

Jiulang! I rode like this for an interminable time in an infinite forest toward the ends of the earth.

Jiuliang! I only vaguely kept track of the sun and the moon as they danced back and forth in the sky above us.

Jiulang! But we did not stop, even though my voice crumbled from calling out his name too many times.

At first, I did not understand how Dama sped so selflessly forward on her own accord, without any urging from me, even though she surely was exhausted, too. Then I realized she was just as enamored of Huang Jiulang as I was. *Jiulang! Jiulang!*

Where were we going? I did not know; all I knew was that we were getting closer and closer to him. How long did we continue like this? I do not know, but my beard was touching my chest when I recognized a familiar object one day as Dama was taking a sip from a babbling stream. I had only seen tree and mountain and river for all this time, and the man-made object looked strange and unearthly at first. But then I recognized it as a temple that I had often visited as a child for special occasions and religious days.

Perched atop a fat emerald hill, the temple's red pagoda roofs glinted in the bright day, their dramatic slopes slingshotting the sunbeams back into space. I dismounted from my horse. My foot had stopped hurting some time ago, but it had healed imperfectly. I limped a few paces toward the temple, wondering if it was a mirage that would fade away as I drew closer.

As the breeze wafted my way, I suddenly smelled the sweet incense burning. The temple did not fade away—it was as real as day. Somehow, I had unwittingly traveled back to my childhood home.

I tugged at Dama's rein excitedly, as this was her birthplace as well, but she let out a weary groan. As I turned back to her, she collapsed in a heap of skin and bones. We had come to the end of our journey together. I stroked her indigo mane and murmured gentle things until she stopped breathing. I thanked her for bringing me home, then buried her under a mound of dead leaves.

Unsure of where else to go, I crept toward my old village.

The sun was setting when I reached the outskirts of town, where my old home was. It was still there, painted red by the magic hour. There was an adult and a child in front of the house, and as I approached I saw that the adult was my mother. She looked very nearly the same to me, perhaps a few more white streaks in her hair, and she was laughing. The child was a sweet girl who looked like family, my little niece I guessed, and she was playing with my mother.

Timidly, I limped toward them, wondering how my mother was going to react, how many tears of joy she was going to cry. But as I drew nearer, the little girl noticed me first, and she cried out in alarm. She motioned at me and my mother turned as well. My mother's eyes widened at the sight of me. She quickly ushered the little girl into my home and followed after her.

Almost immediately, an old man stuck his head out the door. He was my father. He had aged more than my mother; he was balding and stout. He was also holding his old military rifle.

We are honorable people here, he called out toward me. *Leave us be, wild man.*

They did not recognize me. I stood there for a moment, wondering how I should reveal myself. The little girl looked out again through the door. Like her uncle, she was a glutton for punishment, because upon reexamining whatever it was I looked like, she burst into tears. My mother appeared again only to pull her back inside, shuddering as she avoided my gaze.

My father grew enraged. *This is your last warning*, he declared. He raised his rifle and pointed it my way, but as he was aiming at me, our eyes met. He paused and lowered his weapon. I could see it written in pain on his face. He now knew who I was.

As the sun disappeared behind us, my father and I stared at each other. I was reminded of another time my father had stood in this very place, waiting for me as I emerged from the woods after sharing a forbidden peach with a boy named Zheng.

Did you find it? my father finally asked, setting down his rifle. *Did you find whatever it is you were always seeking in the woods at night?*

Father, I replied, *I, too, once thought I was seeking something in the woods. But now I know the truth. When I walk the woods, I am not seeking anything. I am returning to where I truly belong.*

I bowed goodbye and I left them, and returned to where I belonged.

The woods were eerie at night. The air smelled strange and the trees took different forms. I walked to that familiar place, where the trees were denser than the moonlight. I sat there against that old peach tree, waiting. I knew he would come.

Spirit, are you done denying me? I wept to the silence. *Are you done?*

I could already feel his presence next to me before he spoke, his words tickling the helix of my ear.

Yes, Jiulang whispered. *I am done.*

I embraced the fox spirit in my arms.

DONG XIAN
4 BCE

The Emperor was sitting in the shadows when I entered my chambers. I was drenched with rain. For a moment neither of us spoke. Then a flash of lightning from the storm outside lit up his face. He was expressionless.

I kowtowed into the puddle of my own making. *Your Radiance blesses me with your presence.*

The Emperor stood and walked into the light of the window. He was still wearing his magnificent blue robe, emblazoned with nine dragons. They seemed to dance around him when he moved.

Rise, Dong Xian of Yunyang.

Obediently, I stood. He walked toward me. I kept my head bowed.

Look at me, Dong Xian. He was a little taller than me, and I tilted my head to meet his gaze. Still, his face was unreadable. He continued. *I came here because I need to know something.*

Yes, Your Radiance?

You call me Son of Heaven. You acknowledge my sanctity as a living god.

Of course I do, Your—

The Emperor picked up an old vase that was near his feet and flung it against the wall. It shattered, shaking the entire room, including me as I cowered back down to the ground. *Silence, Dong Xian. Look at me.* He walked toward me, his head bowing lower as he approached me, staring deep into my eyes. *If you believe me a god, then why do you play me a fool?*

Forgive me, I do not understand, Your Radiance.

The Emperor towered over me for a moment. Then he turned and sat down on the foot of my mat. Still, he never broke eye contact with me. I felt that I had never had someone look so deeply into me.

You are new to the Endless Palace, Dong Xian. You did not know the late Emperor Cheng, my predecessor, may he reign in Heaven forever. He finally broke his intense gaze, his face softening as he turned to look out my small window. *The Emperor Cheng was my uncle,* he said quietly. A beam of moonlight was projected onto the patch of mat on his side, and he pushed his hand into it, setting it aglow. *The first time we met, I was but a minor prince, yet he said that within me was the same immortal dragon blood that courses through the veins of all the Emperors of the Han. Then he gifted me his most prized ceremonial robe, the very one I am wearing right now.*

Both of us looked down at his splendid garment, its embroidered dragons staring back at us intimidatingly. But for the first time he seemed to me to be drowning in it, in swathes of cerulean captivity. *Son of Heaven, that robe is splendid but it looks heavy, in every sense of the word.*

You are right, Dong Xian. Because a few years later on his deathbed, the Emperor Cheng gave me a second gift: the Heirloom Seal of the Realm. In his last breaths, he told me that it was Heaven's Will that I succeed him. He made me promise that I would uphold our throne and rule justly, bravely, mercifully. But most important to him was that I be a true leader, the true ruler of the Han, bowed to no one. He looked down at the shattered pieces of the vase. *But in two years, I have already failed him.*

Unsure of where this was leading, I began to worry. *May I speak, my Emperor?*

As if startled, he glared back at me. *I don't know if you should, Dong Xian.* His voice was forced and controlled. *I would know not who speaks—you…or my grandmother.*

It felt like the floor was sinking underneath my feet. *P-p-please, Son of Heaven. I will not lie to you. Yes, your grandmother's promotion of my father is one part of a scheme. It was designed by her that you and I meet.*

The Emperor laughed loudly, catching me by surprise as he shook his head. *And this is where you think me a fool.* He sighed as he walked away from me, then looked back, narrowing his amber eyes.

Tell me, Dong Xian, do you think I did not already know the truth? I have known all along that you were sent by my grandmother! Do you think that you just one day stumbled into afternoon wine with the Son of Heaven? You think that the entourage—nay, the institution!—that plans, facilitates and transcribes my life into fine calligraphy would ever simply just allow someone like you to wander into my orbit?

Slowly, the truth of my reality was dawning on me, and it felt as if the floor turned into quicksand. I couldn't even speak, but I didn't need to, because he just continued relentlessly.

Do you think you are the first pretty boy to be groomed by my grandmother? She sent officials to the far corners of my Empire in search of eligible men from respectable families. Do you think I did not know exactly what was going on when I first sat down with you in the courtyard? I had just quarreled with my grandmother that very morning, so my first instinct was to exile your entire clan to the western ruins, just to spite her.

Thank you for changing your mind, Your Radiance, I whispered, looking back down at the floor.

And when you and I started meeting regularly, you cannot fathom the headache it caused! He shut his eyes as he rubbed his forehead at the memory. *My advisers started betraying one another to demonstrate their loyalty to me, blithely unaware of the ridiculous irony. And then there was a full day where a member of my family arranged for me an itinerary made up of meetings with every Wu, Cheng and Gao he could find to assassinate your character. Dong Xian may be handsome but not as much as he is stupid, they all said, and his self-serving ambitions are only rivaled by his depraved sexual addictions.*

He tilted his head, as if suddenly recalling something. *My Prime Minister even tried to have you poisoned at one point.* He looked at me, still cold. *Do you wish me to continue?*

I had never felt so small. *If it pleases Your Radiance, I would like to hear everything that I did not know*, I replied quietly.

The Emperor stiffened at this. *None of this pleases me, Dong Xian.* He sighed, then spoke more softly. *Your father's promotion is his reward for selling his youngest son to the Dragon Throne, aided by his old friend, Yang Xiong the philosopher. It is why you were brought to the Endless Palace in the first place.*

I felt the wind knocked out of me and was unable to speak as all the awful truths fell into place. He then suddenly walked past me to go to the wall behind my mattress. He knelt and lifted a panel out of the floor. Before I could react, a trap door opened and a gust of stale air blew upon us, revealing a stone staircase leading into darkness below!

W-what…is that…? I stammered, peering into the trap door and recognizing the familiar stone on the walls within. I had lived in these quarters for two years, and never had I known of this secret passage right behind my head each night as I slept.

The Emperor nodded. *Yes, your chambers are unique. They are connected to the Shadow. Because this bedroom has been the bedroom of the Emperor's favorite many times throughout history. Because, from the very beginning, even before you arrived to the Endless Palace, your fate had been sealed, Dong Xian.*

Wearily, he sat on my mattress. We were both silent as I knelt in front of him, shaking. Everything I thought I knew about my life had been a lie.

I know the maelstrom in your mind, he finally said. *I went through the same realization when I was much younger. Dong Xian, this whole time you thought that you were playing the game, only to realize you are the game.*

May I speak, my Emperor? I reached my arms toward him beseechingly. I was completely overwhelmed.

You may speak, Dong Xian.

I pressed my palms together in front of me. *I have never been so humbled, Your Radiance. I want you to know that as I walked back here tonight, I was planning on telling you everything. When your grandmother made her announcement, forgive me, but I thought you were as surprised as I was.*

He shook his head, looking sad. *No. I was only surprised that even after I bend to her will, she still revels in humiliating me in front of my Court by parading her plots for all to see. She sends her message to the Endless Palace loud and clear. The Grand Empress Dowager Fu is still very much in power, and I am to be her figurehead until one of us dies.* He put his face into his hands. *I often wish it were me.*

Not remembering myself, I leaped forward and grabbed him by his knees, pressing my face onto his shoes. It was like a floodgate inside me had opened, and I began to weep. *No, please do not say that, my Emperor! I am just so sorry to be a pawn in a wicked scheme that causes you such pain.*

I felt him flinch for a second. Then I heard his robes rustling as he bent forward, as he wrapped his arms around me and rested his head on top of mine.

I do not say these things to be cruel, Dong Xian, he murmured, his warm breath traveling through my tangled hair onto my neck. *I say them because this would be your life. Half the palace would conspire against you, and the other half would only be loyal as long as I am alive. If this is what you want, your life would be inextricably tied to mine, as short as it might be.*

Wiping my hair out of my eyes, I looked up at him. My tears had ceased, and I felt...strangely freed from something. *If?* I asked. *What do you mean by* if, *Emperor?*

Sit beside me, Dong Xian. Carefully, I rose and sat down next to him at the foot of my mat, but he moved back, creating some space between us. *I would never force anyone to be by my side. Now you know the truth, the magnitude of a life before you. If you still wish this life, this life with me, that choice is yours to make. Otherwise, you can walk away, and you have my word that I will make sure you and your clan are protected and comfortable. But you must tell me now, before I can no longer safely exit you out of this situation.*

Deep down I already knew what I was going to say. But I had to know something first. *If it pleases my Emperor, may I ask one question? After all my lies, after all the campaigns against me, after all your grandmother's meddling, why choose me?*

He looked down at his hands, peeking out from within his brilliantly blue sleeves. *When I first saw you, you were exactly what I was expecting: beautiful, charming, eager to please. I have met my fair share of these. But there is something else in you, when I look into your eyes, when our fingers touch—*

His hand reached into mine, our fingers interlocking.

It is a feeling that I cannot describe, he continued gently, *because I have never felt it before.*

Unable to contain myself, I brought his hand to my face, pressing it against my cheek, feeling it bristle against my beard. *I know of this feeling you speak, Emperor, for I, too, have felt it since we first met. It haunts me whenever I am apart from you.*

Yes, he said, nodding as he stroked my cheek, *I cannot bear to be apart from you, either, Dong Xian.*

I do not know what this feeling is, I sighed, kissing his fingertips as they brushed my lips. *All I can say is that it is true.*

A true feeling, he said quietly, as though committing it to memory. He sighed, happily. *I would seek it for lifetimes. That is how wonderful this true feeling is.* He smiled his rare smile at me.

I reached out around his waist, pulling him toward me, feeling a heat begin to course through me. I knew he felt it, too. I took his chin and lifted his face toward mine. He did not resist. *Emperor, I would choose an eternity of lifetimes with you, to be by your side forever, so that you may always experience our true feeling.*

His body now pressed against mine, our hearts encouraged each other to beat faster. I tried to bring my lips to his, but he hesitated and I pulled back quickly.

From now on, Dong Xian, he whispered, *we trust each other unfailingly, and you must never betray this. Please.* He almost begged this of me, both of us knowing that we had already fallen in too deep, that it was too late.

Yes, Liu Xin.

His eyes widened at the sound of his birth name. *What did you call me?*

I nodded as I stroked his face. *I will never betray you, Liu Xin.*

With a profound hunger, he pulled me to him. *Say my name again, Dong Xian.*

My Liu Xin, I said as we kissed.

RIVER
PRESENT DAY

"What is that name?" I demand of Joey. "What did you call me?"

"Liu Xin," Joey says softly, still kowtowing before me.

"And who is Liu Xin?" I ask.

"Two thousand years ago Liu Xin was your name," Joey replies, his face still downcast. "But very few people called you that, because that would be a mortal sin. To everyone else, you could only be referred to by your many titles." He begins speaking in that archaic language again. *Your Radiance. Son of Heaven. My Emperor.*

"But you call me by that name. Why?" I am slowly moving away from him, but his art studio is tiny and I quickly back into the wall. I press against it, because I don't think I can stand otherwise.

Joey moves from the floor to sit wearily on his old blow-up mattress, looking over at one of his half-finished portraits of me leaning against the wall next to it. "It is because I was yours, and you were mine," he says, finally looking up at me. "We were in love."

"And who were you?"

"My name was Dong Xian," Joey says, "and I was just a lowly clerk in your palace, one of your many nameless servants. But I caught your attention, I earned your favor and I became your lover."

"My palace?"

Joey nods. "They called it the Endless Palace, the grandest one ever built upon this earth. Only ruins of it remain today, but back then it was your home, and it was where we met."

I look at the images of my face scattered throughout the studio. "And is that why you know my face? Is that why you created these artworks that look like me?"

Joey smiles at me. "Yes, Liu Xin. I have known your face for two thousand years. It has been the singular image in my mind for so many lifetimes. In this current lifetime, my art is how I express myself and process our situation, because to Remember is a heavy burden."

It all sounds like crazy talk, and part of me wants to run out of here, but instead... I sit next to him. "What's our situation?"

Joey shifts to face me. "To put it as simply as possible, our souls are caught in an endless loop. No matter how many lifetimes we endure, we will not be released from an ancient curse. And once upon a lifetime, I made a promise to you that I would break it."

"Once upon a lifetime... So we have met many times?" I ask. "There have been other lifetimes, before this one, where we knew each other?"

Joey smiles sadly. "In many lifetimes, our souls have reunited in one way or another. And in each of these lifetimes, our reunion has inevitably led to our shared misery and early deaths. This is a fate that we are always destined toward, including in this lifetime, unless I finally end it."

"End it…with the Heirloom Seal?" I ask. "You think it is the way to break this curse?"

"You are connecting the dots," he says, nodding. "The Heirloom Seal of the Realm is the source of the curse. Since Remembering, I have spent lifetimes searching for it. And finally, in this life, it is within my reach. Winston will no doubt keep it close, but I plan to follow him until I have a chance to steal it back, to return it to you."

There's a part of me that dreads the answer to my next question, but I know I need to ask. "And Winston? Who is he to us? Who is he to you?"

Joey's eyes sharpen with a certain intensity. "For many lifetimes, Winston has held me hostage in one form or another. He is part of our curse, what I must endure for my part in it."

"Hostage?" I repeat. "Joey, are you sure there's nothing between you and Winston? I mean…is there any part of you that wants to be with him?"

He looks at me in disbelief, as though the very idea of that is offensive. "Never!" he insists, his dark eyes flashing. "He is my punishment and the obstacle between us and our deliverance, but beyond that he has never meant anything to me."

I nod slowly, wondering how it is that this all seems to somehow make sense. "Just one more question, then," I venture. "How is it that you can Remember, and I cannot?"

Joey chuckles darkly at an unspoken memory. "You used to be the one who Remembered. I was a humble innkeeper, and you were magnificent and terrifying, a nine-tailed magical creature whose vengeance and power was unstoppable."

I scoff, now unsure again. "But in this lifetime, somehow I do not Remember. That seems a bit convenient."

He stands suddenly. "I need to leave. Convincing you is useless if I lose the Heirloom Seal to Winston."

I stand, too, my hands in my pockets. I am wondering if I

should just let him go. Everything he says is utterly unbelievable, yet…

"I'm sorry, Joey," I say to him, genuinely meaning it. "It is all just a lot to take in."

You don't need to apologize, he sighs. *Because I know that you know everything I am saying to you is true.*

How do you know? I ask.

Because you feel it, too, he says. *You might not Remember, but in all our lifetimes, you have never forgotten that feeling.*

That feeling? I ask, but I begin to tremble all over. *What feeling?*

I do not know what this feeling is, Joey replies softly. *All I can say is that it is true.*

I translate his words in my mind, then I realize what he is saying.

"A true feeling," I whisper, as every hair on my body stands on end and shivers run through me. Tears begin to roll down my face. Joey reaches over and wipes them from my cheeks.

"I have been searching," I whisper, almost to myself, "my whole life!"

Yes, Joey whispers back, *for all our lifetimes, Liu Xin. For that true feeling.*

He leans in toward me and we finally kiss.

His lips are full and soft, but his kiss… His kiss is a missing piece of my soul that has finally been returned. We kiss for what seems like lifetimes, and even that is not enough.

When I finally pull back for air, my knees are quaking, weak. "Joey," I sigh, already heartbroken, knowing that soon he will be gone again. "I believe you. I believe everything."

Joey wraps his strong arms around me, holding me close, his dark eyes glistening. *Do you feel it, Son of Heaven?* he asks. *Do you feel the truth between us?*

"Yes," I whisper, cradling his face with my hands. "It is the true feeling. Our true feeling."

We kiss again, and he lifts me into the air, carrying me to his bed.

HE SHICAN
1741

Jiulang sat on my thighs, his nose buried in my hair, as I rested my cheek against his chest and inhaled deeply. I lifted my head to face him and his amber eyes were no longer detached and unreadable—now they burned into me, bright with lust.

Around us, the woods were still and quiet, as though watching.

With a flourish, he was naked. In a blink, so was I. He held out his arms like wings. I felt our bodies levitate into the air. We hovered above the ground, suspended in the atmosphere, which began to pulsate around us.

No, I heard Jiulang say. *Keep your eyes open.* I opened them as he guided me into him. His heavenly warmth wrapped around me. He bit down on my lip and made a strange feral sound, like a pup yipping. I snarled back at him, baring my teeth. He rode me up and down.

In the heat of our entangled bodies, I marveled at his flaw-less skin as it slapped slick against mine. Suddenly, I felt a brush of soft fur. There was a massive glowing amber tail running against my arm, slinking toward me like a luxurious snake.

Then another appeared, swathing around Jiulang's head like a crown. And yet another, this tail running up between us and tickling our chests.

And yet another. And another.

His nine splendid tails, the color and brilliance of raw gold, fanned open around us, undulating in the air. I leaned away from Jiulang to grab at one of them in wonder. Jiulang smiled at me, his small teeth sharp. He pulled me to him and kissed me, as the tails collapsed inward upon us, like a grand flower blooming in reverse.

What are you doing? I started for a moment, but then Jiulang breathed into my mouth, and my eyes rolled up in joyous euphoria. I took another deep breath but mostly inhaled fur. The tails wrapped ever tighter around us, pushing the air out of my chest, as I began to grow dizzy. I was drowning in plush as Jiulang rode me up and down.

Do you love me? the boy asked. His cold breath turned into dew on the tip of my nose.

Yes. I had barely enough air left to rasp out the word.

Still, he demanded. *Say my name.*

I realized I was suffocating. How could I respond? *I love you, Jiulang,* I thought, unable to say the words aloud.

But then Jiulang replied in my head, his voice ringing as clear as if he had spoken aloud. *How much do you love me?* He quickened his pace as he straddled me. I had never felt a pleasure so glorious.

Eternally. The word echoed in my head as I thrusted deeper into him. *I am eternally your servant, Jiulang.*

Would you die for me, Shican? Tell me, would you die for me? He was now shouting in my brain as he squeezed the life out of me. I could feel it in my shaking groin that I was arriving, like a horse on a mad dash toward a cliff.

Yes! I screamed out loud as my entire body burst into a soul-ripping flood. I felt his tails release their hold and flare back open around us, the cool air of night rushing back into my deprived lungs. I grabbed Jiulang by his shoulders and held him down on me as I erupted into him, loading the fox spirit full of my molten love, our bodies convulsing into each other as I cried out into the woods.

Finally, I released him.

I was exhausted from the carnage. My body went limp. I felt our bodies descend to the ground.

But then Jiulang held up my face and breathed into me. I looked at him as his amber eyes burned bright. Enslaved by him, I felt myself stiffen again at his beck and call. Like a bull in crazed heat, I was ready to mount him once more.

Our bodies rose back into the air.

Say my name, Jiulang kept repeating. *Say my name again, Shican.*

DONG XIAN
4 BCE

Say my name again, Dong Xian.

Outside, a clap of thunder answered in unison with me. *My Liu Xin.*

Our lips met, ravenous. I hoisted him up in the air, his legs wrapped around my waist, and carried him to my bed. We both fell upon the mat in a tangle of limbs and tongues. My influence had swollen to its fullest potential, humming with anticipation as I untied his blue dragon robe, which fanned open around us after I pushed it off his shoulders. The Emperor knelt down before me and took me into his mouth.

We were both naked, having flung our garments in all directions. They hung around us like weeping willows.

Is it good? the Emperor asked while taking a breath, looking up at me. His eyes were wide and he was ready to please, ready to consume me. His tongue swirled lovingly around the head, as he eagerly lapped up each sticky dewdrop that beaded out of me.

I leaned down to kiss his forehead. *Yes, Son of Heaven.*

He lay back onto my bed, biting his lower lip. *Please, Dong Xian, call me Liu Xin again.*

With a swift motion, I lifted his legs up and apart into the air. *Only if you are good*, I teased him. He gazed upon me longingly.

Now was my turn to kneel. I carefully spread his buttocks apart and brought my lips to the tenderness between them, the knotted flesh there that was clean and supple. As my tongue pushed into the Emperor, he let out unbridled cries in delirium, his hands finding the back of my head to encourage me in deeper. He tasted sweet and earthy.

Though I still hungered, he soon pulled me upward so that I was on top of him, wrapping his arms around my shoulders in a surprisingly strong hold. Using his hands, he strategically positioned my influence between his spread legs. His thighs were liquid smooth and warm against mine.

Both our breaths calmed, and the room was immediately silent. Even the rain outside had stopped. Like two ships on the sea, we had entered the eye of the storm.

Are you sure? I asked, smoothing his hair off his forehead. I kissed him on the chest, and he let out a stifled moan as I sucked his left nipple.

He nodded. I spat into the palm of my hand until it was slick with saliva and then reached downward between us with wet fingers, readying us both. He arched his back and closed his eyes in tense concentration.

Keep your eyes open, Liu Xin, I ordered. He kept his eyes open as I entered him.

Liu Xin took a sharp intake of breath and gritted his teeth at the initial pain. He dug his nails into my back. He was warm and at first ungiving. I whispered in his ear, something soothing and kind. Then his eyes rolled up and I could feel his pleasure inviting me inside. He relaxed for me and I slid all the way into him in one quick motion. I proceeded boldly as his gasps turned into full-throated moans.

Dong Xian. Dong Xian!
My Liu Xin.

I buried my face into his neck as we moved to an ancient rhythm between men.

I woke the next morning as streaks of hot sunlight splashed across the window onto my bed. After many hours I had been exhausted, and the Emperor had held me protectively, possessively, as we both drifted off to sleep. In the coolness of the night, he had put his ornate blue robe back on and wrapped it around us, its many trinkets tinkering whenever we shifted our bodies. Occasionally, he would gently kiss the nape of my neck, his beard tickling my skin.

Sitting up on my bed, I looked around. He was gone. I lay back, still sleepy, but then felt a cold sharpness against my face. I looked at what I'd been sleeping upon. It took me a second to realize what it was.

Under me was a massive sleeve, which had been severed from Liu Xin's robe. I looked at the impressive piece of brilliant blue silk, studded with precious gems and a now-decapitated dragon brocade. At first, I was confused, until I realized why he had done it.

I had fallen asleep upon his prized heritage robe. And so he could leave without stirring me awake, the Emperor had cut off his sleeve.

RIVER

PRESENT DAY

The next morning, without looking, I already know that Joey is gone. Last night I had tried to stay awake as long as I could, my head resting snugly on his chest as it steadily rose and fell as he slept, my legs entangled with his so that he might not be able to leave without stirring me.

The last thing I heard were his whispers in my ear. *Don't follow me*, he kept saying. *Don't follow me, my Emperor. I will come back for you.*

Don't follow me, Liu Xin.

But soon after that I had fallen asleep, and now he is gone.

Freckled sunlight warms my skin through a paint-splattered window. I take in my surroundings. During the day, the studio is decidedly less romantic, cigarette butts littered everywhere next to half-empty cans of paint. I sit up on the deflated air mattress.

I stand quickly, grabbing my clothes that are strewn all over the studio. I also take the time to see if there are any personal effects or maybe even a note that Joey has left behind. But other than his used art supplies, there's nothing.

I am pulling on my shirt and looking in Joey's dirty mirror when I realize there is something written on my back in red paint. I walk farther from the mirror and I see that while I was sleeping, Joey painted ancient Chinese characters on my back, in a square setting.

And even though I don't recognize them, I already know what they are. The lettering of the Heirloom Seal.

As I climb into my car, I grimace when a sudden sharp pain shoots between my legs, though not altogether unpleasant. Leaning my head against the window, I close my eyes and remember last night.

Joey had lifted me in the air, carrying me to his bed. Kissing me, he placed me on the old blow-up mattress, no comforter except for an old blanket and a single pillow. He took off my glasses and enveloped me with his body. His strong weight on top of me made me dizzy, and instinctively I wrapped my legs around his waist.

With deft maneuvering, he flipped us both over, so I was sitting upright and straddling him. He smiled at me, and I grinned back. *Finally*, he said.

We unbuttoned our shirts as I fumbled with his belt, pulling off his pants. Joey sat back and held me as he kissed my neck. I could feel the true feeling brimming inside me.

"Don't stop," I said, as I reached down between us and grasped him, guiding him until he was pushed against me. The feeling of his head against my hole sent shock waves up my spine.

Joey then reached under the mattress and pulled out a bottle of lube, expertly opening it with one hand and applying it to himself. I tensed a bit, nervous.

"I've only... I've never... This is my first time," I said to Joey, hoping it wouldn't scare him.

Joey smiled and kissed me. *Our first time...but only in this lifetime*, he whispered.

I felt his rough hands sliding upward on my back, until they were clasping my shoulders. He looked at me, waiting. I took a deep breath, then nodded. His hands boldly pushed my body down onto him. I winced at the initial penetrating pain as he entered me.

"Keep your eyes open," Joey whispered, and I did. He lay down on his back, and then in one magnificent motion, he pushed into me fully and firmly. I took a jagged breath as I received him. Joey moaned, trembling as I angled my body so I could take him in even deeper.

His arms swollen with the effort, Joey held me around my waist and guided me up and down, and the initial pain quickly radiated into a searing ecstasy. I gasped loudly as he ran his hands all over my chest and stomach, the friction driving me wild.

"Joey." His pace quickened as he went in and out of me, and the ecstasies multiplied like psychedelic fractals. "Please don't stop."

I won't.

"Please don't stop. Please don't stop." I was now pushing back against him, taking him as hard as he was thrusting into me.

He sat up, wrapping his muscular limbs around me, our sweaty bodies clinging together. Somehow, I could feel him growing even more inside me, pushing all my limits into soul-shaking sensations that I didn't know existed. He raised his mouth to meet my lips once again, his tongue spreading them apart.

I won't ever stop, he promised me. *My Emperor, I won't ever stop.*

And even though I already knew he'd be gone by the morning, I had believed him when he said it.

Liu Xin, I'll never stop. I'll never stop.

I will never stop.

HE SHICAN
1742

We have to stop.

Naked and wet, Jiulang lay on the flat rock next to the river, the moonlight setting his porcelain skin aglow. He was still breathing hard, with feral little gasps that cut into the night.

With great effort, I reached over to him, taking his foot into my palm and massaging it gently. He pulled it away.

Did you hear me, He Shican? We need to stop.

I tried to let out a casual chuckle, but it was interrupted when I started coughing instead. I cleared my throat. *Stop what, Huang Jiulang?*

A centipede crawled onto my chest, and I brushed it off. I was half-submerged in the cold mud of the riverbank, in a putrid buzzing sludge that was alive with all sorts of squirmy and crawly things, but I did not care. *Come over here and let me fuck you again.*

Jiulang sat up, his toes dipping into the water. He cocked his head at me, concerned. *When is the last time you slept, Shican? When is the last time you ate? You look unwell.*

I rolled on my side toward him, ignoring a sharp pain in my gut. *Do you doubt my virility, Huang Jiulang? Do I not pleasure you? Do I not fulfill you? Have I not had you innumerable times in the past week?*

Jiulang reached over and pulled me up onto the rock next to him. I leaned against it, watching the river currents cleanse my body of the filth and weeds. *Past week?* Jiulang exclaimed, looking increasingly worried. *You lose track of time. It has been a year we have been out here in the woods! Look how your bones protrude through your chest.*

I looked down at my own body, and indeed I could see my ribs pushing up against my skin. My stomach was caved inward, and my hands were bleeding. But my manhood was still erect and swollen, like a solitary blossom in a burnt field. It commanded me.

With a grunt, I pulled Jiulang down to me, licking his face and neck. *Please, Jiulang,* I begged, *do not deny me. I want only to be with you.*

Jiulang was still at first, as if thinking. Then he cupped my face with his hands and looked at me deeply. *If we continue like this, you will die, Shican.*

No, I said, pulling him on top of me. *Only if we stop would I die.*

Succumbing, the boy kissed me. His nine tails, sopping wet with our sweat and juice, painted across my body in long, flowing brushstrokes with ecstatically maddening motions that raised every bump on my skin. I felt our bodies float upward like hot steam, hovering above the cold black mud beneath us.

His breath entered me once more, his legs parted for me and the world became beautiful again.

Go. Those voices in my head had urged me my whole life. *Go and look for it.*

Within the woods, deep inside Jiulang, I had found it.

Finally, deep inside Jiulang, I was where I belonged.

And here I will stay forever.

DONG XIAN
3 BCE

Liu Xin chose a bright autumn day to celebrate his birthday. He told me that his father had always refused to celebrate his own birthdays, deeming it as inauspicious to acknowledge one's own aging. Liu Xin's princely father had chosen to celebrate his mother's birthday each year instead, honoring her as the woman who birthed him, the very filial and Confucian thing to do.

But seeing as his father's mother was the Grand Empress Dowager Fu...suffice to say, Liu Xin was happy to celebrate his own birthday instead.

If this bothered Fu, she didn't show it, at least not to me. The morning of Liu Xin's birthday celebrations, she invited me to join her for tea in the Unicorn Pavilion. Looking at the animal skins draped luxuriously around us, I took a moment to marvel about how much had changed for me since I was first roughly pushed into her domain as a scared clerk, more than a year ago.

A true love match, Fu was saying. *That is what they are calling the auspicious union between the Emperor and his Dong Xian. A true love match will shepherd in prosperity and fruitfulness to the Han. It is a blessing bestowed upon us all by Heaven.* She took a sip of the flowering tea, her silver teeth clinking against the black lacquered cup.

The true blessing, I replied, *is that the Grand Empress Dowager had the foresight of such a union.*

Child, how many times have I told you to call me Grandmother now? she chided me with a playful slap on the wrist, though from her it still somehow felt more like an imperial edict.

These teas with Fu had become a weekly occurrence, as I had taken on the role of a conduit peacekeeper of sorts between the Emperor and his grandmother. She would pass her messages to me to bring to Liu Xin, and I would in turn reinterpret them in a way that would not upset him, and vice versa. The successful result was more familial harmony within the Endless Palace than had been seen in generations. And it had made my popularity and influence within the Court—and indeed throughout the Empire—surge skyward.

Her eunuch, Shi Li, approached the table with a pipe. I could see that mysterious metallic dust sprinkled onto the leaves within. I knew better than to refuse. At least now when I smoked Fu's pipe, I no longer had to participate in depraved sexual activities with her eunuch.

Yes, Grandmother, I replied, coughing out the pearly smoke. It still stung my lungs each time, but I had grown accustomed to its heady effects. I had even grown to enjoy them.

Now, a word of advice from Grandmother. She leaned in as my head began to spin pleasantly. *True love alone cannot sustain the Dragon Throne. You must be able to separate your love of Liu Xin with your love of the Dynasty of the Han when it matters. Because sometimes the two will not be so neatly intertwined.*

I took a sip of tea to soothe my irritated throat. *Are an Emperor and his Dynasty not one and the same?*

She sat back. *You can question my advice all you want, but I know more than anyone else that selflessly loving the Emperor is an invitation to one's early demise.*

Is that what happened to the Princess Feng Yuan? Did she selflessly love her Emperor? I had a sudden recall of the tragic end of Fu's archrival and apparent lover, an event that in hindsight I realized had triggered my ascent to these newfound heights.

Fu raised her eyebrows; I had never before brought up to her the Princess turned accused witch whose demise she had masterminded. From a leather pouch procured from his pocket, Shi Li sprinkled some more metallic powder into the pipe. I obediently took another hit.

Who said that Feng Yuan is dead? replied Fu cryptically, startling me. But she would say no more, and soon after that she dismissed me.

I stood to leave and bowed my goodbye, and when I raised my head she handed me a small leather pouch that felt nearly weightless. I looked at her quizzically and opened it to inspect what was inside. The pouch was full of her metallic dust. She had never given something like this to me before.

Our little secret... she purred.

I thanked her, and I pocketed the pouch.

After I slipped into formal robes at my chambers, I opened the hidden door behind my bed and descended into the Shadow, taking the now-familiar underground passageway toward Liu Xin's secret office.

When I entered, he was working at the black marble desk as he stroked Miaomi; the blue cat mewed at me as she sprawled luxuriously over his tablets. Upon seeing me emerge, he set down his jade stamp and rushed to me, leaping into my arms. We kissed deeply.

May you have ten thousand more birthdays, Son of Heaven, I greeted him once we both pulled back for air.

Liu Xin put his hand on my chest. *That sounds exhausting. But if you plan to live that long, I will happily keep you company.*

Ten thousand years with my Liu Xin would not be enough, I replied, stroking his face, meaning every word.

He took my thumb and sucked it hungrily. *Every moment my Dong Xian is not inside me already feels like ten thousand years.*

With a grunt, I lifted him by his firm buttocks onto the top of his desk, roughly pushing aside his work materials. I licked my thumbs until they were sticky wet and reached through his robes to stroke his perky nipples. He shuddered and moaned while I played with their pink tips, his hands wrapping around my influence as it swelled at his beckon. We kissed again, our tongues dancing around each other. He spread open his legs.

Pardon the interruption, Your Radiance... someone behind us said, awkwardly clearing his throat.

Like children caught stealing candies, Liu Xin and I both whipped around, detaching from one another. I crossed my legs and leaned back against the desk while Liu Xin hastily closed his robes. Kneeling at the side of the open door was the head eunuch, Uncle. Next to him, but standing, was Commander Jujun in his heavy uniform. He also kept his eyes to the floor, but his brow was deeply furrowed.

Uncle kowtowed deeply. For some odd reason, one of his sleeves was missing. *Apologies, Holy Child, but we are running late and your festivities are about to start. May you live ten thousand years more.*

Of course, Uncle. Liu Xin nodded and Uncle rushed over to him to readjust his robes. *Cousin, how fare you today?* he called out over his shoulder as Uncle dressed him.

Jujun had turned away respectfully as Liu Xin changed, but I noted that he made sure to avoid looking at me as well. *Twenty one years ago today I held you as a newborn babe. How can I be anything but happy on this day of your birth, Emperor?* he said, sounding anything but happy. *And may Your Radiance have ten thousand more, Heaven willing.*

Not since the night of my father's banquet had Commander Jujun and I spoken, and it was certainly from lack of trying on his part. He still remained Liu Xin's bodyguard and I saw him every day, especially since I had begun spending most of my time with the Emperor. But Jujun refused to ever acknowledge me.

What bothered me most was that I could not figure out why he was slighting me. At first, I thought he was angry about my triumph, as news of Dong Xian's consummation of the Emperor had sent shock waves through the Endless Palace the very night it happened. He had been so vocal about his opposition to me that it was a major loss of face for him. But for him to continue to sulk like this felt uncharacteristically sloppy to me.

Instinctively, I rubbed the scar on my eyebrow that he'd gifted me. I was certainly troubled about his discontent, because if he was so enraged that he couldn't even look at me, then the Commander would prove to be a reckless and unpredictable adversary.

Trying to catch his eye, I leaned to where he was staring off blankly into space in order to enter his line of vision. Finally, we made eye contact, though it startled him. He glowered at me as his cheeks reddened. The rawness of his emotions filled me with fear.

Suddenly, I wondered if I needed to have him assassinated.

Our silent standoff was interrupted as Uncle scurried between us. Liu Xin and the eunuch exited back into the Shadow, with Miaomi tiptoeing after them. Before he left, Liu Xin looked at me. *I won't be long. Meet me at the temple in an hour, beloved.*

I expected Commander Jujun to dutifully follow the Emperor out of the office, but he lingered near the door while the footsteps of Liu Xin and Uncle faded away. Though I was apprehensive, I was glad to have a moment alone with him finally. I needed to alleviate this choking tension between us.

Commander, I'm glad we can finally speak in private because—

Jujun knelt on one knee before me, clasping his hands together as he bowed his head. *Lord Dong, I must ask you for an undeserved forgiveness.*

I was stunned, wondering what genteel demon had possessed Jujun. *Please, rise, sir!*

He stood, though his face was still downcast. *That night at your father's banquet, I had too much drink and I behaved dishonorably toward you. Now, I'd be lying if I said that I never behave like that, because the battlefield can be hard to wash off for a soldier like me. But you did not deserve to be treated that way.*

He lifted his eyes to look at me. Though I was still taken aback, I was relieved. *So that is why you've avoided me all this time?* I replied. *Commander, I meant it when I said we should be as friends to one another, and friends forgive each other for transgressions.*

But Jujun still seemed troubled. *Our problem from the start has been that I don't want to be friends with you, Dong Xian. I never have, not since I first saw you that day at the courtyard.*

What do you mean? I asked as I began to back away from the soldier. A sinking feeling of doom crept into my throat.

He was taking a steady relentless step toward me each time I paced back. *My entire life,* said Jujun, *I have watched as my younger cousin has received every privilege, every pleasure over me, including the Dragon Throne. I've bitten my tongue each time and bowed to Heaven's Will...but I cannot with you, boy. Not any longer!*

My back hit Liu Xin's desk as the Commander towered over me. *Jujun,* I warned, *you lose your mind! Think about what you are about to do.*

Jujun reached out and lifted my chin gently, his jealous eyes penetrating mine. *Oh, but I think about this every night.*

With that, he swooped down and ensnared my lips with his

teeth. Growling, he bit hard into the tenderest flesh of my lower lip. I yelped in pain but like a rabid dog he would not release me as I pushed back at him helplessly. When he finally did free my lip, his massive tongue then invaded my mouth, filling it completely to my cheeks with its wet girth.

His kiss tasted like my blood.

RIVER
PRESENT DAY

There is a trick to hack the long lines to drive into LAX, but I always take the wrong turn.

"No, not left, right, rightrightright—RIGHT!" Garden hollers. I nearly swerve into the parked cop car at the security checkpoint. She groans as we enter the more crowded lane. "Riv, why would you drive into traffic?"

I quickly remind myself that I will not be seeing her for at least a couple of weeks and our last conversation can't be a fight. I put on a big smile. "You know, G, usually when a person offers to drive you to the airport, they're the one driving."

She rolls her eyes. "You know I hate driving. You are lucky I am willing to drive back home during rush hour."

"I'm just trying to spend a little more time with you." I give her puppy eyes.

"Oh, shut up." But she is smiling to herself now.

She may be annoyed, but I'm just relieved we are talking again. After the night of the Reign Incarnate Gala, she had given me the silent treatment for weeks.

I couldn't blame her. It has been a few months since that final night with Joey before he disappeared, and though I remain convinced as ever of everything that transpired between him and me, the passage of time did cool my zealous thinking—enough to regret how I had treated my little sister, who I know only wishes to keep me safe.

A bright yellow Hummer limo straight out of 2009 blares its horn at me for waiting as pedestrians cross. I wonder if drivers are this manic in Thailand.

"So you have your tickets and your passport...?" Garden asks.

I hold them up triumphantly. "Finally, a new stamp! I can't believe this will be my first time in Southeast Asia."

"I still can't believe you're going," she says, shaking her head in defeat. "I mean, I can believe it, but I don't like it."

After we had awkwardly and silently coexisted in the Palisades for those few weeks, I finally broke the ice and apologized to her for everything. To my surprise, she readily accepted, but when I followed it up by telling her my intentions to travel to Asia once I figured out where exactly, she surprised me even more by reluctantly agreeing that I should go. "Clearly, you need closure," she had said. "Go find it."

I maneuver my way through the tightly packed cars, watching departing travelers embrace their loved ones in front of opened trunks. I glance back over at Garden; I can feel her mind working.

On cue she grumbles, "Are you sure you're sure about this? This still feels like it could be an elaborate scam, or a very extra sex trafficking ring."

I sigh. "Listen, we've gone over this countless times. This is no different than if I were just going as a regular tourist. If I get there and I can't find anything, I'll just go sightseeing." The best way to debate my sister is to confuse her by not quite answering her questions.

"Don't do that thing you are doing right now," she says, catching me off guard. "Promise me that the moment it feels dangerous, you are on the first flight back home."

At a red light, I look down at my phone at a screenshot I have saved. It is of an article with a very recent paparazzi photo of Winston in casual clothes getting into a car—unremarkable in every way unless you look closely at who else is inside the car. Sitting inside, there is the figure of a strongly built male wearing a black hoodie. He's turned away from the camera, and just the upper corner of his face is captured. But winking at me like the rings of Saturn, I see that he has an eyebrow piercing exactly where Joey had his.

"Winston Chow arrives in Bangkok to celebrate Songkran," says the caption below it. A quick search on Google revealed to me that Winston attends the Thai New Year festivities in that nation's capital every year "with a cabal of powerful LGBTQ Asian Illuminati types," as *Rolling Stone* had described them.

Garden is glancing over at me. "You are staring at that photo again, aren't you? Everything has changed since you met that boy. I can't believe you are putting off med school for a year."

"Well, here I am going on an adventure of a lifetime, when I used to be afraid of my own shadow," I reply. "How bad are these changes, really?" She scoffs but I'm serious. "Garden, I've felt directionless my whole life, and yes, this is an unusual direction to be going, chasing after some guy who may or may not be my literal soul mate—but it feels good. It feels true."

"Feelings, feelings," Garden groans, defeated. "It's all about feelings with you. You know, Riv, just because something is true, doesn't mean that it is necessarily good. Many truths in this world are dangerous."

We finally pull up to the Tom Bradley International Terminal. April is that time of year when Los Angeles can't quite decide if it is summer yet, but that indecision takes form in an occasional blistering hot day surrounded by cold ones. Today is one of those hot days. The muggy heat smacks me as I pop open the trunk to grab my new traveler backpack. I made the choice to pack light so I could be easily mobile if needed.

Garden is waiting for me on the curb as I sling my pack over my shoulder. I reach out to her and pull her in for a hug, holding her tight. When she pulls back she pushes me. "River, you said I have abandonment issues..."

I wince. "I know, I didn't mean that."

She shakes her head. "No, I will own it. My dad is gone, my mom is gone and now my brother is leaving. I am the literal definition of abandoned."

I push her hair out of her eyes. "I'm not 'leaving' leaving. I will be back before you know it."

She shrugs sadly. "I just worry. When it comes to that boy, all your logic always goes out the window. You are going across the world into another country. You need to be very careful. And when I call or text—"

"Yes," I intercut, nodding my head at what I had promised her countless times. "When you call or text, I will always answer."

With that, Garden hugs me again. "Riv, don't you forget— You're all I've got."

I tuck my chin on top of her head, squeezing her tightly. "I won't forget, G."

She nods, then as she releases me, she looks past me to the side at someone. As her face changes, I turn around and I am shocked to see a familiar face approaching us.

It's Calvin!

Huffing under a crammed traveler backpack of his own, Calvin jogs toward us, a nervous grin on his face. My mouth drops open, and I turn back to Garden. Her face breaks into a smile. "Did you think I was really going to let you go to Asia all by yourself?"

Without thinking, I drop my bag and do a running jump onto Calvin as we embrace tightly. I have not seen him for months, not since that night after the Reign Incarnate Gala. But I had missed him every day.

I pull back and take him in. He has grown a neatly trimmed goatee and his wavy hair is longer, a very dashing look on him. "Surprise," he says, laughing.

"Calvin! Oh, my God! Are you really coming with me to Thailand?" I clap him on the back as he hugs Garden.

He puts up his palms. "For the record, I usually go to Songkran anyway…but also for the record, I wasn't going to go this year until G called me." He begins to talk a mile a minute, amping us both up. "Oh man, River, Songkran makes Peril look like Sesame Street. We need to go shopping the moment we land. I know everyone there and I can't be seen in the same tank top twice. We are going to get so absolutely butt-fucking lit!"

Garden shoots him a look that could wilt flowers.

"Responsibly, of course!" Calvin quickly adds. Then, "With big-dicked Thai boys."

"Okay, I'm definitely good to part ways now," Garden says. I hand her the keys.

After I give my sister a final hug and she drives off, Calvin and I walk into the airport together. "Hey, Calvin…" I begin uneasily.

Calvin groans. "River, I hate when you start sentences like that. What is it?"

"It's just that our last conversation didn't end well, and then you never returned any of my texts. You know that I'm not going to Songkran to party."

We grab our tickets from the automated station and take the escalators toward the security screening. Calvin gives my shoulder a reassuring pat. "Yes, I'm also here to help you look for Joey.

Garden told me you think he's in trouble. If that's true, maybe I can finally put my PR skills to good use instead of bailing out corporate hacks."

I turn to him, speechless with gratitude for a moment. "Wow, Calvin, thank you."

"Yes, and guess what? We can solve a mystery, and we can also party!" The TSA agent checking our passports at the screening entrance gives us a knowing look.

I'm chuckling as usual with Calvin. "With us, the two aren't mutually exclusive. I'm just glad you are here."

"Hey, I figured if I'm not the co-lead of this story, at least I can be the plot twist." He flashes me a devilishly handsome smile as I laugh uneasily, not quite sure what he means.

After we board the plane, I hand Calvin my backpack to cram into the overhead bin above our premium economy seats. He slumps down gratefully next to me and kicks off his shoes, resting his head on my shoulder as we both look outside at the tarmac.

"I think that edible is kicking in," he says happily. "How are you feeling?"

"Excited, but nervous! I just keep thinking about what it would be like to find him over there, how he would react to seeing us."

Calvin accepts a glass of complimentary champagne from the flight attendant and chugs it in one gulp. "You two never just casually bump into each other. You crash headfirst like runaway freight trains. I have a feeling that he's expecting you."

"Or he's hoping for us to come because he needs our help," I reply, fiddling with Joey's green jade bracelet.

"Why are you so sure he is in trouble?"

I sigh. "I mean, I have no concrete proof except that…"

Calvin realizes. "Except you haven't heard from him at all. Damn, not even a dick pic?"

"Nothing."

We are silent for a moment.

Calvin tries to lean back in his upright seat. "Do you ever think about all those visions you had about Joey? The snakes? The blood?"

"How did you put it, our 'magical birthright'?" I reply. "I think about all of it all the time. How can I not? But I realized something these past few months."

"And what's that?"

"Those are all distractions. I understand that there might be something unexplainable between Joey and me, but what can be explained is that we care about each other and we should be together. That should take precedence above everything else, including wild goose chases after legendary stamps and whatnot. And that's what I plan to tell him once I find him."

"I mean," Calvin muses, "some people always need an excuse."

"An excuse for what?" I ask.

"An excuse to disappear," Calvin replies quietly.

I don't know how to respond. The flight attendant comes back to make sure our seat belts are fastened as our plane begins to taxi.

"And what about the Winston of it all?" Calvin asks. He is gingerly applying a slimy peach-scented eye mask with his fingers.

"That's the second piece to this puzzle," I respond, eager to change the subject. "Winston is bad news. I keep replaying in my head that moment at his Gala when he cornered me and confronted me, right before you rescued me. There is something very profound and twisted about his obsession with Joey.

And you saw what happened with the Griffith Observatory. He got off scot-free!"

"Well, he blamed a lot of it on the LAPD. Plus, he pledged to add a new billion-dollar wing to the Griff O," Calvin replies.

"Exactly. Winston wields so much power and money that there's no way that Joey doesn't need our help. Especially be-cause...Joey says he's doing all this for me. That it's a promise that he made me, once upon a lifetime. I can't abandon him, Calvin."

Calvin is casually scrolling through the movie options on screen in front of him, but he sounds a bit tense. "That said, there's one more possibility that you need to be realistic about, River."

"What is it?"

He winces a little, but says it anyway. "There's the possibil-ity that Joey is staying with Winston...because he wants to. I agree that Winston is creepy obsessed with Joey, but the two of them together seem to have a weird toxic codependency as well."

I shake my head. "I asked him about it, and he insisted that the only thing he wants from Winston is the Heirloom Seal. And I believe him."

Our airplane begins to accelerate down the runway, press-ing our backs against our seats. Calvin grabs my hand to give it a quick squeeze as our plane lifts off the ground. "Well," he says, speaking louder over the sound of the engines, "I for one am ready for an adventure!"

I look outside at a rapidly shrinking Los Angeles, saying a mental goodbye to my home. I feel the plane do a U-turn as it ventures out over the Pacific Ocean, heading west toward the East. I press my face against the window as we zoom into the clouds.

But try as I might, I can't extinguish Calvin's possibility from my mind. Even if he denies it, could it really be true that Joey is choosing to stay with Winston? That Joey has a genuine desire to be with him, one that might rival what he has with me?

And if so, how deep does it run?

DONG XIAN

3 BCE

As Commander Jujun's open mouth pressed against mine, his steamy breath scalding the inner reaches of my throat, he released a guttural groan of uninhibited satisfaction. Before I could stop myself, I gulped it down hungrily.

Like a pair of scouts doing wartime reconnaissance, his hands deftly found their way up into my robes, creeping in between my legs. I gasped as I felt his coarse fingers rapidly encroaching upon my pink plum. As he pressed down against the tenderly puckered flesh, my eyes finally shot open.

Commander Jujun! With a scream of fury, I shoved him away. The Heirloom Seal of the Realm was beside me on the Emperor's desk, and I grabbed it, thrusting the heavy jade into his face. *You forsake the oath you swore to the Son of Heaven and the Dynasty of the Han*! I seethed. *But I will not. I will not!*

He pulled away from me as I flinched from him, refusing him. His nostrils flaring, he clenched his fists so tight that I could hear his knuckles crack.

You invoke but a silly oath to barricade me from you? Jujun thundered. *Is that really the only stronghold you have against me, Dong Xian? No lofty declarations of an unparalleled love solely for your Emperor? No chaste exultations of an immaculate body committed only to his pleasure?*

You have gone mad, I growled back, still clutching the Seal in my shaking palm. *These are steadfast truths that need not be said.*

The soldier smiled suddenly, his mustachioed lip curling perilously as his eyes trailed down my body. *As it appears, boy, they are not quite so steadfast.*

Warily, I followed his line of sight down my own body—but already I could feel it before I saw it.

Like a lush tree branch blossoming out from between my agitated robes, my exposed influence was achingly, impossibly, maniacally, exuberantly erect. Its slippery tip glistened along with the flickering torchlights of Liu Xin's office.

When Jujun grabbed me again, I did not resist. As though I were as light as the air, he lifted me upon the Emperor's desk and tore open my robes, exposing my naked flesh to him. I dropped the Heirloom Seal next to me with a clatter.

With a dead-set glare of determination upon me, Commander Jujun stripped off layer after layer of his heavy armor, slowly and deliberately revealing brawny limb after brawny limb, his battle-scarred golden skin rippling with muscle and vein. His chest plate fell to the ground with a crash as he finally took off his helmet, shaking free his long, waving hair that fell wildly about his shoulders.

As I trembled there before him on the desk, my thighs began to spread open of their own accord. He spat into both his hands.

When Jujun finally entered me, I could not tell which feeling was strongest: how much I hated him; how much I hated myself; how much I loved each thick thrust of him into me.

I wrapped my palms around his bouldering backside, pulling him into me, demanding him deeper. That guttural groan of his now an animalistic wail, Jujun laid his powerful body upon mine, blanketing me in his meat as he kissed me again.

This time I returned his kiss, our furious tongues embracing like long-lost flames. Our hands grasped senselessly on our bodies, stroking every touch of raised skin, until they found each other. Our fingers intertwined as he impaled me victoriously again and again.

I could feel myself arriving, and he in turn began to tremor as well.

Jujun! I gasped.

Jujun stood straight again, his puffing chest like twin mountains as his breath went ragged. His eyes, at first daggered into mine, began to roll upward as he released a commanding bellow.

Once I felt the powerful torrents of his hot seed first fill then overflow out of me, my influence burst forth its own exquisite fountain, one that splashed on his quaking body before raining back down upon me in bejeweled droplets. Each of my toes curled and uncurled as I half sobbed out my ravishment, stars colliding in my head as I clenched and unclenched around him, unable to let him go.

After what seemed a mindless eternity, Jujun finally withdrew from me, slinking back, his hulking body still spasming. He reached out a hand to help me up. As I stood, he attempted to pull me to him again.

But I snatched my hand back and bounded away from him, shielding my face with my elbow. *Jujun!* I cried, unable to look at him. *What have we done?*

What we were always meant to do, I heard him reply softly.

I pressed against a wall and sank to the ground in despair. *No!* I protested as I began to weep. *This must never happen again. Never!*

Still, he was as calm as stone. *I think it will.*

I brought down my arm to look up at him. *And what makes you think that?*

The Commander was climbing back into his armor, buckling

the hardened leather and iron lamellar over his body. He did this in methodical silence as I watched him. Finally, he slipped his helmet over his head and turned to face me once more.

Dong Xian, the truth is…you belong to me, Jujun whispered.

With that, he turned and strode out of the office.

I buried my face in my hands. I remained there on the floor for a long time, guiltily savoring the salty musky traces of Jujun left on my tongue.

My legs were still quivering like river reeds and my lower lip still throbbing when I arrived late to the Heavenly Temple. The largest individual building and in the mathematical center of the Endless Palace, the Heavenly Temple hosted all of the Emperor's celebrations, but they never took place inside. In front of this temple was the largest courtyard in the Empire—an acre of neatly polished and laid white stone that could fit tens of thousands of people.

Indeed, there were already throngs of officials and guests assembling in front of the temple for the festivities, but I paid them no heed as I rushed into the building through a side staircase, climbing up the many steps two at a time, grateful the day was cool. At the top of the stairs, Uncle was waiting for me, looking rushed. He ushered me inside.

Surrounded by fanning attendants, Liu Xin was sitting on his magnificent throne, draped in the brilliant blue heritage robe that the late Emperor Cheng had gifted him, the very one upon which I had fallen asleep on our first night together. As would be expected, the robe had been repaired good as new, the sleeve perfectly reattached. The reheaded dragon on its left sleeve danced at me as Liu Xin rose from his throne, his face lit up at the very sight of me.

You might've given Uncle a stroke if you were any later, he teased.

I chuckled weakly, racked with a gaping guilt. *Why would Uncle worry about me? Today is about your people celebrating you and only you, Your Radiance. We can't keep twenty-one thousand of your most loyal subjects waiting.* Outside, the thunderous sound of a legion of drums began.

My thoughts exactly. Liu Xin was walking to the grand entrance of the temple but as he passed me, he grabbed me by the arm and pulled me with him. Before I could react, the temple guards slammed open the massive doors and I was instantly blinded by the direct sun and deafened by the joyous roar of an endless crowd!

Blinking, I saw a sea of twenty-one thousand people below us in the courtyard as Liu Xin and I stood in front of the Heavenly Temple. They were kowtowed before us as they sang ecstatic praises.

Ten thousand years! Ten thousand years! Ten thousand years!

With one bold, swift motion, Liu Xin raised my hand with his, our hands clasped together. With that, the crowd leaped to their feet, cheering and chanting my name, stamping their feet raucously.

Dong Xian! Dong Xian! Dong Xian!

Overwhelmed, I turned to the Emperor, only to see him already grinning at me. He leaned over and whispered in my ear. *Look at their sleeves.*

I looked more closely upon the infinite mass. I saw that every single person had the same exposed arm.

They had all cut off their left sleeves. My mouth dropped open.

Smile at our Empire, beloved, Liu Xin laughed. Shaking off my daze, I broke into a smile so wide that my jaw cracked. The rolling waves of adoration and worship rippled through me like an earthquake. It was magical and intoxicating. I began to laugh, too, squeezing his hand.

Together, we were gods.

Then, out of the corner of my eye, I saw him. I turned my head to lock eyes with Commander Jujun, who stood at his official post a few paces behind his Emperor whenever in public. Unabashed and defiant, he stared straight back at me, his long hair flowing in the wind, his sword set aglow by the pale autumn sun.

No, the soldier had not cut off his sleeve.

When I could not break my gaze upon him, Jujun smiled triumphantly at me, and oh so subtly bit down on his lower lip. Already, he was delighting in the tumults of my mind.

Quickly, I turned away from Jujun, back to my Liu Xin, only to find the Emperor now staring at us as well. Was it possible he had caught our illicit exchange? His eyes shifted slightly toward his cousin in suspicion, his lips parted ever subtly at me in question. Reassuringly, I clasped my beloved's hands firmer than before, and the fraught moment mercifully passed. Seemingly placated, Liu Xin smiled at me.

But as I rejoined his side in front of his Empire, even the booming roar of the exultant crowd could not drown out what I was thinking.

What a cruel irony it was, I thought to myself sadly, that every man in the Endless Palace today had a cut sleeve—except for the three men to whom it mattered the most.

The Emperor, his Dong Xian…and Jujun.

RIVER
PRESENT DAY

Again, feel the beat of a hypnotic bass in your head. A real club banger, one that fingers your soul.

Do you hear it? Good. Let it wash over you like aural pleasure.

Now, imagine a world where we are gods.

Before you is a legendary megacity overrun with multitudes of reveling, delirious, golden-skinned people, freely racing through the streets wielding neon-colorful water guns. They unload indiscriminately upon one another, screaming and whooping and splashing with glee under the bright moonlight. Bodies are showered and soaked with unending blasts of cool water coming from all directions, a blessedly welcome baptism in this otherwise muggy heat that permeates the atmosphere here even at night. Everywhere you look, everywhere you listen, are the ecstatic sights and sounds of this playground of your wildest dreams.

Except it's not your imagination. Welcome to the Songkran Festival in Bangkok.

I am struck by a sudden jet of water right between my eyes, the force and surprise of it jolting me out of my reverie and causing me to stumble. I drop my beer, the bottle smashing on the sidewalk in front of me in an explosion of glass and foam. Laughing as I wipe the liquid out of my eyes, I scan my surroundings, looking for my attacker, cocking my own squirt gun at the ready for revenge. But it is like picking out a single mosquito in a swarm.

I glance over at Calvin beside me and he grins, bewildered, equally overwhelmed as he holds up both hands in surrender. We are outnumbered.

Songkran is the countrywide celebration that dominates every aspect of life in Thailand for a week during the Thai New Year festivities each April. Though the origins of this national water fight started with the pious practice of sprinkling Buddha statues with water to cleanse them, today this holy purification ritual has been democratized into a chaotic free-for-all, where mortal citizens and tourists alike arm themselves with water guns to cleanse each other of any remaining bad luck from the past year. Remix that with Bangkok's reputation for hosting the naughtiest circuit parties in Asia and the end result is a modern nirvana, overstuffed with every vice you can imagine.

I spin around—and quickly dodge another high-velocity stream of water coming my way, just in time. I motion at Calvin to follow as we sprint away from the wet carnage, declaring defeat and eager for another cold beer.

Calvin and I are in a loud raucous network of alleys called Silom Soi, the most famous gay neighborhood of Bangkok. The only thing more colorful than the massive menagerie of brilliant neon signs flickering on every vertical surface are the people who surround me, repping every spectrum of identity and self-expression there is. I'm not sure how the Thai New Year evolved into one of the biggest queer parties in the world, but as I look around at all the wet clothes plastered against tan bodies, I could wager at least one reason.

There is a packed multilevel club called DJ Station that is

playing music whose bass shakes even the concrete pavement in front of it. Squeezing in like a pair of snakes, we work our way through the mass of sweaty people until we are pressed against the bar. "Singha! Two!" I yell at the shirtless bartender, throwing some crumpled Thai baht onto the counter. We are rewarded with ice-cold bottles of slushy lager beer, ambrosia fit for immortals right now.

After I chug down the beer in a couple gulps, I look over at Calvin and smile. He is already staring deeply at me, his floppy bangs dewed with sweat, his dreamy brown eyes twinkling mischievously. Beyond this physical exchange, we don't say anything. We have actually stopped saying much to each other by this point; gone has been Calvin's usual sunny bravado, replaced by a quiet awakening between us. We've been in Bangkok together for more than a week now, and it seems we have reached a point where we transcend words.

Whatever dangers Garden had imagined for me had been greatly exaggerated in her mind. When Calvin and I first landed in Bangkok nearly two weeks ago, I figured that a world-notorious billionaire tycoon like Winston Chow would be easy to track around town. But it was my first time in Bangkok, and I had underestimated the city's sheer immensity and beautiful chaos. I spent the first couple of days jet-lagged and overwhelmed by the different vibrations of Southeast Asia as I took in this Thai metropolis.

Boys, humidity and newly legalized Thai weed swirled all around us. And though our search continually yielded nothing, that initial wave I was riding gradually transformed into an undercurrent between my toes as I dove into this new world. The nightlives of Bangkok were unlike anything I could have even imagined. A pansexual fever dream fueled by lust and poppers. The second night we were there, Calvin booked us front-row tickets to what I thought would be a fairly conventional drag-queen show. And while there were indeed immensely talented performers, including a small legion of dancers who re-created Madonna's Super Bowl Halftime Show beat for beat, the climax of the night happened when all of us in the front row were sprayed by a young man who had a remarkable ability to retain vast amounts of water—just not in his mouth.

As the city began to swell with visitors in anticipation of Songkran, Calvin introduced me to his impressive circuit crew, comprised of nine internationally jet-setting power gaysians who we partied with most of the time. Each night started the same with a light meal at yet another spectacular hole-in-the-wall restaurant— green papaya salad with shrimp is the staple diet of circuit queens here—followed by a club or a party until early morning, then a raunchy homepa at someone's fabulous penthouse suite.

At first, I'd been apprehensive to try ecstasy again, but after a few drinks I accepted the pill offered to me. This one wasn't a pink peach like my first one at Peril, but rather a silver fox on a metallic-colored pill that sparkled at me under the strobe lights. Older and wiser now, I only took half of it, and spent the next four hours being fucked by rainbows on the dance floor. I danced and raved like my life depended on it, kissing every boy who would have me. The next few days were a repeat of that every night, until my poor brain jingled like a bell whenever I moved my head.

But several nights in, I began to wonder about him. Since I was rolling on drugs like I had been that first time at Peril, shouldn't I then bump into him again? What if he could only be summoned, like some sort of mystical spirit, while my mind was on a different plane? Eventually, when the novelty of the stimulant drugs wore out, I stopped dancing and would break away from Calvin and his crew—wandering off to search the crowds, stumbling aimlessly through the sea of men, hoping to catch his face looking back at me. There wasn't exactly a dearth of muscular Asian men all around me, and many a time I reached out to someone thinking it might be him. But it never was. Each night I came back to the hotel room dejected and forlorn, where Calvin was always waiting for me.

Silently, Calvin would hold me protectively under the covers as we both drifted off into a beleaguered sleep, mine devoid of dreams as the specter of that mysterious artist from China grew fainter and fainter in my mind.

When I had awoken this morning, I felt drained in every sense of the word. Songkran would be over in a couple of days, and who knows whether my best lead, Winston, is even in the country anymore? I could feel a depression sinking into me, and Calvin had looked concerned as I dispiritedly poked at the soft-boiled egg in my rice porridge at breakfast.

Seemingly making an executive decision, Calvin waved off our party crew, passing on their plans for an afternoon pool party and instead walking me to the nearest convenience stand. There he bought the two biggest, most obnoxious water guns that we could find. He even filled the tanks with ice so that we might provide deliciously cold gunfire. Then we ran out into the streets, spending the entire day sprinting around Bangkok cleansing everyone of their bad luck, and being cleansed of ours in turn. Because of him, today I had the time of my life, feeling like a carefree kid again.

I lean over to Calvin at the bar and speak loudly into his ear so that he can hear me over the pounding bass of DJ Station. "Thank you, Calvin." I pull back to smile at him again.

"For what?" he shouts at me as a classic Kylie Minogue song about past lovers begins to play.

I lean in and our noses inadvertently touch. "For always coming back, right next to me."

Calvin nods, his eyes twinkling. "That's what love is," he whispers.

Under the bar, I place my hand onto his thigh. When Calvin leans over to kiss me, I do not stop him.

I return Calvin's kiss.

★ ★ ★

The next day is our last full day in Bangkok, as the morning after we head back to Los Angeles. I wake in our hotel room, Calvin's slumbering head on my chest, his smooth arms wrapped around me, our naked bodies fused together by a thin layer of cool perspiration.

Beyond some more kissing, nothing had happened between us last night. But it does feel good to feel his soft skin upon mine. He stirs awake as well, his big brown eyes blinking away dregs of sleep before he looks up at me, bashfully releasing me from his arms.

"Almost time to go home," he says later, as he brushes his teeth.

I nod but don't reply, wondering whether it is truly for the best that I am returning home empty-handed.

We spend the first half of the day chilling at the hotel pool, where we reunite with Calvin's party crew, all of them similarly exhausted and bleary-eyed from our nonstop partying, but also determined to make our final night in Thailand one for the ages. Our ringleader, a swaggering Chinese-Nicaraguan princeling with a three-carat diamond nipple piercing, insists that we forgo the mainstream circuit party for a smaller one, one that is "much more exclusive, much more fitting for boys like us."

Calvin and I look at each other and shrug. "Sure."

The rest of the day Calvin and I load up on mind-blowing street foods like pad see ew and grilled pork satay, and we shop for souvenirs. I buy Garden a beautiful sapphire blue handmade Thai silk bag embroidered with elephants.

By the time we get back to the hotel, the rest of the crew is ready and waiting for us impatiently. I've sweated through every thread of the clothes I brought, so Calvin lends me a neon yellow tank top—an ostentatious piece of skin-tight clothing that I would never choose for myself. But when I slip it on and look at myself in the mirror, I'm surprised that I don't feel like a fraud anymore. I feel like I belong.

At our dinner that as usual is just a drinking pregame with minimal food, one of the crew asks the Nicaraguan, "What's so special about this party tonight?"

"Who knows?" the princeling replies. "But hey, if it's thrown by a billionaire, I think we can have high expectations."

My ears perk at this.

I'm not sure if Calvin overhears this as well, or if I'm imagining it when he seems to tense ever so slightly next to me, but when I glance over at him, he just looks down into his cocktail.

As we all climb into the sprinter van destined for the party, Calvin holds me back. I look at him questioningly. "Come on," I pull at him.

But he shakes his head, his eyes suddenly eclipsed with sadness. "Let's not go."

I'm taken aback. "What do you mean?"

But we both know what he means. We have finally found what I came for.

"You don't have to do this," Calvin implores me, grasping my hands. "You can break the cycle."

A sigh shudders out of me. How many times do I need to break this boy's heart? "I'm so sorry, Calvin." I let go of his hands.

"Lovebirds, we're waiting!" someone in the vehicle calls out to us, oblivious to our crushing anguish.

Calvin laughs bitterly, his cheeks reddening. "Keep chasing him, River. Keep chasing your disappearing man. Because all he'll ever do is disappear on you."

He kisses me goodbye.

After I climb into the van, Calvin walks away without looking back.

★ ★ ★

I stare out the back window as we head farther and farther out of the city. In the seat next to me, the Nicaraguan princeling takes out a small bag of those silver fox pills and everyone quickly clamors for their nightly share.

The princeling raises a finger. "Hold up," he says. "We've been doing this wrong."

"What do you mean?" one of the crew asks. "How else are you supposed to take Molly?"

"Up your butt?" another proposes. "Hey, it's a cleaner high."

Everyone laughs. Through the baggie, the princeling is grinding up the pills with his fingers. "This isn't Molly," he replies. "And it's actually meant to be smoked."

What's left of the crushed pills is now a shimmering metallic powder. Everyone in the van watches as our ringleader lightly licks the tip of a cigarette and then dabs it into the powder. When he removes it, he lights the silver-crowned cigarette and takes a long puff.

When he exhales, the smoke smells like rotten fruit. He quickly dips it into the baggie again and hands it to me next.

As we all take turns toking the glowing powder, that's when I realize we are surrounded by dark jungle, our vehicle bouncing over unpaved road between increasingly dense hardwood trees. We have long left the city. Occasionally, I see the bright eyes of monkeys staring at us intruders, their red pupils eerily catching our high beam headlights.

After about an hour of this and many more puffs of our laced cigarette, the van suddenly stops. Everyone begins to climb out; it is dark and we seem to be in the middle of nowhere in a vast wilderness.

Maybe it is the strangely heady effects of the drug; maybe it is Calvin's warning; but I am full of nerves. I hesitate there in the backseat. The Nicaraguan notices, and leans back toward me, extending a hand.

Curiouser and curiouser, indeed! he comments, grinning slyly.

"What did you just say?" I ask, startled by his odd choice of words.

He only winks at me, his fingers beckoning, his bushy eyebrows arching mysteriously.

Wondering where I've heard that phrase before, I accept his hand, and he pulls me out into the jungle.

RIVER
PRESENT DAY

As I climb out of the van, the stifling humidity envelops me like a heavy robe. There is something ancient yet seductive in the air, coaxing us from all directions.

"Let's fucking party!" our ringleader calls out, singsong shouting into the night. Electrified by our fascinating destination, the rest of the crew jumps and whoops under the glowing moon. I, too, am brimming with excitement, not quite daring to believe where fate has led me. Could it truly be possible that—?

The sound of a nearby bass begins, instantly captivating all of us. As though activated by a siren call, we all quiet and stiffen, entranced by the tremors emanating in the distance. I'm not sure if I imagine this, but everyone's eyes seem to be glowing.

Our direction is clear as we approach the hypnotic beat. We make our way past the dense foliage onto a pathway...then I nearly cry aloud in shock at the sight of a massive face staring back at us, nestled within a cluster of trees.

"Holy fuck," someone gasps as well. "That scared me."

When I catch my breath, I realize that it is a huge statue of the Buddha, completely overgrown by trees, so that only its serene face peeks out from between the trunks.

The rest of the crew recovers and continues walking, but I pause in front of the statue. I am reminded of another statue of a god, one from my childhood, though this one's face was contorted in pain and suffering. And I wonder, have I truly escaped all of that?

There is something folding and unfolding at the corner of the Buddha's half-shut eye. I lean in closer to see it is a butterfly resting upon the statue. Its dusty blue wings flap at me, like a teardrop hesitating to spill over.

When the blue butterfly finally takes flight, I follow it into the clearing. With that, it disappears into the night.

What I witness beyond it I will never forget. Before me are the magnificent ruins of an archaic temple, stacks of blood-red brick turretting into the night sky, intricate carved stone arches flanked by more Buddha idols, all of it reflected eerily into an accompanying lake, still as a moonlit mirror.

And intertwined into this sacred antiquity like an unearthly lattice are flashing lasers of green light from an unseen source, strumming to the pulse of a massive sound system that floods the entire area in rumbling decibels.

I can see that there is a distant gathering of bodies within the ruins. I can't find my crew, but they are not who I am looking for. Cautiously, I venture deeper toward the temple, an odd buzzing sensation washing over me.

I realize then that the buzzing is coming from within my pocket. I take out my phone and look at the screen.

Fuck. It's Garden calling.

Actually, she's been calling for a while now. I just hadn't noticed. I'm sure Calvin has told her everything. I scroll through her missed calls on my screen, wondering if I should pick up, knowing what I had promised her.

I decide against it and put it away, letting it go to voice mail. Once again, she can assume the worst.

I'm sorry, Garden.

My mind now spinning, I timidly walk up the steps of the temple ruins, straining to see what sort of congregation is happening inside. Hiding behind one of the turrets, I sneak a glimpse, and I am stunned at what I see.

In the center of the ruins, there is a group of perhaps twenty-five or so naked men in every form of sexual congress imaginable. I blink, not trusting my eyes, but they are not statues. They are of flesh and cock, engaged in a spellbinding orgy on the cold stone ground that floods our atmosphere with overwhelming erotic energy.

And hovering in the air above them like a north star, the Heirloom Seal of the Realm bathes them in an intoxicating emerald radiance, holding them captive in its power.

Mesmerized by this bizarre occult ritual, I leave my hiding spot, inching my way closer to the group. I can see that the members of my circuit crew are in the carnal mass, as I recognize some of their faces. But as though in a trance, they do not acknowledge me. I see the Nicaraguan princeling's face emerge from the sea of meat, his eyes shut in delirium.

Then a pulse emitted from the Heirloom Seal, and his face suddenly changes.

His face is now my face. I look at all of them, all of the men, and all of their faces are now mine.

Life imitates art, I think, as I remember Winston's ballroom in the Hills. And then, as though on cue...

Emperor, I hear him whisper hoarsely. *I told you not to follow me!*

He is suddenly standing beside me, even if I cannot bring myself to look. The boy I have been searching for all this time, a moment I have dreamed about for months—this is not how I had envisioned our reunion.

I am trembling all over, but finally I force myself to look over at him. He wears a white ceremonial robe, though it is loosely open and he is shirtless underneath. He looks distressed to see me here, but I can tell it is not only my presence that concerns him.

Behind him stands Winston Chow, wearing the same white robe. I am ready for him to be enraged to see me, but he surprises me. Like a tiger cornering its prey, he instead flashes a beaming grin at us. Joey's hand is in his grasp, and I watch as Winston kisses each of Joey's fingers, his eyes glinting triumphantly at me.

Suddenly, as though from distant echoes of time, I hear in my head the ghostly roar of a crowd as it chants a name.

It is that name that Joey had told me was once his, two thousand years ago.

Dong Xian! Dong Xian! Dong Xian!

And that is when I finally Remember the ancient secret between Joey and Winston. It blossoms in my brain like a deadly nightshade flower.

Turning away from them, I run for my life.

As I sprint out of the temple grounds, I frantically try to recall my path, desperately praying that I can find the van, that it is still waiting. I need to get out of here. This is not where I belong.

I can hear him behind me, keeping pace with me, his breath quickening with mine.

I nearly cry out with relief when I catch sight of the massive Buddha head nestled in the trees, and I make a sharp right turn. Instantly, I see the headlights of the van in the distance and I wave at the driver.

"Wait! Please, wait!"

I turn to see him bounding after me. I know that I shouldn't listen to him; he always seems to know exactly what to say to me. But this time, I know how to respond.

"Liu Xin…" he says, his chest heaving, his body glistening with sweat.

"No. Don't call me that." I shake my head. "Don't justify whatever the fuck that was."

He is silenced, his face downcast.

"Don't tell me this is all still part of your plan," I continue, the words pouring out of me in despair. "Don't tell me how you are still using Winston, and don't talk about our past lives."

"It seems like you already know, River," he replies, still emotionless.

"Yes, I do know," I sigh. "I believe all of it. But I don't believe you."

He seems caught off guard and cocks his head at me. "What are you talking about?"

"I Remembered something just then when I looked back at Winston, standing behind us in those ruins. He has stood behind us like that before, hasn't he? I can Remember it now, as clear as though it were yesterday. I Remember that day at the Endless Palace. You and I standing before a crowd of thousands on my birthday. Winston standing behind us, still reeking of you. And that's when I realized the truth. In our first lifetime together, you and he were lovers, too."

His face goes pale, his mouth drops open. But then he speaks.

"Yes," he confirms quietly.

"You loved him, too." I meant to ask it as a question, but it comes out as a fact that we both know intimately.

"Yes," he whispers.

I already knew it deep down, but hearing it aloud from him devastates me. "You lied to me. You told me he has never meant anything to you."

"River, I do not love him anymore," he insists. "He means nothing to me now."

"If that's true, why did you hide it from me?" I demand. "Why did you lie to me?"

He hangs his head low. "I do not know. I was ashamed."

It isn't enough for me. "There are too many mysteries about you. If I can't trust you, I can't be a part of this."

He is shaking his head in dismay. "You weren't even supposed to be a part of this yet. I should never have told you. I should have left you on the bleachers that first night we met. I should have been more patient."

I reach out to place my hand upon his cheek. "You told me that the Endless Palace is in ruins. But it isn't, really. We are still stuck in it. You, me...and Winston. Repeating the same mistakes over and over again."

"You know what's between us is true," he pleads. "You feel it, too."

I feel warm tears on my cheeks. "Just because something is true, doesn't mean it is good. Maybe it is for the best that I don't Remember. Maybe I choose not to Remember. I can't abandon my life for something I don't trust."

"I'm sorry, River."

It's time for me to go. "I'm not going to chase you anymore." Unable to look him in the eyes, I hug him tightly, burying my face into his neck. He shivers at first, but he hugs me back, and then lets me go.

Wiping my eyes, I detach from him and move toward the van. With a sudden grunt of protest, he pulls me back to him by my waist and I turn to fall helplessly into his arms. Knowing that it may be our last, our lips lock into a kiss that tremors through us like an earthquake, our bodies pressed tight to feel our hearts beating against one another.

When I finally pull back for air, our breathing is ragged, our cheeks flushed. I push his hair out of his eyes, giving him a small smile. Then, against every natural instinct in my body, I pry myself out of his embrace.

Without looking back, I climb into the van. My whole body is trembling as the driver backs us out of the clearing. I bury my face in my hands, consumed equally by my doubts about him and by my longing for him. I can still feel him looking at me, even as we drive into the jungle.

A warm glow hits my face from the horizon. The morning sun is rising. Maybe I can forget him; maybe I can erase everything that I witnessed tonight; maybe it will all disappear with the night.

And maybe the sun will never set again. That feels just as likely.

My phone is vibrating again. I will answer this time, and I will reassure Garden that I am okay, that she was right, that I am going to be coming back home to Los Angeles tomorrow. I won't abandon her.

But before I answer, I turn around to look out the rearview window. He remains standing there, his back straight and steadfast, still looking after me. As he disappears into the distance, I realize that I had been right when we first met. Now that I know he is out there, I might be lonely for the rest of this life.

An ambitious courtier in an ancient palace. A humble innkeeper in the woods. An artist obsessed with a singular muse.

A beautiful mystery to the very end.

His name is Joey.

·

JOEY

I watch River drive away into the unforgiving dawn, and he turns to gaze upon me one last time. Unsure if I will see him again in this life, I endeavor to Remember that look on his face, to chisel it into the constant memory of my soul. As I have every time before, I have failed in my eternal quest to break our curse, and I have only myself to blame.

But I will never stop. I will never stop.

I cannot be discouraged. I have failed in the past, and I will surely fail again, but somehow, someday, in some life, I will fulfill my promise to him.

As for tonight, all I can do is Remember his face, with that same look he has given me over and over again in our myriad lifetimes together—from that first time I recited an old poem to him under the wafting shade of a philosopher's tree. His eyes peered deep into me then and have remained there ever since.

That is all I can do. My astonishing ability to Remember over two thousand of my years is the only gift I have, undermined by my many faults. I cannot blame River for walking away. To Remember is a dubious gift, and a staggering burden.

What else do I Remember?

I Remember the final days we shared in those woods, I a mad innkeeper and he my maddening fox spirit, as we rode each other into an insatiable oblivion.

I Remember that whenever I had been inside him, everything was a rapturous blur. When our skin touched and he moaned with pleasure, I felt invincible. When I climaxed, I could feel the very foundations of the earth tremble with me.

I had him in the mud. I had him against fallen trees. I had him on a bed of dead flowers. I came until nothing came out of me except cold air.

At one point, he killed a rabbit and force-fed me its raw flesh. *You need to eat*, he kept insisting, sounding more and more helpless. *You need to rest.*

No, I said, its metallic blood running down my chin. I pulled him back onto me. *Again. Again.*

Finally, after what may have been months, might well have been years, I fell asleep.

When I woke up, it was dawn. I sat up instantly, fearing that he had gone. But he was perched on a rock above the river. His back was to me, and his entire body shuddered as he wept under the overcast sky.

Jiulang, I called out, reaching to him. *Why are you crying?*

He would not look at me as he spoke. *I thought if I freed us from our captors, our curse would be broken. But instead, you are dying. And try as I might, I cannot make you Remember.*

I tried to smile. *What are you talking about? Yes, we freed each other from our captors. And we are together now. What is there left to remember?*

It was then that he turned to me, and he was wearing his true face. His whiskers twitched as he wiped the tears from his downy cheeks. *I am a fox spirit, Shican. You started dying the moment we met. And you are going to die, very soon.*

I shrugged it off. *I do not feel like I am dying.* I looked down at my hands. I realized with dismay that my fingernails had all fallen off, the soft flesh beneath black-and-blue.

With a heavy grunt, I used all my strength to stand, for a moment triumphant. But then my knees buckled, and I fell down toward him, striking my head against his rock.

Shican! I heard him cry out, and I felt him pulling me out of the river onto dry land. In a patch of wild lavender he laid me down, leaning over me as he stroked my face. His fangs were small and sharp and his whiskers tickled my face. *I am sorry, Shican.*

I began to have trouble seeing. *Do not be sorry*, I said to him. I coughed and it tasted bitter.

He cradled my face in his paws. His nine grand tails were swathed around us gently like a golden silk cocoon. *May I tell you a story, He Shican?*

I smiled at the sentiment. *My uncle used to tell us stories.*

He took a deep breath and began his story.

Many years ago there was a king who loved one of his men. He loved this man more than himself, more than his throne, indeed, more than his entire kingdom.

As he spoke, he grasped one of his magnificent tails and pulled at it, straining at the effort.

But nothing was enough for this man—not all the riches, glory, nor power under Heaven—for him to truly return the king's love. As the king grew ill and weak with despair, he realized that his man did not have the capacity to love anyone, not even himself. But by then it was too late.

He was clenching his fangs in anguish as he pulled hard on his tail. I could hear the connective tissue tearing. *Jiulang, what are you—?*

He shook his head, and I fell silent. *It was too late*, the fox continued, *and once the king died, so did his kingdom. Yes, Shican, it was the tragic affair between these two men that brought down a dynasty.*

I knew this story. It was like somehow remembering another person's dream. *Was that really us, once upon a time, Jiulang? It all sounds so very grand and romantic, the stuff of gods and kings. What a disappointment I must be to you today. A sad nobody with a broken mind.*

Ashamed, I began to sink into the black. I could no longer speak.

With a final violent motion, he severed his tail from his body.

And when the king died, he whispered, *he ascended to Heaven, where he was offered sanctuary in that glorious place of fallen kings. But the dead king said no. He rejected eternal peace, because he realized that he had been betrayed. Hence, the dead king chose revenge.*

The fox spirit closed his eyes, lifting his face toward the sky. Burning through, the sun emerged from behind the clouds, bathing us both in radiant light. *After meditating his vengeance in the thin line between life and death for a thousand years, the dead king returned to earth as a fox spirit. And he searched and searched until, at last, he found and reunited with the soul of that man he had loved.*

I could feel my final exhale seeping out of me like a sieve. *Jiulang,* I gasped, reaching for him.

He returned his gaze to mine, his amber eyes shiny wet. *Perhaps now is your turn to Remember. And if you do, you must never stop. Promise me that you will never stop. Promise me!*

It took every last ounce of strength that I had to respond to him. *Promise... Promise!* I whispered, knowing that would be my last word.

He let out a shuddering sigh, kissed me tenderly and then placed his severed tail over my eyes. Darkness.

As I passed away amid the softness of his fur, I felt his cold breath rush into my ear, seeping into my brain.

Do you Remember now? Finally, you know, after all this time, what it felt like to want you, to love you, to die for you. Do you feel it? Do you Remember? Do you Remember now who I am?

Say my name, Dong Xian.

Dong Xian, Remember my name!

I was dying.

I was dying.

I was dead.

I am dead.

Yes.

Yes, I Remember now.

I Remember you, Son of Heaven. My Emperor!

My Liu Xin.

★ ★ ★ ★ ★

ACKNOWLEDGMENTS

Many Thanks

Whereas I wrote much of this book in solitary confinement during a pandemic lockdown fever dream of Summer 2020, these acknowledgements are anything but solitary. As I write them I feel as though I've emerged from my writer cave into a fabulous party full of folks that I love and cherish…and to whom I owe everything.

To begin, I'd like to thank Emperor Ai (born Liu Xin) and Dong Xian, the two very real young men who did indeed fall in love so hard that they brought down the first Han Dynasty, for being the inspiration of this book. Liu Xin and Dong Xian, I hope I captured just how hard y'all loved each other.

I'd like to thank Grand Empress Dowager Fu and Commander Jujun, who also lived actual lives so fascinating that it was quite easy to turn them into delicious villains. Two thousand years into the future, what more could any one of us want?

The preeminent Han philosopher Yang Xiong probably was not a messy lush, but rather was described by his contemporaries as a temperate ascetic, who would have eschewed the extravagance of liquor, so I'd like to thank the real Old Yang for humoring me some poetic license. However, Fu's eunuch henchman Shi Li definitely gave razor blade blowjobs IRL, I'm sure of it.

I'd like to thank the fabulist Pu Songling, as I borrowed the premise and the characters Huang Jiulang, He Shican, and Dr. Qi Yewang from his classic folktale that he wrote in the 1700s. Teacher Pu, I hope you like this remix.

Yes, this party has dead people in it, that's how fabulous it is.

Onto the living, I'd like to thank novelist Jade Chang and screenwriter Nathan Ramos-Park, the sounding boards and cheerleaders of this book—Jade encouraged me start it and Nathan helped me end it. Nathan, cuing you as there's a naughty joke in there somewhere.

I'd like to thank my founding agent Dan Milaschewski, a non-legacy Harvard grad who never stops smiling nor hustling. This young buck cold-called me on an otherwise mundane January morning in 2022 about a largely forgotten manuscript that had been passed to him by his extraordinary colleague Anna Flickinger via her client, the talented screenwriter Lauren Moon. Without this fateful Rube Goldberg of wonderful humans, I would have never found…

Nicole Brebner and Evan Yeong, my brilliant editors at MIRA Books, who politely poked and prodded this book into its final form, which I happily admit is now better. It is not lost on me that they are taking a big chance on a queer love story entirely starring Asian men, and I feel like the belle of the balls.

I'd like to thank the United Talent Agency for bequeathing upon me the legendary Ariele Friedman and the effervescent Orly Greenberg to join Dan as my agents, demonstrating there are few more potent powers than collaborations between gays and women. The four of us also just have a damn good time.

A week before Thanksgiving 2023, I traveled to New York to meet the HarperCollins folks working on this book, and not only are they a powerhouse behind the scenes, they are also the loveliest people you can imagine in person: my publicists Laura Gianino and Sophie James, Lindsey Reeder and the digital marketing team, Ashley MacDonald and the marketing team, Erin Craig and the cover art team, Randy Chan and Pamela Osti and the channel marketing team, and of course the entire Harper-Collins sales team, whose genuine excitement over this book was truly humbling. Thank you to Kathleen Mancini for copy editing the manuscript, and Leigh Teetzel and Joan Burkeitt for proofreading it.

I also owe John Glynn and Eden Railsback a big thanks for being among this book's earliest champions at HarperCollins.

The artist Yixin Zeng took three keywords from me—lush, psychedelic, and romantic—and proceeded to deliver a show-stopper of a cover that knocked the wind out of me the first time I saw it. This is his debut book cover on my debut book, and I feel so grateful to him and his talent.

Incredibly seminal were my years at Pomona College under the influence of scholars like then Vice President-Dean Ann Quinley, Professor Susan McWilliams, and the late great Professor David Foster Wallace. What I will never forget though is the slightly panicked look on my advisor Professor Sarah Raff's face when I told her that I was dropping out of pre-med to become a novelist instead. But that's just how good her Jane Austen class was.

The character Garden is a composite of the women in my life who have lovingly worried about me throughout my years, and like anyone with a blessedly interesting life, I've given them plenty to worry about:

First and foremost, my mother, Lilian Lee, who like me is too Capricorn to malfunction. As a young woman, she immigrated to the United States with almost nothing and then proceeded to give everyone everything. Thank you, Mama, for never giving up on me.

My big sister, Cherise Huang, who taught me how to play pretend when we were kids.

My M2, Lynda Obst, who pulled me off that golf cart on the Paramount lot in the early 2000s and has mentored me endlessly ever since.

My stepmother, Angel Chen, who has painted countless calligraphy paintings in the next room from my writer cave and always imbues my townhouse with her creative painterly energy. (She's a painter.)

My Taipei godmother, Viviane Liu, who saved me from one of the lowest points of my life in 2019, and as if that weren't enough, also found time to teach me about the Buddhist concept of reincarnation, which feels like it might have been relevant here.

My boss turned friend, Kristine Belson, who has selflessly supported my transition from her employee to whatever the hell is going to happen to me next. And my assistant turned friend, Alexandra Cadena-Stempel, for being my best and brightest buddy in the Hollywood trenches.

And to my girl friends, who were my first readers and were so titillated by these gay boys that I realized I might be onto something: Marissa Bivona, Randa Heleka, Zeina Heleka, Amie Karp, Corina Sagun, Dorothy Shapiro, Vivian Wu, and, of course, Mara Sutton-Barnes. Yet it was Caitlin Krier who read this book almost in real time as each chapter was written, and Nina Ofek and Karen Fei who continuously kept me fed with delicious home cooking.

I'd like to thank my dog Swagger, who sat with me as I wrote this book on many otherwise lonely nights. He was a street dog in Shanghai when I adopted him back in 2016, and now he's a retired princeling in West LA. Not bad, Swaggy.

In this book about the sacred bonds between Asian men, I'd like conclude by thanking the Asian men in my life who have shaped both this book and me into better forms:

My brother from a Chongqing mother, Tailin Zeng, who did the deepest reads of this book and provided me with, yes, authenticity checks, but more importantly, raw and unbridled enthusiasm.

My stepfather, Allen Sun, who not only cooks for me whenever I visit, but also picks me up from LAX every damn time I come back home, which any Angeleno would tell you is so sweet but also insane.

My first friend in Shanghai, Calvin Chou, who is as kind as he is tall, and he is very tall. We met the week I moved to China in 2015, and then I cried upon his shoulder many times about various boys...and yes, he is the namesake of the Calvin in this book.

My straight husband, Benjamin Yi, who is not just arm candy, but soul candy. Looking forward to seeing the rest of the world with you, Ben, and thank you for always doing all the planning and carrying all the luggage.

Last yet leading, my father, Charles Huang, who once told me, "I don't care who you love, Justin. I just care that you are a good person, and you are the best person I know." Thank you, Baba, for saving my life with that sentence.

And finally, I'd like to thank every boy who has ever broken my heart, and every boy whose heart I've broken.

I Remembered you as I wrote this book.

xo Justinian